Little

Bird

BLACK VENOM CREW

ALISHA WILLIAMS

This is a work of fiction. Names, characters, places, and incidents are either the product of the author's imagination or are used fictitiously. Any resemblance to actual persons, living or dead, events, or locales is entirely coincidental.

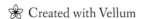 Created with Vellum

AUTHOR'S NOTE

Hello readers! Welcome to the first book, Little Bird, of my new dark reverse harem Black Venom crew. I thought I'd give you a little inside on what to expect from this world! Little Bird is on the lower side of the spice scale, but don't worry, the rest of the series will be sure to be dirty in all the best ways.

These are a crew of killers. There will be semi detailed murder scenes as well as graphic sex scene in future books.

Please note that this is a dark romance filled with men who are unapologetically possessive and obsessed with the main female character. These men are killers, and although their main goal is to rid the world of sick and twisted people, they are still bad guys themselves and do not think twice before doing what they want. Some of the men have been with other woman in the past.

If you are not okay with men being controlling and demanding of the main female character, then this book might not be for you. Don't worry, the main female loves it and even craves it.

Nothing in this series is non-consensual, despite how it might seem. Raven is just as fucked up as the guys and loves anything and everything they do to her. So if you read something and think, hey, she might not like that. Trust me, she does.

I hope you enjoy the start of Raven and her guys' story, and I look forward to bringing you even more dark and dirty goodness as the series goes on.

Enjoy!

TRIGGER WARNINGS

Black Venom Crew is meant to be a dark reverse harem. Although Little Bird is tamer than how the rest of the series will go, here are some of the things with in the book that readers may find triggering or would like to know about ahead of time.

This list includes, but not limited to:

*Violence
*Torture
*Murder
*OW drama not between the main characters.
*Mention of MMC's with OW in the past.
*Offensive language
*Profanity
*Alcohol use
*Voyeurism
*Somnophilia

*Masturbation
*Degradation

LITTLE BIRD

CHAPTER 1

RAVEN

Don't get me wrong, I love the guys, they're my best friends in the whole world. But the thing I hate the most about sharing the top floor with them, is the fact that there's only one communal bathroom.

I'd be getting ready for school while I waited for it to be free, if it wasn't for the fact that my bladder is about to burst.

"Come on, guys!" I shout as I bang on the door. "Pissing my pants isn't how I want to start my last first day of school."

"Just come in!" Hunter chuckles. "There's enough room for all of us."

He's not wrong. It's like a big locker room with multiple stalls and showers, but I'm the only girl who's lived on this floor with these four guys during the past eight years. Well, I guess three now that Link moved out. It might end up being just Hunter and me now that the twins, Travis and Taylor, graduated last year. I assumed they would have moved in with Link over the summer, but they're still here, getting ready for work.

Link owns a car garage that the guys help run. I still to this day have no idea how he could afford to buy the place off the old owner. Link dropped out of high school in eleventh grade, and the only job he ever had was fixing up old cars.

But from the size of his house and the way he lives, he must be doing something right.

The twins just graduated by the skin of their teeth. I think the only reason why they didn't drop out too is because they liked hanging out with Hunter and me.

Black Ridge is a small-ass town, and there's not much to do to entertain yourself, so you make do with what you've got.

Yet, none of us feel the need, nor want, to leave this place. This is our home, and it might be boring as fuck, but it's where we want to be. Plus, as long as I have the guys, that's all I need.

Me? I don't plan on going away to university, but I would like to take a few classes at the community college in the next town over; it's only about a twenty-minute drive.

Link doesn't like the idea, but he's a broody, overprotective fucker and knows I'm gonna end up doing what I want anyway. So, that's why Hunter, Link's little brother, plans on coming along with me.

Not that it matters to me because out of the four of them, Hunter and I are the closest.

He's the same age as me, only older by a month, so since

grade four, we've been in every class together. Even as the others got older and went off to junior high or high school, I was never left behind, always having Hunter at my side. But at the end of the day, we would all end up in the same place. Safe Haven, a boarding home for abused women and children. But that's a story for another time.

Our mothers all have rooms in other parts of the house, but we've always shared the top floor from day one.

My bladder is screaming at me at this point and deciding to say fuck it, I burst through the door. The guys chuckle as I scramble through the steamy room and over to the first toilet stall I can get to. Slamming it shut, I quickly lock it and pull my pants down. My ass just hits the seat before I start pissing like a racehorse. "Fuck. That's better."

"So you're willing to risk a UTI to avoid being in here at the same time as us?" Travis asks. "Come on, Little Dove, don't be so stubborn."

"Yeah, Foxy girl, we're just like you. But... with dicks," Taylor snickers.

Grinning, I shake my head as my body warms at the nicknames they have for me. By the sixth month of me being here, they all had one for me. And I love it. It was like they welcomed me into their little messed up family. A spot I've happily taken.

"Well, as the only one here with a vagina, sometimes it's nice to have privacy and shit," I say as I wipe and flush.

"Dude, you started your first period at school, during lunch while you were sitting on Hunter's lap. I think we're all pretty damn comfortable with each other by this point," Taylor says.

Sometimes, a little too comfortable. I don't know if they forget or just don't care, but my room is between Hunter's and the one the twins share. I hear it, every time they jack off. I know the sounds they make when they cum. As hot as it is, and as many times as I touched myself while they did it, I don't think that's how close friends should be.

"Don't remind me," I groan as I open the door. Still waking up, I rub my eyes with the back of my hands as I head over to the sink to wash them.

I'm in the middle of rinsing when I realize the bathroom has gotten a lot quieter. Looking up in the mirror, I find all three sets of eyes on me. My eyes find what they are looking at, and I have to fight the smug smile that wants to break across my puffy pink lips.

I'm only in a sleep top and shorts, no bra so my nipples are stiff and poking through my thin shirt. My boobs are big and push against the top making my nipples hard to miss. And I know my ass is half hanging out of my shorts; that's where I find Hunter's eyes glued.

These guys might like to act like I'm their best friend, maybe even like a sister to them, but they're not fooling anyone. I know they want me. It's moments like these that it's hard to deny it. But I don't call them out on it, wanting them to come to the admission on their own.

I want them too. Yes, all of them. Have since I hit puberty. I mean, I could be the one to tell them how I feel and stop dancing around the subject, but where's the fun in that? I want all four of these drop-dead sexy, tattooed men to confess their love for me.

Pretending I don't notice, I yawn. Raising my arms above my head for a good stretch, I let out a moan at how good it feels as my shirt rises, showing off the bottom of my breasts.

All three of them curse under their breath, and I do a happy dance inside. But it's taking everything in me not to ogle them all standing there in only a towel wrapped around their waists. Towels that are just barely hiding the stiffie they're all sporting. Morning wood? I think not. That's all my doing, thank you very much.

"Well, I gotta go get ready for school. You three continue your jerk fest or whatever you boys do in the bathroom at the same time," I tease, grabbing a towel off the counter and drying my hands as I give Hunter a playful wink. His electric blue hair is wet and hangs over one of his eyes. Those eyes... fuck, they're stunning. They're so light blue that they're almost white. It's like he's looking into your soul while knowing all your deepest darkest secrets. And I have a lot of those.

He gives me this cat-like grin as I pass. "Brat," he says a moment before I feel the crack of his towel against my ass.

"What the fuck?!" I shout, grabbing my cheek as it starts to throb and sting. Spinning around with a deadly glare in my eyes, I'm ready to rip him a new one, but I stop dead in my tracks when I see that the towel he used is the one that was previously wrapped around his waist.

Holy shit, Hunter is fucking hung! And he's hard as

stone right now. I let out the smallest of whimpers, hoping like hell he doesn't hear it. "Cat got your tongue, Little Mouse?" he taunts in a smug tone.

It's then that I realize my eyes are glued to his dick. They snap up to his, narrowing once again. "You're gonna pay for that, asshole," I huff before spinning around and getting the fuck out of that bathroom before I do something embarrassing like get on my knees and ask for a taste. It's the first time I've seen it, and I hope to god it's not the last. It's fucking tattooed! And the amount of metal on it would set off airport security for sure.

"Can't wait!" he calls after me before the three of them break out into a chorus of chuckles.

I'm way too worked up by the time I get back to my room. *Would it be weird to rub one out before school?* Fuck it.

Throwing myself down on the bed, I get myself off the way I love best. It doesn't take long with how turned on I am anyways. After my heart is done pounding in my chest, I roll off the bed and get dressed.

I showered last night, letting my hair dry before throwing it into a messy bun. So I shake my hair out and brush it before adding some loose curls.

I keep my makeup light, adding a blush colored lipstick as a pop of color on my face. I normally don't spend hours on my appearance but because it's the first day of senior year, I put a little effort into it. I pick out a pair of ripped jeans, pairing it with a long-sleeved black top that hugs my body and shows my tits off perfectly.

Happy with how I look, I grab my bag, my phone, and the leather jacket that Link got me for Christmas last year. It's my favorite thing to wear, no matter what outfit I have on.

My belly rumbles, insisting I grab something to eat before I leave for school. So I make a quick pit-stop in the kitchen.

When I get there, I find the guys and all the moms there. There's no other residents in Safe Haven, and that's just how I like it. I know this place is meant to help women and kids, -and I love that it does- but when it's just us, like it has been for years, it feels like a home. Our home.

Normally, people who come here are gone within six months, safe to go back out into the real world and start their new, safer lives. But we've been here for eight years. The guys, even longer.

I asked my mom why we don't leave like everyone else, but she always just said the home never asked her to leave, and she saw no reason to. She's best friends with Hunter and Link's mom, Rachel, and the twins' mom, Lisa. After a while, I just accepted that this is our home, and I never want to leave. At least not without the guys.

"Morning, baby," my mom, Samantha, says as I enter the room.

"Morning," I reply, giving her a smile as I go over to her and give her a kiss on the cheek before taking the muffin in her hand.

"Hey." She chuckles. "That was mine."

"But it's the only blueberry one left," I say, giving her a pout and puppy dog eyes, batting my eyelashes.

"Fine," she sighs, picking up a banana nut one instead. She turns to the guys, asking, "Does she do this with you to get whatever she wants?"

"Nope," I answer for them, taking a bite. "They just love me enough to already give me what I want," I say around a mouthful.

"That and because that way we don't have to hear her whine about it all day," Taylor says with a grin. I glare at him and give him the finger. He barks out a laugh as his smile brightens.

He's gorgeous. So is his brother. Taylor and Travis are identical twins. There's only two ways someone who doesn't know them, as well as I do, can tell them apart. One is the fact that they have different tattoos, and two is their personalities. They both have the same wavy black hair, blue eyes, black gauges in their ears, and always have slightly stubbled jaws.

But while Taylor is more on the playful cocky side, Travis is quiet and reserved, only teasing me occasionally. And when that grin comes out... fuck, I'm a puddle of goo.

When he's with just me and the guys, he's a little more open. I love that he can be himself around us.

"Raven, behave," my mother chastises.

"Yeah, Raven, behave. Stop being a naughty, naughty girl," Hunter mocks, his eyes lighting up with glee.

"Oh boy. It's not even nine am and they're already going at it." Rachel laughs. "Hunter, be nice."

"I'm always nice! Aren't I, Little Mouse?" Hunter sweet talks.

I grin. "The nicest," I agree. Even though my ass still hurts from his little stunt this morning.

"We better get going," Taylor says to Travis. "Link is gonna be blowing up our phones if we're not there on time."

"Tell that son of mine, I want him home this Sunday for supper. It feels like it's been ages since I've seen him," Rachel tells them.

"Will do, Auntie Rach," Taylor confirms.

The twins move past me, each giving me a kiss on the top of the head. "Be good, Dove, but try to enjoy yourself a little, okay?" Travis says.

"Kay," I reply, smiling up at him. He gives me a little wink before taking off with his brother.

"Come on, Ray, we better get going too. Don't wanna be late on our first day," Hunter says, grabbing his book bag.

We say goodbye to our moms and head out to his car. We get into the front seats, and Hunter already has Skrillix blaring before even starting the engine.

The bass feels amazing as it vibrates through my body. It's the perfect way to wake up for the day.

"Hey!" I shout over the music as Hunter takes my muffin. He gives me a mischievous grin before taking a big bite out of it. He chews, swallows, and then dramatically licks all over the top of the muffin before handing it back to me.

"Thanks," he says, wiggling his eyebrows.

If this fucker thinks that's going to stop me from eating it he doesn't know me that well. Not breaking eye contact, I take just as big a bite as he did and moan loudly like it's the best damn thing I've ever tasted.

Hunter starts cackling as he pulls out of the driveway, and I can't help but grin as we take off to school. Today is going to be a good day.

And it was, up until gym. If I have to hear one more fucking girl cry about how the Cross twins aren't here anymore or how they swear they were going to build up the courage to ask one of them out again, I'm gonna be pulling some extensions out of these fake-ass bitches hair.

Look, I'm not one to be a bitch to other women, but the girls in this school? Yeah, there's nothing classy about them at all; they're all trashy. They love to find any way they can to make jabs at me, whether it be making up rumors that I'm getting gang banged by the guys every night or they're bragging about getting under one of them.

But not one of them has the balls to say it to my face. There's an unspoken rule in this school, hell, even in the entire town- that you don't fuck with me. The guys made sure of that.

It's also why I've never had a guy ask me out and I don't have any friends outside of them. No one wants to risk pissing them off.

Unfortunately, not all the things the girls have said are lies. Hunter and Link don't fuck around. Hunter is always with me and never once shown interest in any girl, no matter the amount of them who have tried while Link has said on many occasions that he has no time for pointless fucks.

The twins, however, have hooked up with a few different girls. I don't like it, it makes me a jealous bitch, and the idea of them touching another woman drives me mad. But they've said it's never more than a fuck. They don't want any of them more than that and always make it clear to the girls before doing anything with them. Some of them just don't seem to comprehend their words.

These stupid bitches like to make a fool of themselves and act like they're going to be one of their next girlfriends. Only thing is, there's never been a previous girlfriend to qualify as the next.

I'm the only constant girl in the guys' lives, and they know it. It's another reason they all hate me.

Giving them all a fake as fuck smile, I walk past them and out to the gym, finding Hunter waiting for me. We spend all of gym laughing and playing around as we fail at badminton.

Every now and then, I have to resist the urge to go over to the girls, grab the volleyball from them and smash it into one of their stupid faces whenever they bring one of the twins names up.

I don't care how crazy it makes me. These guys are mine.

The rest of the day goes by like any other school day. I'm in some classes I hate, like Math and History, and some that I love, like Art and Music.

By the time my last class of the day, English, rolls around, I'm happy it's almost time to go home. Link texted me at lunch saying he was picking me up after school and to let Hunter know.

He already knew what I was going to say from the big dumb smile that was on my face as I read the text. Link drives a motorcycle, and I love going for rides. No one, not even the guys have ridden with him or even sat on his bike, only me and him.

We're about twenty minutes into class when I hear a chatter coming from behind me. I look over at Hunter, who is telling his shirt to be quiet. Raising a brow, I poke him with my pencil. He looks over at me and grins. I give him a *what the fuck* look, and that's when Princess Fiona, Hunter's pet ferret, pokes her head out of his shirt.

My eyes go wide, and I slap a hand over my mouth to hide the giggle bubbling up. Of course this crazy fucker would bring his ferret to school. This isn't even the first time. In tenth grade, he brought her to school for a full week straight just after getting her, claiming he couldn't leave her alone all day. She got out and ended up pissing all over the teachers desk, ruining a few tests she was grading. I was quite proud that one of them was Phoebe McAllister's, a girl Taylor had just hooked up with and who was bragging about it around the school. It was fun to know she had to take a piss stained test home when it dried.

Of course, Hunter didn't get in trouble for it. None of the guys were punished for anything they did. For the longest time, I didn't know why, but I'm starting to gain some suspicions, if the rumors I hear are true.

The final bell rings, and the class starts to gather their things. "Have fun, Little Mouse. Don't give Linky-poo a hard time." He grins. "Also, here," he says, giving me a pink duck the size of an eraser on a pencil. "Find a place on his bike to put this."

"Will do." I giggle as I take the pink duck, and put it in my pocket. Hunter loves to fuck with Link and leave tiny ducks all over Link's work place, house, and anywhere else Link might go.

With a wave of giddy excitement, I quickly make my way to my locker and dump all my shit in there before tossing my bag at Hunter as I pass him on my way to the front door. "Bye!" I shout as he laughs behind me.

Running down the steps, I come to a stop when I see *him* waiting there for me. Lincoln Graves. My eyes roam over him. Fuck, he's so gorgeous my clit can't help but pulse at the sight of him. He's tall, well over six feet, with dark brown hair. He's covered head to toe in tattoos, and I do mean his neck and fingers too. He has two styles. One is a black fitted suit that makes me drool, and the other is black ripped jeans with a black wife tee shirt of some kind. I haven't seen him in anything in between.

Link is the silent, broody, and dominant type. If you

don't know him, you would think he was a raging asshole. He demands, never asks. And he will not take no for an answer. Most people are scared of him, rightfully so.

But me? He could tell me to get on my knees and lick his boots clean, and I'd happily drop like a bag of rocks.

I bite my lip as Link looks up at me from his phone. He stands up straighter as he puts it away. "Little Bird!" he shouts. "Here. Now!"

And like the good girl I am, I obey. I try not to run over there like I want to, enjoying the envious and jealous stares I'm getting from everyone as I walk across the parking lot.

"Hi, Link," I greet in a sweet voice.

"Hi, Little Bird," he says. He reaches up and brushes a piece of hair off my face. The contact has me nearly whimpering. "Get on," he commands as he swings his leg over his bike and hands me the helmet.

As soon as it's in place and he can't see my face behind it, I'm all fucking smiles as I get on behind him. I wrap my arms around him, molding myself tightly to his back. And I almost swear I can hear him growl. Or maybe it was the bike.

He revs the engine before we're peeling out of the parking lot.

I don't even know why Link wanted to be the one to pick me up today. And I don't even care. I'll take any moment with him that I can get. I've been seeing less of him these days, and I hate it. I plan on fixing that though. He just might need a bit of motivation to start coming around more.

CHAPTER 2

RAVEN

Riding on the back of Link's bike with my arms wrapped around his big, strong body is one of my favorite feelings. He used to be the one to take me everywhere but as time has gone by, it's become less and less. I'm not sure if it's work or he just doesn't have time for me.

Well, fuck him because he better *make* time for me. There's no way in hell I'm going to let him put distance between us.

We ride along the highway for a while. I know exactly where he's taking me when I see the big red water tower at the town's edge, where his shop is located. He rarely lets me go there, saying it's not a place for women. Too many men with wandering eyes.

I love that he doesn't want anyone else looking at me in a suggestive way; it makes what I have planned even better.

Pulling up to the front of the shop, Link parks his bike and turns the engine off. "Stay here. I need to do something real quick, then I'll take you home," he states, narrowing his eyes and staring me down.

The idea of him taking me home so soon fills me with disappointment. This is the first time I've seen him in a week. I don't want it to be over so soon. I know he's twenty-three and busy with his own business, but that doesn't mean he can just forget about me.

The guys get to see him all the time, and it's not fair. I miss how it used to be when the five of us did everything together. Now that we're all older and in different stages of our lives, things are changing.

He turns around, heading into the shop. My eyes drop to his ass, and I bite my lip. *Fuck, it looks so damn biteable in those jeans.*

The bell on the door dings when he enters. Once he's inside and the door closes behind him, I do exactly what he told me *not* to do. Taking off my helmet, I shake out my long, honey-blonde hair before placing it on the seat of the bike. Grabbing the little pink duck from my pocket, I grin as I lift the seat on the bike and put it in.

When I'm done, I take a look around, seeing if anything's changed. The same old car sits in the front with the Black Ridge Auto sign next to it. The place looks well loved from the outside, but it's a lot... cleaner than I remember. Like they wanted to keep it maintained without taking away from the original charm.

The front building has a fresh coat of white paint, so is

now no longer falling off in chips. Attached is a small garage with the door open. There's a few cars being worked on, the sounds of impact drills fill the air.

But the thing I never understood is why there's a massive warehouse behind the shop? I'm assuming it's where they keep the rest of the cars, among other things, because there's, from what I can see, no more than three, maybe four cars that can fit in the garage at a time.

Getting bored, I decide to go into the shop to see if maybe they have a bottle of water I can drink or something.

The bell on the door rings as I pull it open, but Link doesn't hear me. He's busy yelling at one of his men.

"I don't give a fuck! Find him so I can deal with him. No one hides from B–"

"Raven!" Quinton, one of Link's workers, shouts in greeting while interrupting whatever Link was going to say next. "Haven't seen you around here in a while."

Link's back goes straight as he lets out a low growl that sends a delicious shiver through my body. He spins around, setting his hard gaze on me. "I thought I told you to wait outside," he barks.

"And when have I ever done what I'm told?" I grin, walking over to the fridge by the desk near Quinton. I open it and grab a water. "Don't worry," I whisper shout to Quinton. "I know the boss."

Quinton laughs, shaking his head. He's cute, like really cute. He's got yummy tanned skin, his hair is short, close to his head, and he's covered in tattoos like all the other guys around here. But the thing that always catches my attention is his eyes. They're the brightest blue, like the ocean, drawing you in and making you want to drown in them.

"Don't encourage her," Link snarls at Quinton before turning his attention back to me. "This isn't a place for kids, get your ass back out to the bike, now!"

"Who the fuck are you calling a kid?" I ask, cocking a brow as I crack open the bottle of water. "I'm going to be eighteen next month. That makes me an adult."

"Yet you can't do shit until you're twenty one. Until then, you're a fucking kid."

"Ewww, that sounds pretty pervy, Link, might want to rethink how you word things," I tease, as I take a drink of water, keeping my eyes locked on his stormy ones. I'm poking the bear, and if it was anyone else they would have hell to pay for it. But I can't help it, I love getting a rise out of him, any of them.

Quinton snorts. "You sure do have balls, Ray."

"Yes, I do, and they're a hell of a lot bigger than yours." I wink.

"Little Bird!" Link warns in a deadly tone, and I decide to stop while I'm ahead.

"Alright, alright." I roll my eyes. "Later, Quinny." I wave to Quinton before heading back out to the bike.

I spend another fifteen minutes waiting, watching the ripples in the water from the lake across the street. Other than the lake, the shop is surrounded by hundreds of miles of forest and mountains. There's a road that takes you through it all, but there's so many twists and turns, most people avoid coming this way and use the highway on the other side of town.

I like it out here. It's secluded and peaceful. At least during the day. At night, that's a whole other story I'd love to know more about.

"About time," I huff when Link starts heading over.

"Don't even fucking start with me, Little Bird," he growls. "Why do you always have to be such a fucking brat?"

"Because it's one of the many things you love about me, duh." I smile sweetly, batting my eyelashes.

"One of these days, I'm going to put you over my fucking knee and smack your ass until you're too sore to sit," he mutters as he swings his leg over the bike. My body flushes with heat, and my clit starts to pulse. *Fuck, please, I'd really like nothing more than for him to do exactly that.* "Get the fuck on, Raven!" he shouts over the rev of the engine.

Putting the helmet on, I get onto the back of the bike, wrapping my arms around him again. We pull out of the shop and onto the road, heading back towards town.

I close my eyes, cursing the gods above because I'm so fucking turned on right now and the vibrations of the bike are not helping at all. It feels good, really fucking good, and I have to resist the urge to grind my pussy where it's pressed up against Link's ass.

My hands tighten in his shirt as the tension starts to build. I feel like I'm being edged right now, teased and tortured. I need friction bad. But I can't start humping Link while we're driving... right? No... Maybe? Fuck.

I'm dying by the time we pass the school. We're almost home, and my body is on fire. I need to move, just a little pressure against my clit. I'll keep quiet, but I really need to cum.

Taking a deep breath, I groan as his smell of gasoline and aftershave hits my nose. One of my hands slip down and I whimper when I feel the hard bulge through Link's jeans.

Link lets out a deep growl, and I know it isn't the engine. He likes my arms around him, he likes me being close, touching him.

Fuck, I'm done for. Not giving a fuck, I try really hard not to be too obvious as I shift my weight slightly, moving my hips in an upward motion, getting just the right amount of friction.

I cum, my clit pulsating in time with the clenching of my empty pussy as a small orgasm hits me. I try to swallow the moan that leaves me, but the curse that leaves Link's lips tells me I wasn't successful.

Taking deep breaths, I try to keep myself from panting while I catch my breath. It's not enough, I need more, something to fill me. But sadly, I'm going to go home and use a vibrator to take away this empty feeling.

We pull up to the house. Link parks the bike, but he doesn't get off. I stay there, my arms wrapped around him for a few more moments, wishing he could take me upstairs and fuck me into next year like I really fucking want him to.

Knowing I have to go inside, I let go of his shirt and climb off the bike. Taking off the helmet, I go to hand it back to Link, but he shakes his head. "Keep it," he grunts, not meeting my eyes.

Did I just fuck things up? There's never been anything we couldn't say or do around the others.

Yes, but how many times did we use one of the others to get off randomly? None.

"Alright, then. Bye," I say, my words having a bit of bite to it.

Turning around, I head inside feeling fucking annoyed. Link isn't the most talkative person. We don't sit down having heart-to-hearts and shit, but he's never once refused eye contact with me.

I'm not one who tends to care about what people think of me nor do I have much of a filter, but any time one of my guys are a little off with me, it bugs me. I can't help but feel like I did something wrong. Do I regret it? No, I was horny, and I got off.

What pisses me off is that I know Link wants me. He can call me a kid, he can say I'm too young, but at the end of the day, that man wants me just as much as his brother and the twins do. That's why him acting like this bugs me more than I'd like it to.

"Hey, Ray," Travis says as I come into the house. Looking to the left, I see him, Taylor, and Hunter sitting on the couch playing video games.

"Oh no," Hunter comments as he hops up from the couch. "What's wrong?"

"Nothing," I spit, putting the helmet down on the coffee table.

"Yeah, sure," Taylor snarks, rolling his eyes. "What did the big brute do?"

"Guys, really it's nothing," I argue, taking a spot between the twins.

"If you say so," Travis says, passing me a piece of pizza. "How was your first day?"

I sit and tell them all about school, even adding that Link took me to the shop. They all give each other a small look of surprise at that.

We play video games, shouting and laughing, making me forget about the odd funk I was in until Hunter's mom said it was time for bed. Seeing it was already eleven, I didn't fight her on it.

"Lucky." I glare at the twins who continue to play.

"Sorry, Foxy Girl." Taylor grins. "Benefits of being adults." He winks.

"And knowing the boss." Travis chuckles.

"I do not miss waking up so fucking early every morning for school," Taylor says.

"You were up early this morning," I point out. The twins look at each other.

"Work emergency," Travis grunts.

"And they needed you two when there's a crap ton of people who work for Link?" I ask, cocking a brow.

"Go to bed, Ray," Travis deflects. "You're making too much out of nothing."

"Fine," I huff, turning to leave. "Night."

"Forgetting something, Foxy?" Taylor says playfully, and I can't help but smile.

Grinning, I walk over to the twins and lower my head. First Taylor, then Travis kisses my forehead and says goodnight.

These fuckers can deny it all they want to themselves, but normal friends, even best friends, aren't like this. Not the way we are. We have such close bonds that no one would ever dare break. And I'd hurt anyone who tried.

LINCOLN

She's pissed at me, but she needs to get over it. She has no idea what she does to me, what it takes for me to not shove her to her knees and push my cock past her pretty puffy lips, making her choke on it until tears are running down her cheeks while she fights for air. The amount of restraint it takes to not bring her to the brink of passing out before letting her breathe and doing it all over again is insane.

My Little Bird used me to get off, and it took everything in me not to pull off to the side of the road to fuck her raw on this bike. Feeling her shudder with her arms around me and hearing the little moan that she made, knowing I might hear it. My cock is fucking stone right now. I'll do something about it when I get back to the shop.

I watch her walk up the steps, her perfect ass swaying in those painted-on jeans. An ass I plan on licking, sucking, and fucking. I can't wait to watch my cum drip from her tight hole.

But not now. I'm not stupid, I know she knows we want

her. She just doesn't know how much. She doesn't know how dark and depraved we really are.

We knew from the moment we met Raven that she was ours. Ours to love, to care for, to fuck, to own.

But she was just a scared, damaged little girl. We didn't want to scare her away. So we made her our whole world, rightfully so. We became her everything like we were always meant to be.

We just never showed her who we are when the sun goes down and the monsters come out to play. And the four of us? We're some of the scariest ones of them all.

She has until graduation to live her life the way she wants. To do as she pleases, within reason. The moment her diploma is in her hands, any freedom she thought she might have in starting her new life is ours.

We already have her future set in stone; she just doesn't know it yet. And she better watch herself or the small amount of time she has left of her life being her own is going to get shorter and shorter.

Keep testing me, and I'll give her everything she wants and more. She might end up regretting it, but I don't fucking care. She's mine and I'm never, and I mean never, letting her go.

My Little Bird is going to be put into a cage, one only we have the key for. *So enjoy your time now Raven, while you still have it.*

CHAPTER 3

RAVEN

I'm in a pissy fucking mood and everyone in the house will know about it soon enough. Last night after the fun night with the guys, I went up to my room and thought I'd settle the empty, wanting feeling left from the orgasm on the bike. Unfortunately for me, I went to the bathroom and found out I was on my period. So I had to settle for some over the clothes play.

So now I'm horny and frustrated, hungry and cramping. Today is going to be a fucking joyful day.

"Oh no," Hunter says as he walks into the kitchen and sees me angrily stabbing at my bowl of oatmeal. "Everyone steer clear, Shark week is here."

"Fuck off," I hiss, giving him the finger before shoving a spoonful of food into my mouth. Brown sugar and cinnamon is usually something I enjoy, but today it makes me wanna puke. Grimacing, I force the mouthful down before pushing the rest away.

A cramp hits me, pain spiking through my belly and making me moan as I let my head hit the table with a thud.

"Hey, Dove," Travis says in a soft tone. Turning my head to the side with my cheek resting on the table, I look at him.

"Hi," I mumble, feeling like death.

He gives me a smile, and my heart flutters. "I'd ask you how you're feeling, but that would be a stupid question."

"Smart observation," I deadpan, making him chuckle.

"Tay and I gotta work tonight, but how about after school, you and Hunter go to the store, pick out a bunch of snacks and spend the night watching movies in your bed?"

"I'd love to. But I don't have any money." I sigh, closing my eyes.

"Here," he says. I open my eyes to see him holding out two twenties. "My treat. Anything for my Little Dove." He winks.

I love you. Fuck, I love you. And I wanna tell you so damn bad. "Thanks, T."

He bends over and kisses my cheek. "Always. Tay is still sleeping, but he told me to tell you bye when he was half asleep."

"Tell him bye." I sigh as I lift my head off the table. Today has been a slow start. I had to drag my ass out of bed, pop a few pills that are finally just starting to kick in and get dressed. I said fuck it and tossed on a bra, hoodie, and some sweat pants with a pair of UGGS. Give me a Starbucks coffee, and I'd be a basic bitch.

"Hey, Ray," Hunter says as I look at him leaning against the island, looking worried. "You sure you don't wanna just stay home?"

"No," I sigh, getting up and bringing my bowl over to the trash. I scrape everything out before placing it in the sink. "Missing the second day of school is not a good idea. I might not be the best student in class, but I do need to keep my grades up to a passing level if I want to go to Stone Ridge Community College next year."

Hunter's eyes flash up to Travis' for a moment. I look between the two of them in question, but Hunter just looks back at me a moment later with a smile. "I don't think a few missed days will hurt."

"I'm good," I say, narrowing my eyes. *What was that?*

"Alright then," he says, slapping the counter top. "Let's get your grumpy ass off to school then." He hops away from the counter and over to grab his bag from by the door before heading outside.

"Wait!" I shout, and he halts but doesn't turn around. "Bag," I say, holding my hand out.

He let's out a sigh, letting his bag fall from his shoulder. He turns around, not meeting my eyes and hands me the bag.

I take it carefully and unzip the top. Out pops a little furry head. "Hunter," I sigh. "You can't keep bringing Princess Fiona to school."

"But why not," he pouts, giving me those big blue eyes. "She gets so lonely. I hate leaving my baby to be all sad by herself."

Taking Princess Fiona out, I let her crawl up my shoulder and around my neck, which makes me giggle. "I know. But maybe we should just get her a little friend or something. It's not safe. She could get out and someone could end up stepping on her, or taking her."

"I'd kill them if they tried," Hunter growls, murder flashing in his eyes.

I don't doubt that he would. "And that's why we need to keep her home. You kill someone, you gotta live with that for the rest of your life. So let's not make a murderer out of you at eighteen."

He snorts. "Fifteen."

"What?" I ask, brows furrowing.

"Nothing." He clears his throat. "You're right. Fine, we'll keep her home. But when we go get snacks, can we stop at the pet store?"

"You have money to just go out and buy another ferret?" I know he has a job, but the way he's been spending money I don't see how he has any left.

"Don't worry about me and my money." He rolls his eyes. "I'm good."

"Alright," I say, grabbing Princess Fiona and handing her to Travis. "Put her away, please. We need to get going before we're late."

"Come on, girl. Let's get you back to bed," Travis coos as he starts heading upstairs.

"Bye my sweet angel!" Hunter calls after her. "Daddy misses you already."

"Come on." I laugh. "She's gonna be fine. You're being over dramatic."

"She's my baby," he says as I push him out the front door. "You can never be too overprotective with your child."

"Oh, yeah? You gonna be like this when you have kids someday?" I ask as we slide into the front seats of his car.

He looks over at me with a deadly serious look. "If anyone so much as looks at my kids wrong, they will regret it."

A shiver takes over my entire body. *Why is that so damn hot?* Knowing he's going to be so protective of our children. Because they will be ours, he just doesn't know it yet.

The morning was tolerable pain-wise once the meds kicked in, but by the time lunch rolled around, I started to feel the cramps once more. Now I'm hangry, shooting daggers at everyone in the lunch line as I huff and puff at how long it's taking.

Finally, when it's my turn, I choose a chicken salad sandwich, and my eyes light up when I see there's one last piece of caramel vanilla cake. It's the kind with caramel drizzle and SKOR pieces on top. *My fucking favorite.*

Just as I'm about to put it on my tray, the person who was in front of me starts to back up, reaching for the cake.

My hand shoots out and grips the girl's hand hard. "Touch the cake, and I'll break your pretty manicured hands," I growl.

"Ouch, you crazy bitch," she snaps. Her eyes go wide when she looks up at me. "You can have it," she says, pulling her hand free before scrambling away with her food.

"Well, yeah, I can have it," I mutter to myself, smiling as I do a happy dance inside, placing the cake on the tray. "Wasn't really gonna give you much of an option."

Hunter texted saying he needed to stay a little longer after class to help his shop teacher. Knowing he will probably miss out on getting anything good, I grab one of the pieces of chocolate cake and ask for another sandwich.

Taking a seat at the table that's been deemed mine for years now, I rip open the plastic wrap off the sandwich and take a big bite. I moan when the flavor hits my tongue. God, I love food.

I'm about half way done when I hear a chair being pulled out from the table across from me. Looking up, I blink as I take in the girl who had the balls to sit at this table.

"Hello..." I say, putting my sandwich down.

"Hi." she says, flashing me a smile. "Hope you don't mind if I sit here. All the other tables are full except this one."

"There's a reason for that," I tell her, sitting back with a grin.

She looks at me worriedly. "Oh no. Is this saved for someone? I'm sorry, I can leave," she says, moving to get up.

"No, it's cool. You can sit here," I tell her, and she relaxes back into her chair.

"So... what's the reason this table is empty?"

"Because it's *my* table," I say cocking my head to the side.

"A whole table to yourself?" she asks, brows furrowing.

"Yup," I say with a shrug. "And Hunter. He'll be here any moment."

"I'm starting to think it wasn't a good idea to sit here," she says, but there's a smile on her lips. She looks around the room and so do I, finding everyone in the lunchroom, watching us like they are waiting for something to explode. "Are they okay?"

"No," I snort. "No one at this school is okay. But if you're wondering why they are looking at you like they're waiting for me to bite your head off, it's because there's a common rule that people leave me alone," I explain. "Hunter and his brothers are very protective, and well, no one has ever had the guts to go against them. Normally, I don't care because I've never wanted to be friends with anyone other than them."

"And now?" she asks with a hopeful grin. I love that she's not turning pale and high tailing it out of here.

"Tell me your name and your story, and I'll let you know after."

Turns out her name is Andrhea. She just turned eighteen, and she's from a slightly bigger town called West

Bridge, just three hours from here. She moved here after her dad lost his job and his friend managed to get him a spot at Black Ridge Auto.

The same shop that my best friend owns. So, if her dad is good enough in Link's eyes to work for him, then she's good enough for me. I like her already. She's not too shy, but not too in your face either. She's a sweet little thing with blonde hair, blue eyes, and her style seems to be a lot like mine. The thing that won me over though, was the fact that she's gay. I don't have to worry about wanting to tit punch her for looking at my guys. Although, if I was into girls, I'd probably be the one snatching her up. But I'm not. I mean, boobs are nice, but I only want dick. *Four dicks to be exact.*

Hunter appears at my side as he takes a seat next to me, halting my conversation with my new friend. "Sorry it took me so long. Mr. Reed wouldn't stop telling me about this nasty growth on his..." Hunter stops talking when he sees we're not alone. "Who's this?"

"This is Andrhea," I answer, waving my hand in her direction. "She's new. And I've deemed her my new friend, who's a girl. Because well, that was on my BINGO card for the new school year, among many other things, making a friend, who's a *girl*." I emphasize the girl part, making sure to get out as much information as I can before Hunter can argue with me. He doesn't like to share me with anyone but his brother and the twins.

"Riiiiight. I know you. You're Tommy's kid," he says. "Saw you come into the shop last week with your dad."

"That's right," she says slowly, looking from me to

Hunter. I narrow my eyes at the expression of confusion on her face. "So... you're the Raven I was told about?"

"Yes," Hunter says. "This is Raven, the girl my brother told your dad about who would be going to school with you." He gives her a hard look. *What the fuck is going on?*

"You two know each other?" I ask

"No," they say at the same time.

"Well, not really. Like I said, she was in the shop on her dad's first day of work. He introduced her to me, Link, and the guys."

"Should I be worried?" I ask him, narrowing my eyes at him as my jealousy seems to wanna come out and play.

His face turns into a bright smile. "Ah, Ray, I fucking love it when you're so possessive of me," he says, pulling me into his lap. He wraps his arms around me and gives me a dramatic kiss on the cheek. "Don't worry, Little Mouse," his voice is low, his breath tickling my neck and making my eyes flutter shut. "There's no other girl for me. Or the guys. Just you, only you."

"Don't worry," Andrhea says. "Remember, I like pussy."

That makes me laugh. I spend the rest of lunch sitting on Hunter's lap, forgetting all about the fact my uterus hates me.

That is until we get into Hunter's car after school. "I wish I was a man." I moan as I lean my head against the cool car door.

"I know, we're pretty fucking amazing, right?" Hunter chuckles as he pulls out of the parking lot.

"Yeah, must be amazing to always get an orgasm." I grin over at him. "Tug at it a few times and boom, cum city."

He looks over at me with a cocky as fuck grin. "Oh, trust me, Little Mouse. If it's going to involve my hands, mouth, or cock, everyone will be fully satisfied," he teases before looking back out at the road.

My body flushes with heat, and I can't help but notice he didn't mention whatever girl he would be with. Leaving it vague and the crazy bitch in me is going to take it as he was talking about me.

"How would you know? Have you had sex?" I ask. *He better fucking say no.*

"Nope," he says, popping the P. He doesn't say anything more, eyeing me out the corner of his eye. *Good. Better stay that way.*

"Alright. Pet store first, then we get all the good shit to make you feel better," Hunter states as we pull into the parking lot of the strip mall.

"Shouldn't it be the other way around? You can't bring a ferret into the grocery store."

"Fucking watch me." He chuckles, getting out of the car.

Smiling, I follow him. We head into the pet store and right to the back with all the caged animals.

"They're all so cute," I comment as I look at the hamsters, bunnies, and guinea pigs. "Oh my god, it's a chinchilla," I whisper.

"I want him," Hunter says as he takes one of the ferrets. I sigh, not bothering to tell him that he shouldn't be taking the animals out without an employee's permission. It's like talking to a wall.

"He's adorable," I say, reaching up to pet the little black ferret. "What are you going to call him?"

He gives me a look as if I'm crazy for not knowing already. "Shrek, of course," he deadpans. "Princess Fiona can't be with anyone else but Shrek."

"Of course." I giggle.

After we get Shrek paid for, Hunter tucks him around his neck where Shrek promptly falls asleep. Hunter, my crazy best friend. *You always do keep me on my toes and nothing surprises me anymore.*

We head over to the grocery store next. Hunter grabs a cart and takes off. *Can't take him anywhere.*

Sighing, I grab a basket and start working my way up and down the aisles. I only have forty bucks, so I gotta pick wisely. Junk food adds up fast.

I really need to get a job, but the idea of standing around a corner store for hours or being yelled at by customers at one of the fast food places makes me okay with being broke.

Only two more months left, then I'll be legal, and hopefully, I'll be making more money than I know what to do with.

I watch porn. I mean who doesn't? And one time an ad popped up looking for cam girls. It piqued my interest, so I clicked on it. Unfortunately, I had to be eighteen in order to sign up. They ask for your ID.

Halloween is my eighteenth birthday, and November first, I plan on starting. I love to pleasure myself, I love orgasms, so why not do it on cam and earn money for it? I'm proud of my body. I already bought the ski mask I plan on using to hide my face.

There's a good chance people in my school watch porn just like me, so there's no way I'm risking one of the asshole dudes at my school recognizing me.

Now, I just need a fun name to go by. I'll worry about it later.

There's a thrill at how pissed off the guys might get if they ever found out. I hope it involves lots of spankings.

"Well, aren't you a pretty little thing," someone says from behind me. I feel the stranger's presence at my back, way too fucking close for my liking. "What are you doing here all alone?"

Spinning around, I regret it immediately when he boxes me in, his foul breath wafting over my face. "I'm not alone," I scrunch up my nose in disgust. "My friend is here."

"I don't see anyone," he says. "I, however, would love to be your friend." He shifts to bring his hand up to my face.

"And I'd love to see how much you'll bleed if I stab you in the neck with my blade," Hunter says from behind the guy, placing his switchblade against the guy's neck.

The creep freezes up. "Woah there, boy. I was only joking around with the pretty lady."

Hunter moves back, allowing the guy to get a look at him. He goes deathly pale, pure terror in his eyes. "Run along now. Don't wanna be out after dark. You don't know what might be lurking in the shadows," Hunter threatens with a grin so wide it makes me shiver.

Hunter is what people around here call nuts, crazy, off his rocker. You never know what form of him you're going to get. I fucking love it. Like I said, he keeps me on my toes.

And right now, I'm so damn turned on.

"You okay?" Hunter asks after the creep takes off running.

"I'm good," I tell him. "I knew I wasn't in any danger."

"You did now, did you?" he asks with his brow raised.

"Duh, you're here. I'm never in danger with you or the guys around."

"Never, Little Mouse," he says with a growl. Then like a switch, he's grinning again. "Look what I got."

My eyes go wide when I see how full his cart is. There's five different flavors of ice cream, ten bags of chips, and god only knows how many bags of candy and chocolate bars are under all of that. "Hunter, I only have forty bucks. This is all too much."

"My treat." He shrugs. "You're the only one of us who's a fucking super human. Fucking bleeding for a week and not dying. The least I can do is fill you with all the sugary good-ness you can stomach."

My eyes tear up at how amazing he is.

"Thank you," I say.

"Now, let's go pay for this, and then we can stop in at McDicks. Get some nuggies in your belly." He winks before hopping on the edge of the cart and pushing himself like a little kid.

How can I not be in love with this man? Impossible.

We pay for everything and head to get take out. After

we get home and everything is put away, we head up into my room.

"Set everything up, I'll be right back," he says as I let out a little moan, my cramps are being a raging bitch again.

Turning the TV on, I set up Netflix and get under the blanket on the bed.

Hunter returns a few minutes later with some of the snacks and a bottle of pop for each of us. He dumps them on the bed. "Hold on," he says, rushing out and bringing in two tubs of ice cream, one for each of us with a spoon sticking up out of both of them.

A smile finds my face at how happy he looks right now. "Thank you," I say, taking the cold, creamy goodness from him.

"Almost forgot. Lay down," I give him an odd look, but lay back into the pillows. Hunter pulls something out of his hoodie pocket. "Hot water bottle, you know, for the cramps." He lifts up my shirt and places it over my lower belly.

Nope, not gonna cry. Fuck off, hormones. This isn't new. This is what he does almost every month. But damn it if he isn't perfect for me.

"Thank you," I manage to say.

He gets into bed and snuggles close to me. We pick a movie and eat our snacks.

Biting my lip, I smile at him. Even though I feel horrible, Hunter helps make everything better.

CHAPTER 4

RAVEN

"What are you doing?" I ask Hunter when he walks into the kitchen looking like he's on the verge of death.

"Going to drive you to school." He groans, then breaks out into a coughing fit.

"No, you're not. Taylor is going to take me," I say, pointing to the half asleep twin sitting at the kitchen table with a mug of coffee in his hand. "You're staying home. You're sick with the flu. And we don't need you infecting everyone at school."

"Who cares. We don't like them anyways," Hunter mutters, leaning against the fridge for support.

"Stubborn man," I mumble and let out a huff as I set my own coffee down. "Let's go, back to bed," I urge, grabbing his arm to lead him back towards his room.

"Stay home with me," he whines. "Take care of me."

"I can't." I laugh at how much of a baby he is when he's sick. "Your mom is off today. She said she will get anything you need."

"She's a good mom," he says.

"The best. Now, up you go," I tell him, pushing him in the direction of the stairs.

"Can you at least tuck me in," he asks with a pout.

Unable to hide my smile, I shake my head. "Come on, you big baby," I tease, swatting his ass while we head up the stairs .

"Careful, Little Mouse. Don't start something you can't finish," he weakly jokes.

My brows raise at his back. *Is that something he's into?* I mean I know the idea of him or one of the other guys doing it to me gets me hot, but I never thought of being the dominant type in the bedroom. I'm willing to try anything once.

"Go," I growl, pinching his ass and making him jump.

"You trying to kill me, woman?" he looks over his shoulder and glares at me. "I could have fallen."

"Get your ass up the fucking stairs, Hunter, and stop stalling. Make me late for school, and I'll push you down the damn things myself."

He gives me a wolfish grin. "Damn, Ray. If I didn't know better, I would think you really were a crazy bitch."

Oh, there's a lot you don't know about what goes on inside my head, Hunter. But you will... someday.

We make it to the top floor and into Hunter's room. I

love his room. He decked out the whole place with everything LED. Including his computer. Everything he owns is black. His walls, furniture, and bedding make his bright blue hair and nearly white eyes stand out.

"Get in," I instruct as I pull back the covers. "If you need anything, text your mom." He gets into bed, and the moment he's under the covers, his head hitting the pillow, he's practically out.

"Thank you, Ray," he mumbles. "I love you."

His words feel like they mean more than two friends caring about each other. "I love you too," I reply, kissing him on the forehead before leaving him.

Making a stop in my room, I change out of my PJ's and into some jeans and a cute top before heading back down to Taylor.

"You're wearing that?" Taylor asks, his eyes widening when he takes in my shirt.

"Yes..." I say, raising a brow. "What's wrong with what I've got on?"

"Raven, your boobs are practically falling out. You're going to have every pervert in your school staring at your tits like a horn-dog."

"So what?" I shrug. "Why should I have to worry about what I wear just because men can't keep it in their pants? They can look, but no one's touching." I grin, deciding to fuck with him and see how he reacts. "Not unless he's hot enough."

Taylor growls, a deadly look taking over his face. He's

fully awake now as he gets out of his chair, storming over to me. He backs me up against the wall, staring me down. "If anyone fucking lays a hand on you, dressed like this, I'll break his fucking fingers. Got it? You wear what you want, it's your body, but know this Raven, you're risking other people getting hurt if we find out anyone tries anything."

My heart pounds as my breathing comes in little pants. Licking my lips, Taylor's eyes drop down to follow the movement, his pupils dilating. "I think that's a risk I'm willing to take," I say, sounding way more breathy than I intended to.

His eyes snap up to mine. "Car, now," he demands, moving away from me. He grabs his keys and heads toward the front door.

The space between us has me missing him already. But it worked. I got a rise out of him just like I wanted. Silly boys think they can hide their feelings. They really do suck at it.

Smiling to myself, I grab my bag from the table and rush after him.

"How are you liking your last year of high school?" Taylor asks me as we drive to school.

"It's okay," I reply with a shrug. It's been two weeks since the first day of school, and life's been pretty much the same as it's always been.

That's not true, I've been hanging out with Andrhea pretty much everyday. But Hunter has been there too. And as much as I love being with Hunter, same with any of the other guys, I'd like to have some girl time and get to know Andrhea on my own. That's why a part of me is kind of relieved Hunter is staying home today.

"How's the new girl? You two are becoming friends right?"

"She's cool. Easy to talk to, likes the same things I do."

"She's not gonna be replacing us, is she?" he asks, shooting me a look.

"Awww, Tay, are you jelly?" I tease.

"No," he snorts.

"It's okay. No one can replace you guys. You're my ride or die." As in, if you even think of leaving me, I will ride over you with this Jeep and you will die.

"Good. She seems like a good kid, but I'm not afraid to go up against a girl to keep you," he warns with a playful grin. Hearing how he's willing to fight for me makes my heart flutter.

"Idiot," I say with a stupid grin.

We get to school and Taylor pulls up by the front door. "Thanks for the ride, see you after school," I tell him, moving to get out of the car.

"Where do you think you're going?" he says, grabbing my arm to pull me back into the car. He leans over and places a kiss to the side of my head. "Have a good day."

Swooning, I get out of the car, watching as he takes off. The twins always kiss me on the cheek, forehead, or temple any time one of us has to leave, or to say goodnight. You would think I'd be used to it by now, but every time they do it, I feel like a giddy school girl.

"So, are you dating them?" Andrhea asks, appearing at my side. "Because I've seen you with all of them these past few weeks and you guys don't look like just friends. Well, except the big scary one. I have no idea where you grew a set of balls to fuck with Link, but girl, I kind of admire you for it."

"Thanks." I snort. "Link loves me. He'd never hurt me." *Well, at least not in ways I wouldn't wholeheartedly enjoy.* "And we are just friends. For now." I grin.

"Oh no. That look can't mean anything good." Andrhea groans.

"You're learning, Andy," I respond, swinging my arm over her shoulder as we head into the school building. "And trust me, nothing that I have planned is a good idea. That's the whole point." I laugh.

"Any of these catching your eye?" Andrhea asks me as we look at the sign up sheets on the school bulletin board for activities and clubs.

"I have no idea," I say. "I've never really been involved with school things like this."

"Really? Like, not even choir?" she asks.

"Nope. Since the moment I moved here, the guys became my whole life."

"You've never had any other friends?" she questions,

looking surprised.

"Nope." I grin. "So, you should feel honored." I wink.

She laughs. "I am! The one and only Raven West allowed me into her friend circle. It makes me wanna brag to anyone who will listen."

We both laugh and continue to read over the lists again. "Well, the only things catching my eyes are Photography Club, Gaming Club, and Book Club."

"Yeah, everything else doesn't sound like something I wanna do. I'll join Photography Club with you. I'm not much of a gamer, so I'm out on that. I think I might take up cooking classes. Couldn't hurt to learn how to make good food." She laughs.

"What about Book Club?" I ask as I sign my name up on the proper sheets.

"Depends on what kind of books. It has to be romance of some kind, and not boring vanilla romance. It has to have some kind of spice. Or at least a good plot. I might be gay, but I don't mind reading about a girl getting railed by a harem of guys." She grins, wiggling her eyebrows.

"You mean my future?" I wink, making her burst out laughing.

"I don't even doubt it," she says, shaking her head.

Using the rest of lunch, we grab some food and head outside to eat under the trees. "You said that you met the guys a while ago. Have you always lived here?"

"No," I say, laying back on the grass. I know a lot about Andrhea, but we haven't talked much about me or my life. "I moved here when I was eight with my mom. Met the guys the first day and the rest is history."

"Is it true you live in a group home?" she asks.

I look over at her. "Women's shelter. It's where women and sometimes children go to get away from abusive situations. They stay until it's safe to get on their feet."

"And that's where you and the guys both live? Still?" If anyone else was asking these questions I would have told them to fuck off by now. But, if we're friends, I don't wanna lie to her.

"I don't know much about the guys and their families' pasts. It's not something I ever wanted to talk about and they never wanted to give that information up. And I'm fine with that. As for me? From what I was told, my dad was a bad man and my mom needed to get us away. She feared for our lives and did what she could do to save us. I've always wondered what he did and who he is. But I could tell that was always a sore subject for her, so I didn't want to ask. I don't remember much about him. He was never home. I know most kids can remember as early as four, but I honestly don't remember much before the guys." I shrug. And I don't care. My life with the guys has been amazing, I don't need to remember anything that might be filled with heartache and pain.

"I'm glad you have each other," she says. "I wish I had good friends like that."

"Family. We're family," I correct, rolling onto my belly to look at her. "And I'm not sure about the guys, they don't really make friends with people. But you have me," I grin.

"And Hunter doesn't seem to mind you all too much." I wink.

"He's not too bad. But he is one odd ball." She laughs.

"The oddest." I agree. "One of the many reasons I love him."

We finish up eating before packing up and heading back into the school. Today is Friday, thank god, but that also means I have gym right before going home. I don't get why they still force you to take this class. It's not like we're going to need this in the real world. If I wanted to skip anything, it would be gym.

Grabbing our gym clothes from our lockers, we head into the locker room.

"Did you see how she was with Taylor this morning?" Rebecca Smalls whines. "I totally knew she was fucking one of them."

"You mean all of them. They live together like some fucked up cult. There's no way they're not slipping into her room and taking turns fucking her," Jenny Franco counters.

Fuck me, I wish. Add that to my dream kink list.

"Sorry to burst your bubble, ladies, no one is getting fucked in that house. Well, maybe a hand or two," I interrupt as I walk around the corner to see them all half naked.

"Get out!" Daisy Thomson says to Andrhea. "This isn't a free peep show."

"Oh no, it's the lesbian. She's totally going to look at our bodies and commit it to memory to flick the bean to later," Andrhea says mockingly, and I snort out a laugh. "Sorry girls, I'd rather think of two old wrinkly people fucking than have any of you on the mind while I finger fuck my pussy. Thanks."

They all look horrified, and I can't hold in my laughter anymore. "Look, I know you all think you did something there, but get the fuck over yourselves. I get it, you're jealous that I can get four guys, and you can't keep yours from fucking your best friend over there." I tell Daisy who gapes, swinging her head over to Jenny. "Oh yeah. Saw her and Matt going at it behind the school last week. You both might wanna get checked out because I saw him raw dogging it with Becky too."

"Liar!" Becky shouts.

"Nah, I wish I was. Sadly this school has more fucking going on than a porn site. And not at all as good." Everyone's getting fucked but me. Fucking boys better get their heads out of their asses, and the sooner the better. I've got needs only they can take care of.

"Girls!" the coach shouts from the door. "Get your asses out here now, or I'm marking you absent."

They all get up and start heading out, sending glares over their shoulders at us.

"Man, they sure have gotten ballsy this year," I mutter, taking my clothes off and putting them in the locker before putting on my gym clothes.

"Have they always been like this?" Andrhea asks.

"Sadly. My guys are some of the most feared but wanted guys around here. Black Ridge isn't exactly full of top grade beef, if you know what I mean. And I've had all the best cuts of steak to myself for the past ten years."

"Why do you have to use food metaphors? Now I'm hungry," she whines, making me laugh.

We get out into the gym and both groan at the same time. "Hell no!" I shout to the coach. "No fucking way."

"Miss West, watch your tone. Your little bodyguard isn't here to save you today," the coach says with a grin.

"Ball hockey is bullshit and you know it. All they do is aim for the fucking face!"

"Then learn to block better," he smirks.

"Fucking dick head," I mutter, flipping him off when he turns around to walk away.

"Coach, Raven stuck up her middle finger at you," Jenny tattles, giving me a cocky smirk.

"Hey, Jenny, want some cheese? I heard rats love that shit," I sneer. "Fucking nark."

"Enough! Split up into two teams and start the damn game!"

We split up, and I end up on the opposite side as Andrhea, but I don't mind because my goal is getting the hard plastic ball into these bitches' faces. Two can play at this game.

With my stick in hand, I go out of my way to make sure I get as many shots as I can, not even bothering to try getting it in the net when I do.

"Ouch!" Becky shouts. "My nose."

"Hope it's not broken!" I call out with a massive grin as she runs off the court with a bloody nose. One down, two to go.

I duck and dodge their hits, making them pissed off and

frustrated. My team does manage to get a few goals before I get the ball again. Giving it all my strength, I slap the ball. It goes sailing through the air, and I watch as it misses Jenny. She gives me a smirk like she's won, but I grin in shock as the ball bounces off the net, hitting Jenny hard in the back of the head. She's taken by surprise, causing her to trip over her own feet. She goes down hard, smashing her chin on the ground. For a small moment, I almost feel bad. Almost. Karma's a bitch and so is Jenny.

She starts to cry as the coach helps her off the ground. "I'm taking Miss Franco to the nurse. No more foul play while I'm gone, or so help me," he glares at me, and I grin.

When he leaves, the game starts back up. Daisy gets the ball, managing to get it pretty close to our net. I try to get in the way to intercept her, but she's got an opening.

That is until Andrhea takes the ball from her and slaps it back over to the other net.

"What the fuck!" Daisy shouts. "We're on the same team!"

"Yeah, well, I don't like you. So, let me know when you find the fuck I should give." Andrhea shrugs.

"I'm done," I announce, tossing my stick in the pile. "Coach can suck it."

"Same," Andrhea agrees. "Wanna skip the rest of class and go get some ice cream at the store across the street before the twins come and get you?"

"Fuck yeah." I laugh.

Who knew I could have such a fun day without Hunter.

Not something I plan on getting used to, but it's definitely needed every once in a while.

This year is about trying new things, and I'm kind of excited.

I can't wait to tell the guys about gym. Best day in a hell of a long time.

CHAPTER 5

RAVEN

"**Y**ou're home!" Hunter says from his place on the couch when I walk into the house.

"I am." I laugh, looking at his mom. "He on the good stuff?"

"Yup." She grins. "He was complaining about a headache so I gave him something for it. Worked a little too well I guess." She giggles.

"Ray. Ray-man. Little Mouse," Hunter rattles off, sounding out of it. "You're my favorite person."

"And you're one of mine," I respond with amusement. Drugged out Hunter is fun. I wonder what drunk Hunter is like. It's crazy that in all these years, I haven't seen any of them drink. I don't drink, never have, but that's something I plan on changing this year. It's on my bucket list. Get shit faced and experience what a hangover feels like. One might think that's a stupid goal, but hey, life's short and I wanna do it all if I can.

"Riiiight. You love the others too. It's okay, I can share," he says, giving me a wink that makes me snort a giggle at how silly he looks.

"Hunter. You okay there, buddy?" Travis says, him and Taylor appearing at my sides.

"I'm fucking amazing. How can I not be amazing? My girl is back." Hunter looks at me and his face goes serious. "We've been bad, bad boys."

"What?" I ask, still grinning as I raise a brow.

"He's being stupid," Taylor says. "Aren't you, Hunter?"

"No! We've been keeping something from you. Something big," Hunter admits, then groans. "I don't feel so good."

"Get some sleep, man," Travis says. "Come on, Ray, let's go out to eat tonight. Less time in this germ infested house the better."

"Wait, I wanna hear what he has to say," I complain.

"He's out of it, he doesn't even know what he's saying," Taylor retorts as he wraps his arm around my shoulder, guiding me back toward the door.

"Hey! Someone call the police! He's kidnapping my woman!" Hunter shouts.

"Shut the fuck up, man. We're just taking her to get food," Travis hisses.

"Oh. Can you grab me a pizza? Maybe some chicken wings too," Hunter mumbles.

"Yeah, whatever you want man," Travis says.

"What was all that about?" I ask when we get into the car. "You guys aren't keeping something from me now, are you?"

"Ray, that was the ramblings of a sick man. Before we came to get you, he was going on about little rats making homes in his sneakers."

"Fuck." I laugh. "We should all get high together. Sounds like it would be a good time."

"You want weed, Foxy Girl?" Taylor asks, grinning at me over his shoulder. "I can hook you up."

"Tay..." Travis says in a warning tone. "Link would kill us if we got her high."

"Link isn't my dad," I snark back. "He can't tell me what to do." He might not be my dad, but fuck me if I don't want him to be my *Daddy*. Link oozes Daddy vibes, and it's fucking hot.

Travis snorts. "Whatever helps you sleep at night, Dove."

I stick my tongue out at him, earning a chuckle from both of them.

"Where are you taking me anyway?" I ask as we reach the downtown area. "Better not be Bobby's Burgers. I almost got food poisoning last time we went there," I grimace.

"No." Taylor shudders. "I remember that. God, it's like war flashbacks. I thought my gut was going to explode."

"I think they shut down, last I heard," Travis comments, giving Taylor a look.

"Wherever you're taking me, it better be good," I say. "I'm starving."

"Thought you would be full from all the ice cream you and your little friend got. You know, when you skipped school," Travis chides.

"You're kidding me right?" I snort. "As if you guys should be saying anything about skipping. You guys skipped more school days than you attended."

"She has a point." Taylor grins.

"But she's better than us," Travis counters.

"And now *he* has a point." Taylor shrugs.

"It was gym, it's not going to effect my overall grade. It's not a big deal. I'll still get into college," I confirm as we pull up in front of Annie's, one of the best home cooking restaurants.

"You still wanting to go? It's a shitty school. Not worth the time," Travis says.

"I could always apply outside of state." I shrug. They both look at each other and burst out laughing. "What the fuck is so funny?" I ask, annoyed.

"You're so fucking cute thinking you can move away from us. Not happening, Foxy Girl," Taylor states before getting out of the car, Travis following after him.

I sit for a moment, blinking while watching them out the front window. A slow smile creeps across my face. Most girls would be pissed at some man trying to control her by telling her what she can do or can't do. Not me. Knowing that they get all possessive over the idea of me leaving fills me with excitement. I fucking love it.

Getting out of the car, I follow after them with a little pep in my step. Annie's just opened over the summer, and

I've only been here a few times, but I'm already addicted to their food. Rachel and Lisa both work here so they're always bringing home something delicious.

"Go grab a table, and we'll go order. Mom's working so I'm gonna ask her to put a rush on ours," Taylor says.

"Travis!" Patty, an older woman who works here, calls out.

"Hey, Patty." Travis says, giving her a wave. "I'm gonna go say hi. Be right back." He gives me a kiss on the temple before heading over to Patty.

As I look around to see where I want to sit, my eyes catch on a table of girls. "Lovely," I sneer as some glare at me while others look behind me in the direction of the twins.

We could sit at a table away from them, allowing them to stare at us like a bunch of weirdos. But... I choose the table right behind them. If they're going to talk about me, I'd like to at least hear what they're saying.

Slowly, I walk toward them, making it look like I'm going to confront them. A few of them shift in their seats uncomfortably, while some others' eyes widen.

Just as I reach their table, I take a few steps forward to the table behind them.

And, of course, I don't sit with my back to them, how can I meet their eyes with an amused grin if I can't see them?

That's exactly what happens when a few of them look my way. They don't talk to me, but I do hear them whispering.

"Where are you going?" one whisper shouts as a blonde

girl gets up. She doesn't say anything, but smirks at me before walking over toward Travis. I sit and watch as Patty goes into the back.

The blonde girl goes up to Travis and starts talking to him. He stops and listens, nodding his head before a smile breaks out across his face. Blondie bats her eyelashes as she reaches up to run her hand up and down the muscles of his arms, coming back up to trace his tattoos with one finger.

A growl rumbles in my chest, and it's taking everything in me to not go over there and tell the bitch to fuck off for touching *my* fucking man.

Travis plays with the scruff of his beard as he listens. When she's done, he lets out a little chuckle, running his hand through his shaggy black hair.

I'm halfway out of my seat when he leans over to whisper something in her ear, but then her face turns annoyed, followed by pissed. So I sit back down. She walks back over to her table, that smug persona gone. She casts me a nasty look before sitting back down.

"Whore," she mutters, and I know it's directed to me. *What the heck did Travis say?*

A moment later, Travis is walking over to our table with drinks in his hand. "Miss me?" Travis teases as he places the drinks down before sliding in next to me.

"Only a little," I smile with a playful wink. Leaning in, I whisper, "What did she want?"

"She pretty much asked if I wanted to go into the bathroom so she can suck me off," he snorts.

"What the fuck?" I say. "Oh, that's so sad." I sigh shaking my head.

"Yeah, I told her no thanks. That my girlfriend does it better."

That has me going stiff. *Keep your cool, Raven. Murder in a public place is a bad idea.* "You have a girlfriend?" I ask, trying not to sound bothered by it.

"No," he says. "But I told her you were."

My eyes go wide. *Good boy with the no girlfriend.* I'd hate to start the year off with charges on my hands. "That would explain the nasty look she gave me. She really looked like she wanted to claw my eyes out." Then it hits me. "Wait... you told her I was your girlfriend?"

"Yeah, why?" he asks. "You don't wanna be my fake girlfriend, Dove? I'm hurt." He glares playfully at me. *No, not your* fake *girlfriend anyway.*

"Didn't say that. I'm surprised that's all. This is a small town and people talk."

"So," he shrugs. "Let them talk. But that's not the only thing I said." He grins.

"And the other thing would be...?" I ask, taking a sip of my soda

"I told her Taylor was dating you too." He drops that bomb while trying to hold back laughter.

I choke on a mouthful of my drink. "You did not!" I screech coughing a few times.

He pats my back and shrugs again, looking proud of himself.

"What did he not do?" Taylor asks, appearing at the side

of our table with food. I didn't even look over a menu. But everything he brought looks amazing.

Taylor leans down to listen to what his brother has to say. When he straightens up, he's beaming ear to ear. "Oh, I like this."

He takes a seat next to me, and the girls choose that moment to turn around to gawk at us.

"Tay," I say in a fake breathy tone. "I loved that thing you did with your tongue last night." The girls eyes widen. "I think it would be even better while my mouth is busy with Travis, if you know what I mean."

"That can be arranged, baby," Taylor agrees, cupping my cheek. "Anything for our girl," Travis says, gripping my chin and bringing my face to look at him.

The girls let out annoyed sounds as they all get up from the table.

Travis's mouth is close enough to mine to kiss me, making my heart pound while my eyes flick between his. He looks like he wants to, like it's taking all his restraint not to. But he doesn't, pulling back, he chuckles. "That was fun."

"Yeah," I reply, sitting back in my seat properly and shoving an onion ring into my mouth. *So fucking close, damn it!* I wish he would just get over himself and do it. All of them are stupid idiots. But they're my stupid idiots.

"I'm bored." Andy sighs, rolling over on the bed to look at me, "Wanna go do something?"

"Like what?" I ask. Normally, the guys and I just hang out at home on the weekends, watch movies, play video games. But the twins and Hunter have been taking on more shifts at the shop, leaving me to entertain myself.

Hunter is still feeling like shit, sleeping most of his day away, so I asked Andrhea to hang out. Only thing is, I've never hung out with a girl before, so I have no clue what to do.

"Wanna go shopping?" she asks, wiggling her eyebrows. "I can drive us into River Valley, and we can hit up some strip malls."

"I don't know," I say. "I mean, yeah, we could go, but I don't really have money to be shopping."

"Can't you ask your mom?"

"I can, but she already does so much. She gives me money for lunch everyday and that adds up," I tell her shyly, picking at the blanket.

"Let's just go, get out of the house. We can blast music and just look around. Maybe you'll find something you could come back for," she suggests.

"Yeah," I smile, the idea sounding fun. "Let's go."

Tossing my hair up in a messy bun, I slip on one of Hunter's sweaters that I stole and a pair of jeans, matching it with some black and white Vans; a gift from Taylor last Christmas.

"Where are you two going?" Travis asks as he walks into the front door, looking behind him, where I can see Link outside on his bike talking to Taylor. I haven't seen much of him since the bike ride incident. He came over that Sunday for supper like his mom asked, but he was quiet and still wouldn't meet my eyes. I don't like how he's been treating me, and it makes me wanna do shit just to piss him off.

"Andy and I are gonna go for a ride to River Valley. We're gonna go to the mall and window shop."

Travis looks at Andy, then me. "I don't know if that's such a good idea."

"Why?" I ask, brows furrowing. "We always go to River Valley."

"Do you have any money?" he asks.

"No," I snap.

He narrows his eyes at me, his stubbled jaw ticking. He reaches into his pocket and pulls out two one hundred dollar bills. "Here."

"What? No." I protest, shaking my head. "I can't take that kind of money."

"Take it, Ray. You're not going almost an hour away with no fucking money," he growls. Damn it, a shiver runs over my arms and down my back.

"Fine," I concede, snatching the money from his hand.

"Good girl." He grins, proud of himself. My body heats at the praise. I love that I made him proud. I hate taking his money, but if he's happy to give it to me, I'm not gonna fight it. I just can't wait until I have my own money.

He steps into me, wrapping his arms around me. I sigh, hugging him back. "Have fun, Dove. Be a good girl and don't do anything that will set Link off, please."

"Can't promise anything," I murmur into his chest.

He sighs. "One of these days he's gonna reach his breaking point."

"He won't hurt me," I assure him, knowing that for a fact.

"No. But this is Link we're talking about. Anyone else acts the way you do with him, and they'd be d- in big fucking trouble."

"I'm just that awesome." I laugh.

"No lies there," he chuckles. He kisses me on the top of the head and lets me go. "Have fun."

"I will now," I say, waving the money and wiggling my eyebrows.

"Get." He laughs before taking off up the stairs.

"Ready?" Andy asks me.

Patting my pocket, I find my phone. "Yup."

"Don't you need a purse or something?" she asks, looking at the money in my hand.

"Don't have one." I shrug. I never really carry anything other than my phone, and I have pockets for that.

"We're going to change that today. I'll help you pick one out."

Heading down the front steps, I can feel Link's eyes on me.

"Where are you going, Little Bird?" Link's gruff voice asks.

"Going shopping," I reply, not bothering to look at him.

"And who said you could do that?" He questions. That has me pausing and turning around.

"I fucking did," I sass back. "Because I'm my own person and can make my own choices."

He snorts, a cruel smile taking over his lips as he shakes his head. "How fucking wrong you are," he says cryptically.

"What was that?" I ask, putting my hands on my hips.

"You're not leaving without one of us. Taylor can go with you if you want to go."

"No," I object. "I'm going with Andy. She can drive. She's my friend, and we wanna go shopping."

"Ray, I don't mind Taylor coming with us," Andy relents from behind me.

"No, it's okay," I tell her, looking at her over my shoulder. "We're having girl time."

"Raven," Link growls.

"Link," I say back, raising my brow.

"One of these fucking days," he hisses to himself as he runs a hand over his face. "You piss me off, little girl."

"I'm not a little girl. I'm going to be eighteen in a month. So fuck you. You're not my dad, not my keeper. You haven't even talked to me in two fucking weeks. So don't be coming around here and thinking you can tell me what to do."

The look he gives me would kill anyone else. He's

pissed, jaw ticking, but I don't care right now. I'm still pissed at him.

"Anything happens to her, I'm blaming you Andrhea," he says pointing at her.

"Don't threaten my friends." I glare at him.

"Ray. I think you need to calm down," Taylor says, looking at me with concern.

Link storms over to me, crowding me until I'm pinned against the car. "Listen here, you little brat," he sneers down at me. "Don't push me. Just fucking don't. You mean the world to me. That's the only reason why I haven't strapped you down and punished you for that mouth of yours. Disrespect me again, Ray, and I'm gonna have to show you who's in charge."

He's so close I can feel his warm breath on my lips. My heart is going a mile a minute, and I feel light headed and dizzy.

With a low growl in his chest, he pushes away from me, turning around and going back to his bike. He doesn't look back as he starts it, peeling off down the road.

"Foxy Girl," Taylor says in warning. "You need to stop."

"Why?" I ask. "He's been an ass to me the past few weeks by ignoring me."

"He's had his reasons, trust me. He's not mad at you. Just stop testing him. It won't end well for anyone. It's one thing when no one else is around, but you know he hates it when you two have an audience."

"Fine," I huff. "I'll try," I mutter as Taylor comes over.

"Thank you, Foxy. Now, go. Have fun, and be good."

"You sound just like your brother." I roll my eyes.

"You love it." He chuckles.

"Maybe." I shrug.

Taylor kisses my cheek before heading inside. We get into the car and just sit there for a moment in silence.

"So..." Andy starts after a few minutes. "How wet are your panties right now?"

We both look at each other and burst out laughing.

"I knew there was a reason I liked you," I say, turning on the radio.

"I have a ton of things you're gonna like, just wait."

"Try this on," Andy demands, holding up a really cute brown top.

"Oh, I like that!" I say, taking it from her, adding it to the pile of things. I'm not going to get all of them, but the fun part is trying them on.

"Ok, I think I got enough, what about you?" she asks.

"Yeah, I think I'm good too," I agree, holding up everything with a laugh.

"I'd say." She laughs back. "Just make sure to show me everything after you try them on!"

We each pick a changing room, and I lock mine behind me, placing my things on the little bench. One after the next, we try on different shirts and pants, coming out to show each other.

Some fit amazingly, and we compliment each other, others make us burst out laughing because they just aren't our style or don't fit quite right.

I save the cute brown top for last, pairing it with some jeans that I've already decided to buy because they make my ass look fabulous.

My brows shoot up as I adjust the top to put into place properly. "Holy shit," I breathe as I check myself out in the mirror. I fucking love this top. It's a long sleeve crop top that shaped my breasts perfectly, with a little hole in the middle that shows off some extra cleavage. It's just revealing enough, and it makes me feel sexy.

"What? You okay?" Andrhea asks from the other side of the door.

With a smile on my face, I open the door to show her. "What do you think?"

"Holy shit!" she repeats my statement with a smile. "Damn, babe, you look fucking hot! I don't know how these boys managed to keep their hands off you this long." She eyes me up hungrily. "You sure you don't swing my way? Even just a little?" she asks, wiggling her eyebrows.

"Sorry," I laugh. "Sadly, I don't. But if I did, you would be at the top of my list."

"I'll take it," she says with a giggle. "But you need to get that outfit."

When we're done changing back into our clothes, we pay for the stuff we want before heading to the food court to grab some iced coffees.

"There's a sale going on at the new lingerie store. I wanna stop there before we go home," Andrhea tells me.

"Okay."

With our bags on our arms and coffees in hand we go check out the store.

"Wow," I say, looking at all the mannequins. "They all look hot."

"Right?! I wish I had someone to wear all of those for. Sadly, I need bras and panties for only me to see." She sighs dramatically, making me laugh. "But you should grab something. You live with Hunter and the twins right? Put something on and walk around, accidentally bump into them." She grins wickedly.

"If I didn't know any better, I'd say you're becoming a bad influence. I love it." I laugh.

"I'm a genius, I know." She winks.

We break apart to browse around. I do end up grabbing a few really cute pairs of bra and undie sets because, come to think of it, mine are all from Walmart and aren't the best when it comes to support. I have a bit of the money left and with the sale, I could get a few more things.

Just as I'm about to go pay, I stop next to one of the mannequins. The lingerie it displays is gorgeous, black lace with stunning patterns. The cups are padded, and I know they would push the girls up nice and high. And the back would show off my ass in such a sexy way.

"Fuck it," I say, grabbing one in my size before stepping up to the counter.

"Yes, girl!" Andrhea cheers as the worker puts everything into a bag nicely. "You could even wear that as a bodysuit with some jeans."

"Yeah like the guys would let me do that." I laugh. "Hunter would toss me back in my room and make me change while Travis and Taylor stood outside the door to make sure. I don't even wanna think about what Link would do."

The girl at the cash register goes pale as she hands me the bag. "You okay?" I ask, brows furrowing.

"Y-yeah. I'm fine. Have a good day."

"You too," I say, giving Andrhea a look. She shrugs, hooking her arm with mine.

We leave, heading back to Andrhea's car. As soon as we get in, my phone dings. I look at my text messages and see it's from Link.

"What's up?" Andrhea asks.

"It's Link. He wants you to bring me over to the shop. I guess I'm staying at his place until Hunter gets better because he doesn't want me to catch what he's got. He says Taylor went home from work with a stomach bug. Do you mind?"

"No, that's okay. I had to go there anyway to pick up my dad. He's getting the guys to do some work on his car."

"Thanks," I tell her. The idea of staying at Link's place, just the two of us, gets me excited. I might be annoyed with him, but I still miss him. Some might think because of the way he talks to me that he's an asshole, but they have no clue how hot it gets me.

Once he mans the fuck up, I'll happily stop pushing his buttons and do whatever he tells me. Until then, I'm gonna have my fun.

CHAPTER 6

RAVEN

Something Andy said earlier gave me an idea. Now, I'm not about to walk into the auto shop in my lingerie. But that top I bought would definitely get a reaction out of Link.

Just as we round the side of the mountain, the shop comes into view.

"Can you pull over for a moment?" I ask.

"Sure," she says, pulling onto the side of the road. "Why?" she asks, putting the car in park before looking at me. I climb over into the back seat and grab my bag, digging through it until I find the shirt.

"Because," I start, holding it up with a grin, "I feel like wearing this."

"Girl," Andy laughs. "You're just asking for that man to tan your ass red."

"God, I wish," I huff, taking the tag off. "Also, sorry about this."

"About what?" she asks, turning around in her seat to look back at me just as I take my top off and give her a face full of boobs. She stares at them, blinking in shock. "Never be sorry if this is what you're offering," she comments under her breath.

Laughing, I put my new shirt on, and Andrhea pouts, turning back around in her seat. After I'm done, I crawl back into the front, practically shoving my ass in her face.

"Damn girl, first the titties, now that sweet ass. What did I do to deserve such a wonderful sight?" she jokes.

"Just drive," I grin, shaking my head as I put my seatbelt back on.

We pull up into the parking lot of the shop and park. I go to get out of the car but Andrhea stops me. "Hey, I got you this," she tells me, reaching over to grab one of the bags from the back and hands it to me.

"You didn't have to get me anything," I say, looking at her with surprise.

She shrugs. "I saw it, and... and thought you would like it."

Hesitantly, I open the bag to find a black purse. It's not too big, just small enough to fit some cards, money, and my phone. "Thank you. It's perfect."

"You're welcome. Now, I can stop worrying about your phone falling out of your ass pocket and breaking," she grins.

Rolling my eyes, I smile and get out of the car, leaving the bags for later. We head into the front of the shop, the bell ringing as we enter. "Hey," Andrhea says to some guy at the counter.

"Andy!" He grins. I've only been here a few times, and none of those times do I remember seeing him. He looks at me, his eyes lighting up as he takes in my outfit. I wanted to get someone's attention but it wasn't his. The side of my lip lifts slightly in a sneer as he licks his lips and grins wider. "Who's your friend? Hey, mama, name's Tony. But you can call me daddy if you want to."

"Tony," Andrhea says in a slow and serious tone, "This is Raven."

The moment she says my name, Tony's grin drops into a look of panic as his eyes shoot over to Andrhea's. She nods, and he turns white as a ghost. "Look, I'm sorry," he says, standing up, giving me pleading hands. "I was only joking. Fuck, I was only joking. Please, don't tell Link, I'll do anything."

I should be wondering why he's so worried about what Link would do to him for hitting on me but I'm not. Would Link beat him up? Threaten him? Maybe worse? From the way Tony is acting, it's like he's ready to get down on his knees and beg me to keep my mouth shut, maybe it's a possibility. And the thought of Link killing someone for hitting on me or looking at me the wrong way turns me on.

But he would never... right?

"Relax," I say. "As long as you never look at me like that again, nothing happens."

His eyes drop and he quickly mutters, "Thank you."

This man looked like he could make a grown man piss

himself, and here he is looking like he's the one who pissed his pants. He must really be afraid of Link.

"Where is everyone?" Andrhea asks.

"Garage," he answers.

"Thanks." Andrhea looks at me. "Wanna meet my dad?"

"Sure," I reply.

Andrhea leads the way, like she knows her way around the place. A part of me gets jealous that she's clearly here enough to know where everything is. Yet Link won't let me come around, and if I do, he mostly makes me wait outside.

"Hey, Dad!" Andrhea yells as we walk into the garage.

"Hey, Andy," an older man responds, pulling his head out of the front of a car. He's in coveralls stained with grease and oil. "And this must be Raven. It's a pleasure to meet you," he says, giving me a warm smile, but he won't keep eye contact for long.

Andrhea starts to talk to her dad, and I use the chance to wander away while they're distracted. My eyes take in the garage, the few cars in here, the massive amount of tools, and the smell that reminds me of the twins when they get home from work. A part of me is going to miss them. I know it's stupid, I just saw them a few hours ago, but hanging out with Andy took the time away that I would normally spend hanging out with them.

Other voices catch my attention, causing me to look toward a door at the very back. Looking over my shoulder, I don't see anyone watching me. Maybe today is the day I'll find out what's really in the warehouse because it can't be just cars.

"I don't give a fuck!" the shouting voice spits, and I recognize it as being my man. "If he doesn't talk, we make him talk."

"And what exactly do you want him to say?" I ask as I step into the room. We're not in the warehouse but a room in the back of the shop. I've never been in here before, so it's a start. I have no idea what they're talking about, but I play along. The room full of guys turns to look at me.

But they're not the eyes I want on me. Link slowly turns an annoyed glare on me that turns downright murderous.

"What the fuck, Raven?" he growls.

"What's wrong?" I ask, giving him a smirk as I put my hands on my hips.

The other guys start whispering to each other, casting me hungry glaces. But they're quick to regret it when Link pulls a fucking gun out and points it at them.

"Next person to look at Little Bird dies," he snarls.

My brows shoot up as my body fills with heat. *Shit, I wanted a reaction out of him, but I didn't think I'd be getting this.*

Everyone looks away, some even ducking their heads like they can hide.

Link looks at me again, this time his eyes slowly looking me over. I see the hunger in his eyes, and I feel pretty fucking proud of myself right now. "You really do love to test my fucking patience, Little Bird."

"Wouldn't you need some for me to be able to test?" I taunt, keeping my face blank as I try not to laugh at the vein near his temple throbbing. I want nothing more than to bend to his every will, but not until he tells me the truth when it comes to how he feels about me. He just needs to tell me he wants me, loves me, and I'm all his.

But he won't.

He turns back to his men, clearly dismissing me. "We're done here for now. We'll deal with the issue later," he announces as he puts his gun away. He turns around and before I know it, I'm tossed over his shoulder.

"What the fuck!" I shout as he carries me through the door I just came through.

"Quiet!" he barks, his hand coming down hard on my ass. The slap makes a cracking sound that echoes through the room.

I can't help the small moan that slips between my lips. I guess I love being spanked. *Learn something new about yourself everyday.*

Link growls, storming through the garage.

"Raven?" Andy asks.

"Say goodbye to your friend, Little Bird," Link states.

Raising my head and hand, I wave at her with a massive smirk on my face, giving her a wink. "Bye!"

Andy and her dad both try not to laugh as they shake their heads.

"Wait!" I object as Link tosses me into the front seat of his car. "My bags are in Andy's car." I look up at him, fluttering my eyelashes at him like I wasn't just set on getting him going.

He glares at me before slamming the car door. Turning around, he strides over to Andy's car, rips open her back seat door and grabs my stuff, before slamming it and coming back.

He gets into the driver's side and shoves the bags into my lap.

"Are you mad at me?" I ask, wondering if I went too far.

He closes his eyes, jaw ticking as he breathes through his nose. "Don't fuck with me around my men, Little Bird. You're the only person in this world who doesn't get punished for the way you talk to me. Just don't do it around my men."

He looks over at me, his eyes softening. "Sorry," I offer.

He lets out a breath as he starts up the car. "You're with me tonight. We can order in, watch a movie or some shit. Not sure what's up with Taylor, but with Hunter sick, I don't want to risk you getting sick too."

Link might be a scary fucker to everyone else, but he's always had a soft spot for me. He cares in his own way, like right now.

We drive the rest of the way in silence as we head toward his house. I smile when it comes into view. When Link said he was moving out and buying a place, I asked him if I could help him pick a house. He allowed me to look at some listings, and I found this place.

It's a five bedroom, three bath house with a big back-yard. And a wrap-around porch. It's not at all what Link would have gone for, but when I told him it was the house of my dreams, he didn't bother looking at it, choosing to go with it based on my want alone. It meant a lot to me. I love coming over here, I spent half of this past summer in the back under the big willow tree, sitting in a lawn chair reading.

We pull into the long driveway. As I gather my things to exit the car, Link is already at my door, opening it for me. "Why thank you, kind gentleman," I say in a bad southern accent.

Link grins, shaking his head "Trust me, Little Bird, I'm anything but a gentleman."

That's what I'm counting on, big guy.

We get inside the house, and Link takes off, leaving me in the living room. He doesn't tell me what he's doing or to make myself comfortable because he knows I'm going to do it anyway.

Wanting to put my bags somewhere, I head upstairs towards the room I use when I'm over here. Opening the door, I let out a little gasp when I take in the room. It's not the same as it was this summer. Before it just had the basics, nothing fancy, but now? It's my dream room. I'm not even kidding, it has everything I ever mentioned I wanted for my room. Floor to ceiling bookshelves, fully stocked with every book by every single one of my favorite indie authors. I step inside, going over to the books as happy tears fill my eyes, and I run my fingers over the spines. I can't believe he did this, for me.

Taking in the rest of the room, I see a king size bed with a galaxy bed set, a pink fuzzy mat, and a cute as hell reading chair in the other corner of the room. There's a desk with a whole computer set up, dressers with tons of knick-knacks on top of them, and a TV mounted to the wall.

Tossing the bags on the bed, I take a seat on the edge of it. I'm about to lay back and relax for a moment when Link yells out. "Raven!"

Getting up, I go over to the door, open it and shout back. "Yeah?"

"What do you want, Chinese or pizza?"

Damn, both sound good, but sadly the only good Chinese food place shut down a few months back. A new one took its place but it's not the same.

"Pizza, e-" I start to tell him my order but he cuts me off.

"Extra cheese and mushrooms with a side of honey garlic chicken wings. I already know, Little Bird."

Grinning like a fool, I giggle. "Thanks! Be down in a minute." Ducking back into the room, I look at my bag. This top and jeans aren't meant to be relaxing and comfy. So, if we're going to sit and watch a movie, I wanna be comfortable.

Checking the dresser and closet, I see there's no clothes. Good, that means my idea is doable. Stripping out of my shirt and pants, I grab the bag and dump it on the bed.

Looking at my new bras and panties, I pick a cute black lace set. I grimace when I look down at what I'm wearing now. The pink bra has a few pulled strings and the straps are loose even though they are adjusted to be the tightest they can go. I'm gonna have to thank Travis again for the money. I never knew how much I needed new undergarments until now.

"Eww," I groan when I take in the fact that I'm also wearing baby blue panties, which are not cute at all. Taking them off, I toss them into the trash bin by my bed and put the new set on.

Spinning around, I take a look at myself in the mirror that's behind the door. "Damn, I look good." I grin, pushing my boobs up and checking myself out. "Even did my ass justice."

I spend the next few minutes using my brand new makeup to add some mascara to my eyelashes. Nothing too obvious but something to make my eyes pop. Not sure what to do with my hair, I end up tossing it up into a messy bun, letting a few pieces of my bangs hang loose to frame my face.

Lipstick would be trying too hard, so I settle for a slight shine on my lips with some lip balm. "Perfect." I grin.

The bell rings and I cackle as another idea slips into my disturbed mind. With one last look at myself, I leave the room and head down the stairs. I reach the bottom just as Link opens the door.

The delivery boy is a teenager, maybe around my age. He hands Link the food, but his attention is only on Link for a moment when he realizes I'm here. His eyes go wide as his face turns pink, swallowing hard.

I can see the side of Link's face, and his expression is confused as he turns to see what this dude is looking at. "Is that our food?" I ask, as if I don't know the answer.

A deep, primal growl emits from Link's chest. He turns to the guy and snarls, pushing him out the door, making him let out a startled sound before slamming it in his face, not even paying the poor dude.

"That wasn't very nice." I glare at him. "He was only doing his job."

"His job isn't to fucking perv on you!" he shouts as I take the final step, ending up a foot away from Link. "What the fuck, Raven?" he says.

"What?" I ask. "I didn't want to sit in jeans and that top to watch a few hours-long movie. I don't have any other clothes, so I thought I'd just wear this. I mean it's almost like a bathing suit anyways."

"Trust me, it's nothing like a bathing suit. No fucking way I'd let you around anyone but me and the guys if you had a bathing suit that looked like that," he scoffs. "Now, go get changed. Dear God, woman, you're gonna give me grey hair before I'm twenty-five," he huffs. He sounds annoyed, but he can't hide the hunger in his eyes or the bulge in his pants.

"But I just said, I don't have anything to wear," I point out.

He curses, running a tattooed hand over his face. "Hunter left some clothes here, go see if anything he has will fit. Just cover the fuck up before I lose my ever loving mind," he demands.

I pout. "Fine. You're no fun."

"And you're a brat. Go!" he yells again, pointing up the stairs.

"Whatever you say, Daddy." I roll my eyes and turn around to start up the steps.

Link let's out a string of curses as I take my time going up the stairs, knowing my ass is flexing with each step. It's so much fun fucking with him. But I want more than anything for him to punish me for being a bad girl. Just got to get him to crack. *All in good time, Raven.*

Getting to the top of the stairs, I pass Hunter's room and go right to Link's. I've never been in here before, and I'm almost expecting it to be locked, but when I turn the door handle, it opens.

Looking over my shoulder, I make sure Link isn't there watching me before slipping into the room.

Once the door is closed, I flick on the light. I'm a little disappointed to see his room is so... boring. I was hoping for something a little more exciting, but his room is a light grey, his bed set is a darker shade, and all he has is a dresser, side table and a computer desk with a monitor on it.

A part of me wants to check and see what's on his computer, but I know Link would have it password protected. No way I'm risking getting locked out and Link knowing I was snooping.

Remembering why I'm in here in the first place, I go to his dresser and open the drawers. Top is socks and boxers. Grinning, I hold up a pair. "I can't wait to see what his cock looks like hard and standing at attention for me in these," I mutter to myself, putting it back and going for the next drawer. It's his shirts. I search through until I find one of his older band tees. It's worn, some of the image on the front is fading, but it's one of my favorites. I hope he doesn't miss this because I will be taking this back with me.

I have something from each of the others, but the only clothing from Link that I have is stuff he gave me as a gift.

Placing the shirt on the bed, I take my bra off, groaning at how good it feels to have the girls free. Nothing better than taking your bra off at the end of a long day of having them suffocate.

I put the shirt on, letting it fall to my knees. Grabbing the fabric, I bring it up to my nose and take a deep breath. I have to find out what he uses to wash his clothes with because, fuck, it smells so good. I moan as I snuggle into the fabric.

Going to grab my new bra, I smirk and decide to leave him a little present. I'll ask for it tomorrow before I leave.

"Come down and eat, Raven, now. The food is getting cold!" Link shouts.

I make a pit stop in my bedroom to see what I look like. I love it. Being in his clothes, smelling like him. These guys have no idea just how obsessed I am with them.

"That smells so good," I moan, stepping into the living room. Link has the pizza halfway to his mouth when he turns to look at me. Well, more like my breasts because my nipples are hard, pressed against the fabric of the shirt. It might be big, almost down to my knees but my boobs are big enough to fill most of the top part. "You gonna eat that?" I giggle.

His eyes slowly lift to mine, and I almost whimper at the look in them. Pride swells in me. He looks like he's five seconds away from bending me over this couch and fucking me until we break the damn thing.

But he doesn't, and disappointment fills me as he takes one more look down my body. He lets out a grumble, pushing the box of pizza on the coffee table towards me. "Eat. Start with the wings first. You hate reheated chicken, and I don't like those kind of wings. So let's not let this go to waste."

"Not like you paid for it," I snort as I plop down on the couch next to him.

"You're lucky all I did was slam the door in his face before paying. Now, eat!" he commands. A thrill fills me, and I move to do as I'm told.

"Yes, da—"

"Raven," he warns, shooting me a deadly look.

"Fine," I sass, bending over to grab the chicken wings. Now, I could have easily kept my ass on the couch, the wings were well in reach, but where's the fun in that?

I make sure to stick my ass in the air, angling it towards him. I can feel his eyes on the roundness of my backside, and I bite my lip. *Is he hard right now? Does he wish he could command me to take care of it for him?* Because I'd gladly do so.

He groans, but I let out a bark of surprise when his hand comes down on my ass hard. "Sit. Now."

I shiver, my panties unmistakably growing wet. Grabbing some food, I sit down, bringing my knees up and using the tops of them to place my plate on. But I make sure to have my feet apart, leaving the wet patch on display.

His eyes find it with no issue. This man has amazing will power because just when I think *this is it, he's had enough and he's going to give in,* his face shuts down, giving me nothing.

Yet again, he gets himself in-fucking-control, and I'm getting pissed. There was a part of me that wondered if I should just suck it up and tell them. None of us are stupid. But now? Fuck, that shit. I plan on fucking with him just for the fun of it. I know it gets to him and that's the main point. I will get his stubborn ass to crack.

Link tears his eyes away, muttering angrily to himself as he rents a movie. He puts on *Smile*, the psychological horror movie, and I whimper.

The dick chuckles. "What's wrong, Little Bird? I thought you loved scary movies."

"I do. Like Scream, all of the Conjuring movies, and anything within that world. Not some creepy as fuck smiles and get the image burnt into my mind, giving me fucking nightmares," I huff.

He rolls his eyes and grabs my food. "Come here," he mutters, pulling me over and into his lap. He hands me back my food and says, "Don't worry. If anyone ever tried to hurt you, even in your dreams, they're dead. And their blood will be proudly on my hands." He says it so seriously, like it's a done deal.

My heart pounds in my chest with his face so close to mine. *Would he do that? Would he kill for me? Stain his hands red for me?* A part of me really wishes he would.

I want to lean in, kiss his soft pink lips. I'm so sexually frustrated right now, but I don't want to ruin this moment.

We used to be this close all the time. But as I got older, it became less and less. I miss this, I miss him, and how we used to be. I know things will never be the same as before, and I don't want them to be. I want so much more now.

The sounds of the movie starting breaks our little stare down. "Eat," he whispers, kissing the side of my head.

Lowering my head, I smile as I take a bite of my pizza. Any pissy mood I might have almost found myself in is gone now.

We watch the movie and eat. When I get distracted with the movie or I wasn't eating fast enough, Link would bring the pizza up to my lips, silently telling me to take a bite.

There are a few times during the movie that I turn my head into his chest, hiding from the creepy faces. Every single time that happens he chuckles low and deep, making me want to squirm in his lap as he holds me tighter, whispering, "I got you, Little Bird. Always."

The last time I turn my face in, I end up staying there, falling asleep in the arms of a man who owns not just a part of my heart, but my soul. I'm all theirs. They own me.

CHAPTER 7

LINCOLN

Raven fell asleep in my arms toward the end of the movie. It's been an hour now, and there's some random show playing in the background. I haven't moved her, and she hasn't woken up.

She's where she belongs, safe in my arms. She's fucking gorgeous all the time, but I quite enjoy her like this. Sleeping peacefully and not running that sassy mouth of hers.

I know what she's doing. She knows I want her, and she's trying to tempt me into admitting it. But she doesn't know what she's asking for.

She doesn't understand that I not only want her, I want to *own* her. To make her bend to my every will and have her eager to do it.

I see the fire in her eyes when I demand something of her. Even though lately, half the time she's a fucking brat, she's having to stop herself from giving in.

Soon she will understand, I won't allow that.

There are different sides of myself that I show the world, compared to what I show her. But the only time I'm truly myself is in the dead of the night when I'm doing what I do best.

Sometimes I wonder if she will see us differently when she finds out what we really do at the shop. That it's just a front for something much bigger, much more sinister.

Not that it matters, even if she hates us and wants nothing to do with us, she doesn't stand a chance. I wasn't kidding when I said I will cage her to keep her if I have to.

I don't think it's going to come to that. She loves it when our dark sides slip out. I saw the lust in her eyes after I almost exposed everything earlier today when I threatened to kill my men for even daring to look at her. They're not allowed to until I can show them all who she belongs to.

Looking down at her sleeping face, I smirk at how adorable she is. Half the time, I wanna bend her over my knee and turn her ass red, but the other half, I want to pull her close and fuck her until she can't breathe. Right now, I can't fucking do either.

Her lips are parted, her breaths coming in soft and steady. She's snuggled into me, with her cheek on my chest. But what has me smug as fuck is the way she's gripping my shirt, like she doesn't want to risk letting go of me.

Speaking of shirts. When I saw her standing in nothing other than my shirt, her nipples hard, pressing against the fabric, I nearly went feral.

I've been hard as a fucking rock practically the whole

time with her perfect, tight ass sitting on my dick. Every time she wiggled, I growled in warning. And of course my Little Bird just took that as a challenge. *Brat.* I can't wait to fuck that out of her.

Knowing I can't sit like this forever, I lift her, taking her up to her room. Laying her down, she mumbles something sleepily, then settles under the covers. After tucking her in, I take a seat in the reading chair in the corner.

I didn't just get the chair so that she can read. I got it so I can sit here and watch her, like the sick fucker I am, while she sleeps.

This isn't the first time and sure as hell won't be the last.

My cock is still throbbing, needing a release. Leaning back, I unzip my jeans, pulling out my thick, hard cock.

I stroke myself as I imagine all the fun and twisted things I'm going to do with my Little Bird.

Legs parted, I tighten my grip to a nearly painful level. My cock is already leaking, precum dripping down my length. Using it as lube, I pick up the pace.

More than anything I wanna walk over there, spread her thick creamy thighs and bury my face into her sweet cunt until her voice is hoarse from screaming as I drive her fucking mad.

When she's had too much, her body spent and she begs for me to stop, I won't. I'll pin her down and make her cum over and over again until she passes out.

Then I'll wake her up with my cock. Fucking her until the only thing she can think about is my cock deep inside her cunt as her walls squeeze me, begging me for my cum.

And I'll fucking give it to her. I'll give her every last drop, filling her up, marking her as mine, putting a baby inside her. Fuck, just the idea of her belly swollen, pregnant with mine or one of the other guys' baby, drives me crazy.

She's going to beg me for more, so I'll take her ass, hard and fast. She'll be crying out into the pillow, asking me to never stop.

I'll play with her clit, drive her mad until she's gushing, dripping with my cum and her juices. When I cum again, it'll be deep in her ass. Pulling out, I'll be hard and ready to go again, all fucking night, as I watch my cum drip from her tight holes.

Raven will be passed out, and I'll go again and again until my balls have nothing left to give her. Only then will I be done with my Little Bird.

Letting out a low, deep groan I cum, my cock twitching in my hand as it shoots out onto my hand, some landing on my jeans.

Grabbing some tissues off the table next to the chair, I clean my hand off and toss them into the trash bin.

With eyes on my Little Bird, I stand up, cock still hard and wanting more. Raven is a heavy sleeper, she always has been. There could be a tornado, hurricane, and earthquake all happening at once outside her bedroom window and she wouldn't even stir.

Slowly, I walk over to her bed, cock bobbing between my legs, pointing at the one thing I crave more than anything in this world.

Carefully, I get up on the bed and brush her hair up and out of the way before straddling her head.

Hovering, I lean over, balancing some of my weight on one arm while I use my free hand to grip my cock, angling it towards her mouth. With the cum still on the tip of my cock, I smear it against her lips, painting them with a layer of my release before slipping the head of my cock through her parted lips.

My cock meets her hot, wet tongue. Gritting my teeth, I clench my fist as I stop myself from ramming my cock down her throat and fucking it until she's choking on my length.

Pulling my cock out from between her lips, I look down at my cum glistening against her skin in the moonlight. "My pretty Little Bird," I murmur as I stroke her cheek with my thumb. "You have no idea what I have in store for you, baby doll. I can't wait to show you the monster locked in his cage. He can't wait to trade places, and I'll watch you from behind those bars."

CHAPTER 8

RAVEN

As my eyes flutter open it takes me a moment to realize I'm not in my room. Well, I am, just not in the house that I actually live in.

Groaning, I sit up and rub the sleep from my eyes. The last thing I remember was being in Link's arms. I must have fallen asleep during the movie and Link brought me up here.

Looking over at the alarm clock, I see that it's eight in the morning. "Why the fuck am I up?" I mutter to myself, voice cracking. Licking my lips, I throw the blanket off me. My nose scrunches up as something salty and bitter hits my tongue. "What the fuck?" I say, my hand reaching up to touch my lips, but there's nothing there. Must still have something on my face from the pizza or the wings last night.

Needing to pee, I get out of bed with a frown. I'm used

to getting up in the morning for school, but if I'm up early on a weekend, I'm almost always tired and cranky.

Padding my way over to the bathroom, I do my thing and wash up. When I get back out into the hallway I perk up at the smell of coffee and the sounds of something cooking.

"Morning," I grumble as I take a seat at Link's kitchen table.

He looks at me over his shoulder and gives me the smallest smirk as he takes in my morning appearance. "Morning, sleeping beauty."

"Nothing beautiful here. I feel like a zombie and look like one too." I caught a glimpse of myself in the mirror upstairs. My eyes look sunken and my hair is falling out of my messy bun.

He turns back around to flip an egg. "Gonna have to agree to disagree," he states.

My eyes roam his back. He's not wearing a shirt, showing off his back full of tattoos. There's a mix of skulls, snakes, and other epically dark things. So fucking hot. They stop when I reach his ass. He's in boxers, holy shit. *Turn around, please!* I plead in my head.

"Disagree about what?" I ask, eyes never leaving his bubble butt.

"About you not being beautiful," he says, answering my prayers as he turns around. My eyes practically bug out of my head when I see what he's packing. I've seen the twins in their boxers as well as Hunter, but Link was always more careful around me. Maybe it's the age gap. *Doesn't seem to be an issue now.*

He fills out his boxers all too well, and he's not even hard. Fuck me, that thing is going to destroy me in all the best ways.

"Raven," Link growls. My eyes flick up to his and my cheeks heat.

"Sorry, what?" I ask, biting my lower lip.

His eyes flash with heat as he sets a plate of food down in front of me. "Eat," he says, his voice a low rumble. *Well, I'm awake now, no coffee needed.* Okay, lie, coffee is much needed because even though I'm ready for a good dicking, that's about all I'm ready for until I get some coffee in me. "And, what I said was that I need to go to work today. Do you need anything before I go?"

"Ahh, yeah. A ride home would be nice," I say, taking a bite of some egg.

His brows furrow. "You're not going home. Taylor and Hunter are sick. It's better for you to stay here for now."

"I know they're sick, but I'm not going to just sit around here bored all day while they're at home feeling like crap. I'm gonna go home, take care of them, and keep them company."

"No," he says, crossing his arms.

"Yes," I reply, raising a brow. "Who else is going to take care of them?"

"My mom, the twins' mom," he counters.

"No." I shake my head. "They would have to call in sick from work. You know how much they hate doing that. They actually love their jobs. I'm going home, and I'm helping the guys. You know that if it was me at home feeling like shit, you all would be there to help me."

He glares at me. "Stubborn fucking woman," he mutters. "Don't come bitching to me when you get sick."

"I promise to tell everyone else but you if I get sick." I grin.

His jaw ticks, and I take that as my cue to go up and get ready. I'm done with my eggs, so I snatch the bacon off the plate and stand up. "Thanks for the food. I'll be right back."

"What about your coffee," he asks, holding it out to me in a travel cup.

"Thanks." I grin, leaning up on my tiptoes to kiss him on the cheek. I freeze as soon as we make contact, his body going tense. This is new. The twins are always the one to kiss me, and I've kissed Hunter on the cheek, but never Link.

I pull back, but not fully away. Link turns his face, his lips now so close I can feel his breath against my lips. "Get dressed," his voice is low and raspy, and I bite back a whimper.

Without another word, I turn around and head upstairs.

After I'm done getting changed, I find Link waiting for me at the door.

"I'm keeping this," I tell him with a grin, pulling at the shirt.

"Fine," he grunts, "Let's go."

We head outside to his car. When we're inside and buckled up, I turn to him. "Are we good?" I ask him.

"Yeah, why wouldn't we be?" he asks me as he pulls out of the driveway.

"Because you were ignoring me for way too fucking long up until last night," I tell him, raising a brow.

"We're fine," is all he says.

"Good. We better be. I don't like when you're mad at me."

"I wasn't mad at you, Little Bird," he sighs.

"Then why were you acting like that?" I ask.

"Don't start," he tells me.

"Why not?"

"Raven!" he snaps, shooting me a warning look.

"Okay," I concede.

He grabs my hand, lacing his fingers with mine as he drives. We're quiet the whole way home, and I don't care, happy to take this contact with him over words any day.

We pull up to the house, and before I get out, I look at Link. "Last night was fun. I missed you," I say.

"I'm right here, Little Bird," he responds, brows furrowing.

"But are you really?" I counter, giving him a sad smile. I give his hand a little squeeze before pulling it away. But he doesn't let go, pulling my hand toward his lips. He kisses the back of my hand.

"Be a good girl, Little Bird."

"We both know that's not possible." I grin, and I love the small smirk he gives me as he shakes his head.

Getting out of the car with my bags in hand, I get a rush of excitement at seeing the others. I missed them.

Turning around, I give Link a little wave. He nods his head before backing out of the driveway and taking off to do whatever the hell he really does in that garage. I need to find that out and soon.

"Oh, thank god you're home, Raven," Rachel says as she rushes over to me.

"What's wrong? Is everything alright?" I ask.

"I need to go to work and that son of mine, as much as I love him, he's reminding me of what he was like when he was eight and sick. I need a break." She gives me a desperate look.

"Go," I say, bursting into giggles. "I'll take care of him."

"He's feeling better, but three days is enough," she sighs, kissing the side of my head before rushing out the door. "Good luck!" she shouts before closing the door.

Grinning, I head into the kitchen to make another coffee before going to find Hunter. I didn't see him in the living room when I first came in so he must be in his room.

"Hey, sweetie," Lisa greets me.

"Hey, Auntie Lisa," I say as I grab the pot of already brewed coffee.

"How was your time at Lincoln's?"

I shrug. "It's Link, so it wasn't full of heart to hearts and long conversations," I laugh.

"True. But your friendship is different with each of those boys. I don't think you two need that to still be close."

"No." I smile. "We don't."

"They're some lucky boys." She gives me a smile. "I couldn't have imagined anyone so perfect for them."

My eyes widen. "What do you mean?"

"Oh, sweetie. Us mothers aren't blind. We know how they feel about you and you for them," she chuckles as she takes the cup of coffee I was making and adds some things to it.

"And you're okay with that? If I was to be with all of them?" I ask, my belly doing cartwheels as I wait for her answer.

"None of our lives are what one might call normal. We all have something that society might think is wrong or doesn't agree with. But not me, Rachel, or your mother. All we care about is that all of you are loved and happy."

"I love them. They mean the world to me," I admit to her. "I can't imagine my life without them."

"And you're their whole world too. You have been since you and your mother came here. That's never going to change," she says, placing her hand on my arm as she hands me the coffee.

I take a sip and hum in approval. Rachel makes amazing coffees, always adding the right amount of everything. "Yeah, well, first I have to get them to actually admit their feelings."

"They will. Just give it time," she says.

Taking my coffee, I make a pit stop at the snack cabinet, grabbing some goodies for me and Hunter.

"Hey, do you mind checking in on Taylor? I gotta get going to work too. He's been a lot better about being sick than Hunter has been," she laughs. "I don't think it's the flu because no one else has gotten sick. We think it might have been something he ate, but he's been living on the toilet for most of yesterday and last night," she informs me while grimacing. "He's sleeping right now though. Travis left not too long ago to open the shop before Link brought you home."

"Yeah, of course," I tell her. I hate that Taylor was so sick, and I wasn't here to help.

Heading upstairs, I go to Taylor's room first. Putting the stuff on the floor outside his room, I crack open the door. "Taylor?" I whisper. When all I get back is a snore, I grin, holding back a laugh and step into the room.

He's sleeping, his face looks pale and clammy. Concern fills me as I brush some of his sweaty black hair out of the way. It's sad to see this big tattooed man look so weak and helpless.

Putting my hand to his forehead, I feel that he's a little hot. "I'll be right back," I whisper, not that he can hear me anyways.

Going to the bathroom, I grab a washcloth and wet it in cold water. Bringing it back to him, I place it on his forehead.

"Raven," he moans out in his sleep, causing me to go still. "That's it, baby," he says sleepily, "Look at you taking two cocks at once."

My eyes go so wide they're about to pop out. I don't know if I should laugh or shake him awake and ask for that dream to be reality. I'm gonna put this little bit of information away for later.

Grinning, I still can't help but blush. I'm going to guess

the other cock I'm taking in his dream is his brother's. And I very fucking much love that idea. I can't wait to be fucked by both of them any way they wanna take me.

"I missed you. Get some sleep," I laugh softly, giving his cheek a kiss.

Leaving Taylor's room, I pick up the things I left on the floor and head toward Hunter's room. I frown when I open the door to find the room empty.

"Where the heck are you?" I mutter to myself. I check Link's old room and don't find him there either, so I try my room next.

Opening my door, I grin and shake my head. He's in my bed, cuddled up with one of my shirts, sleeping.

Closing the door behind me, I place my bags on the floor next to the dresser and bring the coffee and snacks to the side table.

Pulling back the comforter, I get into bed. Hunter rolls over, his arm snaking around my waist and pulling me into him. "Don't leave me again," he mumbles. "Life is hell without you."

"It was only for a day and night," I tell him, snuggling into him.

"Way too long to be away. No more, promise?"

"Promise," I reply, grinning like a fool.

"Raven," he says, his lips against my neck.

I shiver. "Yeah?"

"I love you," he says. He always says those words to me, we're best friends. But right in this moment, I feel like it's a little bit more.

"I love you too," I whisper.

I end up falling asleep for a few hours. When we wake up, it's lunch time. I make us some grilled cheese and soup, eating it in my bed as we watch TV. Hunter looks a million times better than he was on Friday. I still think he should stay home for another day, but he's not having it. He said he can't go another day without me. He's fucking adorable.

"Hey," Taylor says from my doorway as Hunter and I eat popcorn. We should be heading to bed soon because of school tomorrow, but we can't seem to leave the other just yet. "Got room for another?"

"Always," I say, patting my free side. Taylor walks over like a zombie, still looking like he could use a good week's worth of sleep.

"Never, and I mean never, get the tacos at Ricky's. Ever," he groans as he lays down next to me.

"Dude needs to be shut down. Why would you even go there?" Hunter asks, leaning over to get a look at Taylor.

"Because they have amazing milkshakes. But fuck the meat, I don't think that's beef."

"Eww," I laugh. "I don't even wanna know."

"I'm talking both ends," Taylor continues, making Hunter crack up.

"Okay, fuck off with the nasty talk." I cover my ears. "Boys are so gross."

"Hey, we might be gross, but at least we're hot." Hunter wiggles his eyebrows at me.

He has a point.

The rest of the night is perfect. We talk, laugh, and I tell them about my time with Andy. I swear Hunter is jealous, and it's cute. He has nothing to worry about though. Because next to my mom, they will always come first in my life. Nothing will ever change that.

The guys end up falling asleep in bed with me, giving me the perfect ending to the night.

"And he lives!" Andrhea screams dramatically as Hunter and I walk into school.

"Look, you might think it's not a big deal, but I felt like I really was dying," Hunter grumbles.

"It was a cold," Andrhea deadpans, blinking at him before looking at me. "Is he for real?" she asks, hooking a finger over at him.

"Oh, he was totally close to death. You should have seen him. He was delirious and everything," I say, laying it on thick.

"I hate you." Hunter glares down at me, his blue hair covering one eye.

"Nah, you don't," I retort, booping him on the nose. He nips at my finger before lunging at me. He tickles me, making me break out into a laughing attack.

"Stop!" I shout in between laughs. "I'm gonna piss myself."

"Say you're sorry first," he chuckles as he continues.

"I'm sorry!"

"Now, tell me I'm your king and you're gonna do everything I tell you." He stops tickling me, giving me time to repeat his words while looking at me with a smug grin.

Licking my lips, I try to steady my breathing. Locking eyes with him, I take a step toward him. Crooking my finger to beckon him closer, he brings his face next to mine. I lean in, my lips right next to his ear. "You're my king," I say in a sultry tone. "And I'm going to do everything you tell me to do."

"Fuck me," he groans.

I grin as I pull back. "If you ask me nicely." I wink.

He growls, taking a step forward, making me step back into the lockers.

"Watch what you say, Little Mouse. I'm feeling the need for a little hunt," he growls. *Fuck.* My belly burns with need. I want to beg him to kiss me, for him to tell me his feelings now, so we can stop dancing around this shit.

"So, were you two planning to fuck in the hallway? Because if you are, do it quickly. The bell just rang and we don't have all day," Andrhea says, stepping next to us and breaking this little sexy intense moment.

"I have to go meet with some teachers to get the work I missed, so I can catch up in my free period. I'll see you next class, okay," Hunter tells me, tucking a lock of my hair behind my ear.

"Okay," I say. I love, but hate how easily I can go from a playful friend to a lovesick puppy in seconds when around these guys.

"Girl, I don't think you're going to have to wait much longer," Andrhea says as we watch Hunter take off down the hall. "That boy looks like he's ready to cave now."

"I wish," I sigh, closing my eyes as I take a moment to get myself together. "Alright, we better get to class."

The next few classes go by fast, but when we get to Math, I have a hard time paying attention because Hunter keeps poking me with his pencil.

"Would you fuck off," I hiss.

"Miss West," Mr. Carton says, "No talking."

Hunter snickers like a fucking kid, and I shoot him a glare. I go back to doing our questions when I feel the pencil poke lower. Then before I know it he's fucking shoving it down the crack of my pants, making me jump up and out of my seat. "What the fuck!" I shout at Hunter who breaks out into a fit of laughter, tossing his head back.

"That's enough, both of you, detention after school," Mr. Carton reprimands.

The whole class goes deathly quiet. "I'm sorry, what?" Hunter asks.

"You heard me. I will not tolerate these childish interruptions in my class." This dude is new, and although I do agree with him, it's Hunter's fault. The other teachers always let the guys get away with anything, and are pretty lenient with me. Not that I really did anything that warranted getting in trouble.

Hunter is used to getting what he wants and I don't want him to be a spoiled brat about this.

"We'll be there," I say, sitting back in my seat.

"The hell we will!" he whisper hisses at me. "I don't do detention."

"You do now," I whisper back, giving him a challenging look.

He glares at me for a moment before sitting back in his seat. "Fine," he mutters.

Big baby.

Even though we've moved on, the whole class keeps shooting Hunter looks like he's gonna blow up or some shit.

Wanting them to mind their own damn business, I shoot them all glares.

The rest of class, Hunter keeps his hands and pencil to himself. I can't help but feel bad for getting us in trouble. Hunter was just being himself, and what he was doing didn't actually make me mad. He startled me and I reacted, getting pissed in the moment.

When class is done, we gather up our things before heading to our next class. "Stop with the pissy mood," I tell Hunter, poking him in the sides.

"Kinda hard when I'm pissed," he responds as we walk down the hall. I don't like this. Hunter is normally like a golden retriever on crack. He's almost never in a bad mood.

Grabbing his arm, I pull him to the side in front of some lockers. He looks down at me, his face a mask of irritation. Jetting out my bottom lip, I give him my best pout and add on some puppy dog eyes for added effect. "Please, don't be mad at me," I say in a small voice, my lower lip quivering.

His face softens and he lets out a sigh. "I'm not mad at you," he says. "I'm just pissed because I know the whole fucking school is talking."

"I'm sorry," I say, stepping closer. His stunning blue eyes shine bright. "What can I do to make it up to you?" I ask, blinking up at him.

His face breaks out into a grin. "You're a sneaky Little Mouse."

My lip quirks up at the side. "I don't know what you mean."

"Come on," he says, wrapping his arm around my shoulder, leading us toward our next class.

Snuggling into Hunter's side, I grin to myself. He can't stand being mad at me for long. I hate it when any of the guys get mad at me, not that it happens often. I'm spoiled, and I fucking love it.

CHAPTER 9

HUNTER

I don't fucking do detention. And I was ready to tell this new fucking teacher exactly why that is the moment he opened his mouth. But Ray was there, so I had to shut up and accept it.

After school, I was going to tell him where he can stick his fucking detention and take my girl home, but then she was all fucking adorable with her cute fake pout. Then, when I caved like always, she pointed out at least we would have time together since we haven't seen much of each other the past few days.

It takes a lot to admit defeat but whatever kind of cold I got, I swear it must have been some fucked up mutated strand because I felt like I was dying. And I've been fucking shot before. I'd take that over having that cold again. *Dramatic?* Maybe.

The part that sucked the most was not being able to be

around Raven. The guys didn't want her to get sick, rightfully so. I would have hated myself to see her with that pain.

Every moment away from her slowly drove me insane. So, when she went to Link's for the night, I stayed in her room, cuddled up with her blanket. Just being able to smell her made it bearable. Did I later use that same shirt to jack off with as I pictured her smothering me with her perfect tits while pumping up into her pussy and making her scream out my name? Yes, yes I did.

With each passing day, the deal that the guys and I agreed to years ago becomes almost impossible to uphold.

The moment we laid eyes on Raven when she arrived at Safe Haven, we all knew we would do anything to protect her. We all fell hard and fast. She became one of us, our best friend. But that quickly turned into an obsession none of us are ashamed about.

We do everything with Raven, never needing anyone else but her and each other.

But the deal, this deal, can go to hell. Once we all realized we were so far gone for this girl, we came up with a solution. Let Raven live as normal of a life as we could. School, friends, anything she wanted. Then the moment she walked across that stage and accepted her high school diploma, she was ours.

We don't plan on giving her a choice. She is ours because none of us will ever let her go. And trust me, of all the things that make us the bad guys, not giving her a choice in this is the lesser of two evils.

If she found out now, the twins and I could work with

making her life still as normal as we can, but there's no way Link could.

Once she knows everything, Link wouldn't be able to hold back any longer. He would want her with him all the time. To bring her into our world and officially make her our Queen.

I can't fucking wait. We've only kept two things from Raven, and neither are small things some might look past.

But we know Raven, and I'm confident in saying I don't think she's going to care. She already knows we want her, none of us have exactly hidden that fact. It's just none of us have said it out loud yet.

My eyes never leave Raven as we sit in detention after school. We're forced to write about what we did that earned us detention and what we need to do to make better choices.

My piece of paper simply says 'Get Fucked' with a very well drawn hand giving the reader the middle finger.

But Raven is hard at work, her hand moving fast as her pencil works. When she bites the end, stopping to think about what to write next, her brow furrows in concentration, and I imagine those lips wrapped around my cock. Fuck, if she wants to bite it too, I'd be down for that.

She's fucking gorgeous. A vision. The sexiest woman to ever walk on this planet. And it's taking everything in me not to put her on her desk, lay her down and eat her like the starved man I am.

Sadly, I can't. I mean don't get me wrong, if this was after she knew everything, my tongue would already be buried deep inside her sweet pussy. None of us plan on keeping our hands to ourselves once we get the green light to cross that line.

So, I'll just suffer the hard on that is painfully tenting my pants right now and jack off later to the camera feed I have saved from last week, when Raven finger fucked herself into one hell of an orgasm.

Sometimes I like to think she knows about the cameras I put in her room. Like she's putting on a show just for me.

The twins hate me for it. Not because I put one in there, but because I won't share the feed with them.

We're all fucked, okay? We each have our own things to deal with, especially not being able to have Raven the way we want.

Link sits in the corner of her room and jacks off as he watches her sleep. I have the camera and the twins... well, they're the only ones who've fucked other girls.

But it's not like how you're thinking. Honestly, I think they're the most fucked up with what they do. Every girl they've ever fucked, the whole time they're with them, they degrade them and tell them they're never going to be good enough, never going to be Raven. That this is all they will ever get from them because they might get their cocks, but they belong to Raven.

It's why the girls in our school hate her. It's their own fault, it's not like they didn't know what they were getting into.

God, I'm so fucking bored. I thought since I'd be here with Raven, it would help, but anytime I try to talk to Raven, I get shhhed or a dirty look.

"I'm going to the bathroom," I say, feeling restless.

"No, you're not," Mr. Carton says, not bothering to look up.

Jaw ticking, I look at Raven who gives me a small smirk. She knows I'm done playing nice, and she's sitting back to see what I'll do next.

Giving her a wink, I get up and walk over to his desk. "Hey," I say, making his head snap up. He gives me a glare, opening his mouth to talk, but I raise a hand. Whispering, I lean in to say, "You're new here, so you gotta learn. I'll give you a free pass. But I'm gonna assume if you moved to Black Ridge, you've heard the rumors." He looks confused for a moment, but when I pull down the collar of my shirt to show him the tattoo over my heart, his eyes widen in understanding. "So, like I said. I'm going to the bathroom."

He clears his throat. "O-of course," he nods.

Giving him a cat-like grin, I turn on my heel and leave the room. The moment I'm out, I take out my phone and call my brother.

"What?" he grunts, sounding out of breath as the screams in the background filter through the phone.

"Aww man! I'm missing out. Fucking detention," I mutter.

"Don't worry, there's always next time. Now, what the fuck do you want, I'm busy."

"So, is there anything I can do to persuade you to forget about the deal we made?"

"Hunter," he growls. "How many fucking times do I have to tell you no?"

"But fuck!" I whine. "I want her so bad. My dick is gonna fucking fall off at this point from being hard so much. I don't even know how I'm alive because, clearly, all the fucking blood in my body lives in my dick!"

"You're not the only one who has to wait. Trust me, the way she's been testing my fucking patience, I'm honestly surprised I haven't snapped," he mutters.

"Okay, then get Raven to keep being a brat so you break, got it," I say, grinning like a fool.

"Don't make me shoot you," he sneers.

"Relax. You really need to get laid," I tease. "Where is Quinn?" I chuckle.

"Hunter, I swear to god, I'll kill you in your sleep," he snaps.

"Alright, Mr. Grumpy," I huff. "You're no fun."

"Fuck off."

"Tell my little friends I said hi!" I say before hanging up the phone.

I love to fuck with Link as much as Raven does. When we were kids, I bought this bag of mini ducks. They were so cute, and there were hundreds of them. Link was in a bad mood that day, -not much different from any other day really- so I thought I'd give him a laugh by putting one of the ducks in his room on his pillow.

As time went on, any time he was extra broody, I'd leave a little duck somewhere he would find it. Years later, and I still do it, always having one of them on me at all times.

I have no idea what he does with them, but they're never where I left them, so I know he's seen them.

They're probably rotting in the landfill. Poor little duckies.

Looking at the time, I realize detention is over, and I've drifted away from the classroom, never going to the bathroom while I talked to Link.

Running back to the room, I find Raven stepping out. She glares at me. "Traitor. You abandoned me."

"Never!" I chuckle. "I just really had to pee."

"What did you say to him that made him change his mind?" she asks me as we start walking down the hall toward the parking lot.

"I was just my sweet, charming self," I respond, giving her a confused look.

"Right," she laughs, her gorgeous eyes captivating me like always as she looks up at me. "You might wanna work on that then because he looked like he was about to shit his pants."

"He really is a dick," I say as we reach the exit.

"You're a dick," she teases.

"You like my dick," I tease back, grinning wide when her cheeks grow red. "Ahh, Little Mouse, are you thinking about my dick, now? I can give you a repeat of the first day of school if you want."

"It wasn't that impressive," she shrugs, and my mouth goes slack.

"Take that back!" I shout as she starts walking towards my car. "My dick is fucking amazing. It has tattoos for fuck's sake! And not to mention pretty much every cock piercing you could ever think of."

Raven stops, bursting into giggles as we enter the parking lot to find a few of the teachers still here, standing by a car. They are all gaping at me in horror.

"Don't be acting all prudish. A cock like mine is in all your dirty old lady dreams," I grin. Okay, they're not that old, maybe in their fifties but the teachers here are just as sketchy as the students. I have no doubt most of them let some of the guys fuck them for better grades. I've seen it myself. "I'm looking at you, Mrs. Pen." I wink.

"Hunter!" Raven yells. I look over to see her leaning against my car, her honey blonde hair shining in the afternoon sun. And there goes the very cock we're talking about, getting hard as stone for the only person in the world who knows how to activate it. "You left them with a nice visual. Now get your ass in this car and drive me home."

"Sorry ladies, my woman is calling." I give them a charming smile and a wink before running over to my Little Mouse. "Anything for you, baby," I say. She laughs and gets into the car.

It's so hard to act like I've always acted without doing every single thing I really want to do. But much like my brothers, even one little taste of temptation, and I'd fold, unable to hold myself back. So for now, I gotta stay strong, and keep my dick to myself.

CHAPTER 10

RAVEN

I'm swinging in the backyard of the house on the swing set we have for when there's kids staying here, when Andrhea walks through the back gate. "Hey," she says.

With one last swing, I jump off, landing on the ground with a thud. "Hey," I answer back. "What are you doing here? I thought you had a date?"

It's been a week since Hunter's been back at school after his weekend of hell, as he calls it, and he's been up my ass any chance he gets. Not that I mind, I love how he's always there with, at least, one of his hands on my body at all times.

But now he's at the shop with the guys working, leaving me home to be bored out of my mind. I knew Andrhea had a date and mine and the guys' moms are working, but I never realized how much I hated being alone; too much time to think. So seeing Andrhea here perks me up.

"Ugh," she scoffs. "Yeah, about that bitch. Caught Kandy making out with Kyle Rigger when I went to go pick her up. She lied to my face, said they were just talking and Kyle was over to hang out with her brother. Yeah, sure, if talking means gagging on each other's tongues." Her lip peels back.

"I'm sorry," I say, pulling her into a hug. "She sucks and you can do way better than her. There's gotta be at least one decent woman in this town."

"Highly doubt it," she replies, pulling back. "Whatever. Her name was Kandy, what did I expect?"

"Fair point," I laugh. "You have me. Let's do something."

"Yes!" Her eyes light up, and I feel like I might have made a mistake. "Let's go get a tattoo!"

"What? No!" I let out a shocked laugh. I'm all for tattoos, but I haven't found any designs I like enough to get put on my body for the rest of my life.

"Come on!" she whines, giving me a pout, her blue eyes pleading. "Pleeeease?"

"No." I shake my head but give her a grin.

"Fine, how about a piercing then? Do you have any?" she asks me, looking me up and down. Her eyes linger on my tits, and she smirks. "What about your nipples? I bet the guys would fucking love it." Her eyes grow even bigger. "Oh my god, you should totally get your clit pierced."

"Whoa there, girl. Slow down!" I laugh, holding up my hand as her blonde curls bounce with her as she vibrates with excitement. "The nipples I could do. But no ones touching my vagina unless it's one of my guys."

"Fine. I'll take it. Free the nips!" she shouts as she grabs my hand and pulls me out of the backyard toward her car.

"Wait!" I object. "I need to go grab my purse."

"Nah. I'll pay for it," she says, bringing me to the passenger side.

"No." I look at her with wide eyes.

"It was my crazy idea, the least I can do is pay for it." She shrugs. "Plus, it's for my benefit too. If you don't think I'm gonna be staring at your tits to see if you're wearing a bra so I can see them poke through, you're dead wrong babe." She grins wickedly at me.

"You're such a bad influence," I laugh, shaking my head as I get into her car.

"You fucking love it."

"You sure this place is sanitary?" I ask as we step inside the shop. Looking around, things seem on the up and up. But this is Black Ridge, so I can't be too careful.

"Yes. I made sure," she says as we walk over to the desk and look at the man behind it. "And if they aren't, and you get an infection, they will be in big shit."

"We make you sign a waiver before we do anything." The man looks smug. "If you don't sign it, we don't do shit."

Andrhea wraps her arm around my shoulder, pulling me to her side. "This sexy bitch here is my bestie, Raven. She also happens to be best friends with Link, Taylor, Travis and Hunter." The look on his face drops as his eyes widen. "Ah, so you've heard of them. Wonderful. So, we're not signing shit. You're gonna give us your best piercer and tattoo artist and everything *will* be sanitary. That means, keep your food and shit away from us," Andrhea states, pointing to the guy who's tattooing someone. He stops to reach over and take a drink of his coffee with his gloved hand, then proceeds to continue the tattoo without changing gloves.

"Yes, of course. I'm so sorry about that," the guy stammers before rushing over to the gloved dude.

"What's all that about?" I ask, looking away at the two guys, who are having a harsh, whispered conversation.

"You know your guys are scary. Everyone knows them." She shrugs.

I do know that. But I also think there's a lot I don't know. Having people back down or run the opposite direction when they see one of my guys isn't something new, I don't think I've ever really questioned it; I'm just used to it.

But lately, I've been wondering how much there is that I'm unaware of.

"I'm starting to think they might have something to do with Black Venom Crew," I tell her. "It would make sense why people are afraid of them," I joke. If they actually were, they would have told me. We tell each other everything. And that would be one massive thing to keep from me.

"Maybe," she laughs.

Black Venom Crew runs this town, but I don't think I actually know anyone who is a part of that crew. They're like ghosts that only come out in the dead of night when everyone is sleeping.

Everyone knows about them, but no one knows who they are exactly.

The front desk guy comes back. "Who's getting the tattoo, and who's getting pierced?" he asks us.

"I'll be getting the tattoo. She's getting pierced. I think it would be best if she was pierced by a woman," Andrhea states. I raise a brow at her in question.

"Look, just in case the guys aren't too happy about this impromptu trip, I don't want to add the fact that a man touched your tits on top of it," she says, giving me a look.

"Smart." I nod. "Yeah, better make it a woman."

"Of course," the guy nods. "Come with me."

We follow him, and he leads us to the first room. "This is Tony, he's one of our best artists."

"Hey," Tony says, giving us a wave from his chair inside the room.

"And this is Angie. She's going to be the one doing your piercings." He gestures his hand to the room directly across the hall.

"Ahhh. I think I wanna get something pierced too," Andrhea announces, blinking at Angie, her eyes wide as she takes in the beautiful woman. She has long black hair and is covered in bright tattoos.

Angie laughs. "How old are you, doll face?" she asks Andrhea.

"Eighteen," Andrhea answers, a slight blush taking over her cheek.

I can't help but grin at how adorably smitten she is with Angie.

"Call me," Angie flirts, handing Andrhea a business card. "If you ever want to get something pierced. Or whatever."

"O-okay," Andrhea says, then pulls me into the room where she'll be getting a tattoo. "Oh my god. She's so fucking hot!"

"She is," I laugh. "And you should totally call her."

"You need to get as much information about her as you can," she demands, giving me a pleading look.

"Got it." I nod.

"Umm. We good to start?" Tony says, interrupting our girl talk.

"Oh, right, you," Andrhea sighs. "Yeah, fine." She sounds so disappointed.

"I'll be done before you, so I'll come and sit after," I tell her as I leave the room and go into Angie's.

"Hey," I say, stepping into her room. "Sorry about that."

"It's okay," she laughs. "Your friend's cute. What's her name?"

"Andrhea."

We talk while she sets everything up. Angie is twenty-one. Lives in the next town over. Single. She takes care of her elderly grandma. *How sweet is that!* And is 100% gay. That's points for Andy right there. I'm not getting any vibes that have me on alert, so I'm happy to relay this little tidbit of information back to Andrhea.

"Alright. You don't have to take your top off, but I do need you to take your bra off and lift up your shirt."

Nodding, I unclasp my bra and take it off through the arm holes. I can't believe I'm actually doing this right now. I feel like I should be more anxious about getting my fucking nipples pierced, but I'm actually excited. I told myself this was my year to try new things. So far it's been tame by making a new friend and going shopping or to the movies.

Why not go a little more wild?

Lifting up my shirt, I give her a full view of my tits. I love how professional she is because she doesn't even bat an eye. She clamps one of my nipples, bringing up a big needle. "Alright, big deep breath in. Exhale when I tell you." I take a deep breath in as she places the needle. I start to freak out at the exact moment she says 'exhale.'

Too late, I say nothing. Breathing out as she shoves the needle in, my eyes go wide as pain spikes through my boobs. "Fuck!" I shout. "Holy shit, oh my fucking god that hurts," I sob out, my eyes stinging with tears.

"You're doing so good," she encourages, "Look, the bar is already in."

Through blurry eyes, I look down and see the little silver bar. "Okay, be quick with the next one before I chicken out," I tell her while I'm still feeling the adrenaline of the last one.

Again she tells me to breathe in, and on the exhale, she stabs me again. It takes everything in me not to curse her out and punch her. But I asked for this. *Now, I just need to remember why.*

My nipples throb, but the tears stop after a few moments. I didn't cry, but fuck.

She eyes up the piercings and nods. "They look awesome. Take a look." Standing up, she moves out of the way of the mirror behind her.

I walk over to stand in front, getting a good look at them. "Okay," I grin. "I do have to admit these are sexy as fuck."

"Right! You were made for these."

I can't wait to see what the guys think. I can't just lift my top up and show them my boobs. I mean, I can... *maybe I should?*

Angie goes through the care instructions. She said I can wear a padded sports bra for gym, but I wonder if I could use this to get out of that class? *Is this considered a medical thing?*

I do love the idea of having an excuse to go braless. I fucking loathe them, even if they make me look good.

Thanking her for everything, I go over to watch Andrhea get the rest of the tattoo. When I walk in, she's chatting away to Tony. "Oh, you're done!" she says when I walk in. "Let me see."

"Ummm, Andy..." I start, grinning as I look over at Tony.

"Right. Yeah, not a good idea. The guys would lose their shit," Andrhea says. She's not wrong.

Tony stops and looks at us both. "I don't want any problems with those guys," he says.

"Nah, don't worry. You're fine," I say. "No flashing you my titties."

"Thank god," he sighs. "I'm sure they're nice and all, but I don't even roll that way," he chuckles.

Andrhea is a fucking champ, it's like she doesn't even notice the tattoo as she talks away the whole time.

When she's done, she shows me her tattoo. "It's stunning," I compliment her, looking at the kitsune on her arm.

"I love it," she says, and thanks Tony. Andy loves Japan and its folklore, so it's perfect for her.

Once we pay, we head out to her car. "I want to get a tattoo," I sigh, looking at her arm again.

"Then get one," she retorts. "We can spend hours looking online to find something you like."

"I mean, it wouldn't hurt," I say.

When we get into the car, we crank the music and roll down the windows. I'm all smiles as our hair blows in the wind and the sun sets off in the horizon.

I'm glad Andrhea came over today. I've noticed the guys have been a lot more absent lately. Tomorrow is October first, and it's my birthday month. The five of us go on a camping trip every year on the weekend before my birthday, and I'm starting to wonder if we're even going to continue that tradition this year.

I hate it. Call me needy, but I miss them. At least when the twins were in school, I could see them everyday. Now that they're working with Link, Hunter is the one I see the most. And even nowadays it's only in school. As soon as we get home, he's off with the guys, coming home late. Sometimes I even wake up in the middle of the night to find all three of them gone. I text them, asking where they went, and they always answer that they have been called into work.

Who the fuck has to fix a car at two in the morning?! I know they're keeping something from me, and I plan on finding out what they're really up to.

We pull up to the house, and I'm surprised to find all the guys waiting out front. *Shit.* I look down at my phone to turn on the lock screen, but it's black. "Fuck," I hiss.

"What?" Andrhea asks. "Ahh, Ray," she says, seeing the guys too.

"I know," I groan. "I forgot to text them to let them know I was leaving the house and my phone is dead."

She parks the car and looks over at me with a concerned look. "Shit."

"Yeah. Shit," I sigh. Looking out the front window, I find them all staring at me now. They look pissed. Is it wrong that their murderous looks turn me on? Might not be the right time, but fuck me please.

"Good luck," she offers as I get out.

"Thanks. I might need it." I give her a forced smile.

"Text me later to let me know you're still alive."

"I will. See you," I say and close the car door.

"Where the fuck were you?" Link snarls, his lip pulling back in a sneer. My nipples harden, and not because of the cool breeze. I wince because of the piercings.

"Why the fuck didn't you pick up your phone when we

called or answer your texts?!" Travis demands, his nostrils flaring.

"You know the rules, Foxy Girl," Taylor says, his arms crossed as he glares at me.

"Naughty Little Mouse," Hunter tuts.

My mind blanks. I haven't seen them this pissed off at me in... well, ever. *How am I going to get myself out of this with the least amount of* yelling?

An idea forms quickly and I pat myself on the back. What better way to distract boys than to show them boobs?

"I had a good reason," I tell them.

"Better have been you were dying in a ditch. But seeing you're standing here in one piece, that's not the case," Link growls.

"My phone died," I told them. "I didn't see any of your texts or calls."

"Where were you?" Link demands again.

Hooking my thumbs under my shirt, I lift it up over my tits, giving them one hell of a show. "Went to get these."

All of the guys go stiff. "Fuck," Hunt hisses, his hand going right to his dick. He doesn't even bother trying to be discreet while he adjusts himself.

The twins both have their eyes locked on each boob, and Link's eyes are devouring the view.

"Is this a good enough reason?" I ask.

"For fuck's sake, Raven," Link hisses, finally snapping out of it.

"What? I like them." I shrug, putting my shirt down.

"Me fucking too," Hunter groans, and I can't help but

grin at him. His face breaks out into one of his own as he shakes his head, his blue hair falling over his forehead. He runs his hand through it, getting it out of his eyes as he lets out a deep breath.

"Who the fuck let you get that?" Link snaps, taking a step forward. "You're not eighteen yet. Did your mother consent to this?"

"Nope," I say. "Andy went to get a tattoo, it was a spur of the moment thing and seeing how this year is meant for fun and living life outside my comfort zone, I thought why not get some nipple piercings."

"I approve of this list," Hunter says. "I didn't get a good look, can I see again?"

I giggle as Taylor slaps Hunter upside the head.

"Well, I don't approve of this," Link counters.

"Too bad it's not your body," I snark, giving him a challenging look. I'm tempted to tell him it could be if he just tells me how he feels, but I keep my mouth shut.

Link slowly walks over to me, and I stand my ground. Jaw ticking, his large tattooed hand grabs me by the neck. I'm taken by surprise, my eyes widening in shock as a little gasped moan slips out.

He leans in close, his lips brushing against my ear as he adds a little pressure to the grip on my neck. "When will you realize, I own you, Little Bird?"

It's all he says as he nips at my ear before letting go. He doesn't look at me, stepping to the side and walking away without another word. Spinning around, I see him hop on his bike and take off down the street.

"Fuck me," I whisper to myself.

"Dove," Travis says, getting my attention. "For everyone's sake, make sure your phone is charged before you leave the house. We were ready to tear this town apart. Don't let it happen again, understand?"

"Yeah," I let out a breath. "I'm sorry," I say, walking over to them.

Taylor pulls me into his arms. "We just want to make sure you're safe at all times, okay? We might live in a small town where nothing exciting really happens, but the world is still a fucked up place where anything could happen."

"I know," I say, holding him tight. "Are you done with work?" I ask, pulling away enough to look at them. "I miss you guys."

They all look at each other, a guilty look taking over their faces. "Yeah, Foxy Girl. We're yours for the rest of the night."

I'm excited to finally get them to myself again, but as I look over my shoulder in the direction Link left, I can't help but wish he was close with me like the others are. I know he's not the cuddle in bed type, but I feel like a piece of me is missing every time he's not with us.

"Come on, Dove. Have you eaten yet?" Travis asks, rubbing his hand up and down my back.

"No," I answer, looking up at him.

"Let's order something and watch a movie. It's officially October tomorrow, so I think we can start our month-long Halloween movie binge a day early."

"Sounds perfect." I smile up at him.

We head into the house, and Travis pulls out his phone to place an order. "Little Mouse," Hunter says, stepping up behind my back, his lips close to my ear. "Those piercings? So fucking hot."

I shiver as he steps away and jogs up the stairs, calling out that he's going to check on his babies and will meet us in my room.

Biting my lower lip, I smile. As much as I love hanging out with Andy, I'd pick spending my free time with these guys over everything. They will always come first, no matter what.

CHAPTER 11

RAVEN

Hunter is going to be late for lunch again today. He's the best in his shop class, so I can see why his teacher always asks Hunter to help him with stuff. But today isn't the best day for that because Andrhea is out sick, meaning I'm all alone. It's rare these days, and I'm finding myself not a fan of it. Call me needy or spoiled, but it's true.

I could try to make more friends, but I also hate that idea. Plus, at this point any possible connections would simply be for them to get closer to my guys. So, it's going to be a no for me.

As I head down the hall toward my art class, so I can turn in a late assessment, I pass the guys' locker room. There's laughter and banging of the lockers that has me shaking my head. *Jocks.*

It's hard to ignore when I can still hear them a few doors

down. When I get to the classroom, I can see my teacher talking to another student, so I wait.

After another minute, I blow out a breath of annoyance. I know it's my own fault for not handing it in on time, but when the twins wanted to hang out the other night, I couldn't just say *no, sorry I have school work.* I mean, I could, but I'd much rather spend time with them, even if I like art.

I'm starving, and it's making me a little cranky. And I'm really thirsty right now. I look over at the water fountain next to the locker room. Feeling like I could use a drink, I walk over.

As I take a quick mouth full of water, I'm glad it doesn't taste too bad.

The guys in the locker room are still chatting away. I'm bored and nosy, so I open the door just enough to hear what they're saying.

"Hey. You know Raven, right?" someone says.

"What about her?" someone different responds.

"She's hot. I'd fuck her," the first person says. *Eww, barf.* Maybe they're talking about a different Raven.

"Yeah, and then her guys would kill you," another one barks out a laugh. Okay, there's a good chance they're talking about me. Now, I really wanna hear what they have to say.

"There's a reason no one has tapped that," someone new interjects.

"I bet I could," I recognize that voice. It belongs to Jeff Peterson, captain of the football team and the school's resident man-whore. I'm pretty sure he's fucked every girl in this school apart from me and Andy.

"Oh yeah? What makes you think that?" the guy who brought me up in the first place asks.

"The only one she hangs out with is Hunter. She doesn't have the others around to intimidate everyone," Jeff says.

"Yeah, but Hunter is still fucking crazy and not someone I'd wanna fuck with."

"True, but I think if I can get her alone, I could ask her to hang out. I'll take her somewhere private, sweet talk her. Make her feel pretty and whatever bullshit girls want to hear. I've never had a girl turn me down, and I don't plan on starting now. I could get her to fuck me if I wanted to," Jeff brags, sounding smug as fuck.

Ah, no you fucking can't. It's taking everything in me not to burst through this door and laugh in their faces until I can't breathe with how fucking pathetic he sounds. There's no way in hell he would ever be able to get me alone in the same room long enough to fuck me.

"Let's make a bet out of it. If you can get in Raven West's pants, we'll all put up a grand," first guy says.

Damn, a grand to get in my pants? That's a pretty penny around here. So I'm not surprised when I hear Jeff agree. They all start hooting and hollering.

The door to my art classroom opens, and I quickly step away from the locker room door.

So, Jeffy-boy thinks he can fuck me. I'd love to see him try. Grinning, my mind comes up with its own plan. I've been wanting to step up my game when it comes to getting the guys to spill their feelings for me.

What better way than making them jealous by making them think I'm interested in someone else. Call me petty, but hey, it could be fun.

They would never believe I'm actually interested in Jeff, or anyone else, really. But I could swing it as being part of my senior year bucket list. I've never dated or even kissed a boy. Not that I plan on kissing that asshole.

As I think more about this, I get excited at the thought of how the guys are going to react. I probably won't be able to get away with it for very long, but even just getting a reaction out of them is enough for me.

After I turn in my art assignment, I head to my locker to trade in my books for my gym clothes for my next class after lunch.

"Hey," Jeff says, leaning on the locker next to me as I stand in front of my open one. Well, that didn't take player-boy long. Guess he's really determined to get that money.

"Hi..." I say as I close my locker door. He's grinning down at me with what I think is supposed to be a flirty smile?

"How are you?" he asks me. *Really?*

"Hungry," I say, raising a brow. Look, I'm not gonna fake a smile and bat my eyelashes like I'm swooning for this fucker. We both know that wouldn't be how I'd react if I didn't already know what he had planned. But I don't worry about being myself and scaring him off because I know he wants that money, and he won't back down so easily.

"Good thing it's lunch time, then," he chuckles. Jeff isn't unattractive. He has blonde wavy hair and bright blue eyes. He's your average fuckboy jock. I could see why girls are drawn in.

Me? I'm gonna have to fake it because even if I didn't hear rumors that he does more fucked up things with girls than sleep with them as a game, he isn't my type.

I like my men tatted, possessive, and crazy for me. Or, well, just crazy would do.

"Yeah. And that's what I plan on doing right now," I retort, taking a step away from him.

"Wait," he says, grabbing my arm. Biting the inside of my cheek, I try not to turn around and dick punch him. "Sorry," he says, taking his hand off me when I glare at him. "Look, I know we haven't really talked much."

"Or at all," I clarify. I've never had a conversation with him in my life.

"Yeah. Well, there's a reason for that. Your best friends, the guys... well, they are scary people, not gonna lie," he laughs, rubbing the back of his head. "It's the reason why no one has ever asked you out before. We were all afraid they would lose their shit on us."

"Fair judgement call," I nod.

"I have to ask, are you dating any of them? Because I've heard some of the girls talking. And they seem to think you're... involved with the twins."

"Not that it's anyone's business, but no, I'm not dating them. Or anyone," I admit. It's technically true, I'm not. For now. All in due time, though. They will be mine and only mine.

"Good. That's good. Because... I wanted to ask you out." He smiles shyly. *Oh, he's better at this than I thought.*

"You do, do you?" I ask, giving him a smirk of my own.

"I've had a crush on you for a long time now. And well, it's our last year, and I thought I'd shoot my shot before I never have another chance at it," he says. It's sad how easily he lies. He's good, too good. "What do you say, would you like to hang out sometime? Maybe go on a date."

Biting my lower lip, I make him wait. He stands there, shifting back and forth from one foot to the next. "I'm not looking for anything serious." I narrow my eyes at him.

"That's fine. We can just hang out and go from there." He grins like he's got me hooked.

"Alright. I guess it couldn't hurt," I say with a shrug. His eyes widen like he can't believe I actually said yes.

"Really?" he asks, looking all too happy with himself.

"Sure. What's your number?" I ask. He exchanges numbers with me, and I don't give him any more of my attention, turning around and heading toward the café.

Now, the question is, how much can I get out of this before he realizes he's not going to be able to get me alone?

HUNTER

As much as I like my shop teacher, -and I do, he's a good man- I can't keep staying after class. He's been making up excuses to have me stay and help him. I think he just wants someone to talk to, and I feel bad for the guy, but he needs to get some friends his own age.

And this is taking away my time with Raven. Sure, I live with her and have almost all the same classes as her, but that's not enough. If I could handcuff her to me, I would.

Looking down at my phone, I see a text from Raven that she sent just a minute ago, telling me she's going to her locker then heading to the café. I wonder why she's not already there. She did mention something about having to hand in an assignment.

Rounding the corner, I stop dead in my tracks. I see red as Raven stands there, talking to fuckboy Jeff. *What the fuck does he think he's doing talking to my girl!?*

Vibrating as my hand twitches to grab my blade and fucking stab him for even looking at her, I wait for her to laugh in his face and tell him to get fucked.

When she doesn't, I get more fucking murderous. And when she takes his fucking phone to give him her number, I fucking lose it.

She walks away from him, and I duck back around the corner. The moment she turns, coming into view, I grab her and shove her up against the wall.

"What the fuck, Hunter?" she snaps.

"Why were you talking to him?" I ask, my chest heaving.

Her eyes light up. Fuck, fuck me. She likes that I'm pissed. She's one naughty Little Mouse, one I'd very much like to punish right now.

"Because he came up to me," she answers.

"What did he want?"

"To go out with me. It's kinda sweet, really. He confessed that he wanted me for as long as he could remember and wanted to take his chance before he lost it forever. It's right out of a hallmark movie if you ask me," she says with a wistful sigh. I see through her bullshit. I know her better than anyone else. She's full of shit. "I have to admit, it's nice to hear someone admit they have feelings for me. It's better to tell the person you want them, than to keep it to yourself and make them wonder," she taunts, raising a brow.

I don't think she's talking about Jeff anymore.

She has no idea. No idea how much I want to get down on my knees, to worship her body, to feast on her cunt. To make her scream my name and know who fucking owns her.

But my brother is standing in the way of all that. And now my cheeky Little Mouse wants to play games. I don't fucking like this one bit.

Running my tongue along my teeth, I think of what to say next. Now that I know she's just doing this to get a rise out of us, I have to think before I act. I hate doing that.

"You're right," I nod, taking a step back.

"I am?" she asks, looking surprised by my answer. *Two can play this game, baby girl.*

"Yeah. I mean, why not? If he likes you so much, why not go out with him. You're single."

Her breathing starts to pick up as her face drops. She's pissed, really fucking pissed. I hate that I've upset her, but she doesn't understand the kinds of games she's playing.

I know she wants us to admit our feelings, and we want

that too. But she doesn't know the severity of what she's asking.

"You know what? You're right. I am single. And this year I'm doing all the shit I've never thought of doing. So why not go out with Jeff? He's not exactly who I thought I'd have for my first kiss but hey, I don't seem to have anyone else lining up to be with me," she sneers. She pushes me away from her to walk away, but I don't let her.

Grabbing her again, I shove her back up against the wall. With a low growl, I slam my lips to hers. She gasps in surprise, her body tense for a moment, but as I move my lips against hers, her sounds turn into a needy moan as she parts her lips. Taking that as my opening, I slip my tongue in and over hers.

Fuck me, she tastes like heaven and hell rolled into one. I want to devour her here and now as my cock gets painfully hard.

When I break the kiss, we're both breathing heavily. Her eyes are wide, pupils dilated. She looks so fucking sexy with her pink lips all swollen.

"What was that?" she asks, her voice in awe. I wanna kiss her again so bad, but if I do, that's not all I'm going to be doing. I won't be able to stop. I've already tested myself too much.

"You're my best friend, Raven. There's no way in hell I was going to let that fuckboy, who's probably kissed a thousand lips, be the one who gets your first kiss. That was always meant to be mine," I growl. She whimpers, her body relaxing in my hold.

I've said too much, and my cock is painfully hard. I need to get the fuck out of here.

It takes everything in me to rip myself away from her and turn around.

"Where are you going?" she asks, calling after me.

"I need to take a walk."

As soon as I take a step outside, I see the slime bag himself. He's chatting with one of his buddies, laughing like he doesn't have a fucking care in the world. I'm about to blow his whole day to shit.

I crack my knuckles as I storm over to him. "Hey," I bark. His head snaps over to look at me just in time as I cock my fist back, sending it right into his face, hitting him in the eye. I grin as he shouts, grabbing his face.

"What the fuck was that for?" he demands, his hand covering his eye.

Grabbing the shithead by his shirt, I pull him close. "I don't know what your motive is, but whatever bullshit you spewed to Raven is just that, bullshit. We both know you only want one thing. If your dick goes anywhere near her, I'll fucking cut it off. Do. You. Understand?"

"Yes. God. Okay!" he says.

"You think you would have been smart enough not to fuck with her. You were doing good all these years. Stay away from her," I warn before shoving him to the ground.

I need to get out of here before I fuck up, and Link has to save my ass. Grabbing my phone, I call him.

"What's up?" he asks.

"I'm not going to last until graduation," I tell him, pacing back and forth as I try to rein in my need to kill someone.

He lets out an angry sigh. "What the fuck happened now?"

"Some fucker asked her out. And she said yes."

"What!?" he says, his voice deadly now.

"She's trying to get under our skin. I know she's been messing with you. And well, it's fucking working. She's not stupid. And this little song and dance we're all doing? Yeah, it's not going to end well."

"I'll talk to her," he says. "If she thinks she can go out with another guy, she's sorely mistaken."

"And what? You tell her no, she tells you to fuck off and goes and does something she might regret just to spite you," I growl. "Link, this isn't going as we planned. We thought Raven was happy with just the four of us. That things would stay the same until we chose to change things. We were wrong. Raven is doing what she wants, when she wants, just like we do. And right now, she wants to get us to crack. I'm pretty fucking close."

"You will do nothing. We play her game. She's bluffing. She won't do shit with him. Not when she knows she's ours. Because she knows, even if we haven't said the words. She's not stupid."

"I know. It's why the little brat is so damn good at getting to us," I say, grabbing a fist full of my hair. "I'm skipping the rest of the day. Do you have anything I can do to work off this anger before I stab the next person who looks at me funny?"

"Yeah. Come to the shop. I'll call the twins, get them to pick her up after school."

"Link," I say, before hanging up.

"Yeah?" he grunts.

"I kissed her. I couldn't risk him being her first." The line goes quiet as I wait for him to respond.

"Good," he says. "It was your kiss to take."

Letting out a breath, I say my goodbye and hang up. Looking back at the school, I feel guilty for leaving her alone for the day. I know she hates not having someone with her, but there's no way I'm going to make it through the rest of the day without losing my shit.

Sending her a quick text to let her know I'm leaving, I turn and head toward my car. I have my keys and wallet, so I don't need to go back inside.

As I drive away from the school, I feel like I'm leaving my heart behind.

CHAPTER 12

RAVEN

With a shaky hand, I touch my lips. They still tingle as I watch Hunter storm out of the school.

Did that really just fucking happen? I can't even find it in me to be pissed that he didn't admit his feelings, that was pretty damn close. I didn't think getting under their skin would work so fast, but holy shit.

Biting my lower lip, I smile. "Oh my god," I breathe, letting out a little squeal as I do a happy dance.

Needing a moment to process everything, I lean back against the lockers with a dopey smile on my face. It might not be my end goal but it's something.

My stomach growls, reminding me that I'm starving. Not wanting to waste any more of my lunchtime, I head to the café to grab something to eat.

As I'm waiting in line, my phone buzzes. Checking it, I

see Hunter's name. I click on the text, reading what it says and disappointment fills me. I know he needed some time to cool off, but I was hoping he would come back.

Yeah and do more of that tongue fucking he did to your mouth.

The rest of the day lagged. I couldn't concentrate at all. All I could think about was Hunter's lips on mine, the way my body lit up like a fucking Christmas tree. I was shocked at first, but I never wanted it to end. That was my first kiss for fuck sakes! And it was better than anything I could have hoped for.

You see movies with girls talking about how clumsy and awkward their first kiss is. That was not the case for me. I don't think Hunter has done anything with anyone, but the way he kissed promised me our first time is going to be unforgettable.

The final bell rings. I grab my bag and rush out of class to my locker. After tossing the books that I don't need inside, I lock up and head toward the front door.

That's when it hits me... if Hunter left, how the fuck am I going to get home? *Note to self, when I start making money, save for a car.*

As much as I love the guys driving me everywhere, mostly because they don't give me a choice, I'd like to be able to have my own way around if needed.

Grabbing my phone, I'm about to call one of the guys to come get me when I notice two very pissed off identical tattooed men leaning against a Jeep. Guess my ride is here after all.

"What's got your panties in a bunch?" I ask with a chuckle and a grin.

They continue to shoot me glares.

"Get in the Jeep," Travis grunts, turning around to get into the driver's side.

"Tough crowd," I say to Taylor.

"Car. Now," he commands, turning to get into the passenger's side.

Well, fuck you too then.

Getting into the back, I buckle up before speaking. "Alright, who pissed in your corn flakes?" I ask them, getting annoyed with their demeanor.

No one says anything as we pull out of the parking lot. The moment we're on the road, Taylor speaks.

"How are your nipples?" he asks casually.

"Really?" I snort. "That's what we're going with. Alright, well, they are tender but doing good. But I could use some help keeping them clean, wanna volunteer?" I ask, trying to sound playful.

I can only see the side of his face as his jaw ticks.

"Why don't you ask your new boyfriend?" Travis spits.

That surprises me. Excitement fills me at the fact that Travis is clearly jealous. I've never seen him act like this. I love it.

"I guess Hunter has already told you," I say. "And he's not my boyfriend,"

"It was Link, who by the way, is fucking pissed." He snorts a laugh. "So good luck with that one, Ray, because Link can only take so much of your bratty attitude."

"Excuse me?" I question, brows furrowing in shock.

"Don't sound so surprised. You've changed, Ray," Travis looks at me through the rearview mirror, his baby blues filled with fury. "There's joking around, and there's just being a fucking brat."

Not going to lie, I'm kind of hurt. This isn't how I wanted them to react.

"Why? Because I'm having my own thoughts. Doing things to my own body. Making friends like I have every right to do?" I say, my voice rising. "Not one fucking thing I've said to Link was to be a brat. I was in the right. It's my life."

"No, it's not!" he snaps, his nostrils flaring.

"What's that supposed to fucking mean? You don't own me. You don't get to tell me what to do. We're friends, right? That's all!" I spit the last words, knowing it's a lie. We've never been just friends, always destined to be so much more.

"Let's just breathe," Taylor says. "We're just looking out for you, Foxy Girl." His nickname settles the panic I didn't know I was getting from Travis. He not once used his nickname for me in his whole rant, referring to me as Ray. "Whoever you agreed to go out with, he doesn't deserve you. You're better than him."

"You don't even know who asked me out, do you?" I ask.

"No, that was left out. Why don't you enlighten us," Travis taunts.

"Jeff from the football team."

The car comes to a screeching halt. It happens so fast

my body jolts forwards. "What the fuck, Trav!" I shout, feeling my stomach roll.

"You have got to be fucking kidding me. Little Dove, please tell me this is some fucked up joke," Travis says, spinning around to look at me with wild eyes.

"He asked me out," I start. "I'm trying new things. I've never been on a date so I thought why not. I'm not gonna make him my boyfriend or anything. I'm not that stupid."

"This fucking list of yours," Taylor says, shaking his head. "I need to fucking burn it."

"You do know that he's a fucking player right? That he's fucked every girl in that school as well as the next fucking town over. He's scum, Raven. Lower than low."

"I'm not going to sleep with him!" I snap back at him. "I don't see anyone else lining up to ask me out, so fuck you." I take my seat belt off and throw open my door.

"Where the fuck are you going?" Travis shouts out the window.

"Walking home!" I shout back. *How dare they!* I didn't expect them to be happy about it. I knew they would be pissed, but this isn't how it was supposed to go.

They can't fucking tell me what to do and not tell me why they think they have the right to do it. They're not my boyfriends, no matter how much I want them to be. God, I just want to shake them.

"Get in the fucking car, Raven," Travis deadpans as he pulls the Jeep up behind me.

"Fuck you!" I yell while giving him the finger. "You don't have the right to tell me what I can do with another person. You think I like hearing from all the girls you fucked about how big your cock is, or how hard you made them cum? Fucking hypocrites, the both of you!"

Travis and Taylor curse. They say nothing for a minute as Travis drives behind me. I'm shaking with anger, trying to hold back tears. And that pisses me off because I'm not one to cry over much.

This whole thing with Jeff was stupid. I never should have even agreed.

"Little Dove," Travis' voice comes out softer. "Please, get in the Jeep. I'm sorry. You're right. We had no business acting that way. Please, just get in the Jeep."

I stop, swinging my gaze to him. He brings the car to a stop. Storming over to him, I get in his face through the window. "You're my best friends. My whole fucking world. But why do you have to be so fucking stupid?"

My voice cracks, and I really want the ground to open up and swallow me whole.

"I know," he says, the look on his face telling me he knows what I really mean. *Ah, then why don't you just say the fucking words!* "Can you get in the Jeep, please?"

Not wanting to walk home, I listen and get in the car.

The rest of the ride is quiet. But I can feel their eyes on me the whole time. When we pull into the driveway, I get out as soon as it's in park, slamming the door behind me.

"You have got to be fucking kidding me," I murmur when I see who is waiting for me. *Well, my plan is totally backfiring.* I'm the fucking stupid one for doing this in the first place. But with what happened just now with the twins, I really don't want to deal with Link on top of it.

I don't have a choice because he's standing there on the front step. I've seen him pissed with this murderous look but never has it been directed at me. Fuck.

"Not now," I say as I walk toward him. He's blocking the way up the stairs and when I move to walk around him, he blocks my path.

"Yes, now," he snarls. We stand toe to toe. "You think you can just act like a fucking brat and get away with it? I've been far too forgiving for how you've been these past few months, but that stops now. I don't know what the fuck has gotten into you, but you better start acting like yourself."

"Or what?" I shout. "Are you gonna stop being my friend? Are you going to kick me out of your life, this house?"

"Of course not," he spits.

I let out a humorless laugh. "Fuck you, fuck all of you." I shake my head. "I need some space. My head hurts." I'm drained both emotionally and physically.

Link reaches out, gripping my chin. He brings his face close to mine. "You will not go near that boy, do you understand me? You will not talk to him, look at him, nothing. Do you understand me?"

"Let go," I demand. But I didn't want him to. Fuck, I'm getting all hot and bothered right now. What a fucking time to get horny, but I can't help it. The way Link is with me, the way he demands things of me, handles me... well, my pussy is a fucking river right now. And I hold back a wince at my newly pierced nipples tightening in response.

He chuckles low and deep, not helping my state at all. "Oh, Little Bird. You couldn't handle me. I'd ruin you in all the best worst ways."

A part of me wants to scream that I don't care, that that's what I want. To do it already. But I just grind my teeth and rip my chin out of his hold.

"Get back here!" he roars as I dart around him, running into the house.

"Suck my left tit, dickhead," I shout. Not the best thing to do, I really shouldn't be talking to him like that, but gah, I just can't help it! He's so infuriating. I hate these little mind games, and I'm not doing anything to help it.

At this point I don't even think if I admitted to how I felt that they would do the same. They seem determined to keep their mouths shut. But why?

Running up the stairs, I go to my bedroom. Slamming the door shut behind me, I start to rip my clothes off, wanting to get into something more comfortable.

I'm so over today. I fucked up. Playing games was stupid and childish. Teasing them and pushing their limits are one thing, but going as far as agreeing to go out with some loser just to piss them off, it wasn't the right move. I'm big enough to admit that.

I've let my need for them to admit to wanting me cloud my judgement.

"Don't you fucking walk away from me!" Link bursts

through my door. It bounces off the wall, leaving a hole behind.

"You better fix that!" I yell, waving my hand toward the damage. I'm standing in only my bra and underwear. When he doesn't answer, distracted by my tits, I shake my head and turn around.

He's there in a flash, pushing me down onto the bed so that my face is shoved into the mattress.

His hand comes down on my ass, hard, the contact making a cracking sound. The pain splinters through my body, and I suck in a surprised gasp that turns into an involuntary moan. "Brat!" he shouts. His other hand grabs a handful of my hair, wrenching my head back so that I'm looking at him upside down. "From this moment on, you will not push me. You will not egg me on. No sassy words will come from these sinful lips. When I tell you to do something, you will do it, no questions asked. Enough is enough. Don't play little girl games when you're supposed to be a woman," he sneers, his voice low and dangerous.

My breathing is short and choppy as our lips hover less than an inch apart. I want him more than anything to kiss me, harsh and demanding. Like I'm the air he needs to live.

His grip tightens, and my eyes close as I try to resist the urge to moan again. "Do. You. Understand. Me?" he says slowly, deadly serious. I know better than to argue with him or test him anymore.

"Yes," I whisper.

His eyes flash with heat, loving the fact that I'm doing as I'm told and not fighting him.

He brings his lips so close to mine, I can feel the heat of his skin. My heart stops as I hold my breath, waiting to see what he does next. "That's a good, Little Bird," he praises, and I fucking melt into the hold he has on my hair.

Letting go of me, he moves away and is out the door in seconds.

I let myself fall onto the bed and lay there, trying to wrap my head around what the fuck just happened. Now, I'm sexually frustrated and dripping, lovely.

Something inside me ignited, a need I knew was hovering on the surface. I just learned two things about myself; I love being dominated, and I love being praised.

The rush I felt pleasing him was so much better than the thrill I get fucking with him.

They know how I feel, and only a fool couldn't see what I was doing. So I'm gonna lay off on trying to get the truth out of them.

For now.

CHAPTER 13

RAVEN

Since the moment all hell broke loose with the guys, when Link slapped my ass, pulled my hair, and demanded I stop being a brat, -which I fucking loved by the way- things have gone back to normal. The guys and I hang out, joking around like nothing happened.

And that's the problem. I don't want things to stay the same, I want them to stop keeping secrets from me and be honest. Yeah, yeah, call me a hypocrite all you want, that's not the point.

I guess I wouldn't say everything is how it was before, because now I have Andrhea. She's probably the only thing keeping me from going insane from my frustration with these guys. She says to give it time, that they probably have their reasons. But we're family, closer than anything, whatever reasons they have they should know I can handle them.

I'm hoping maybe some time alone with just the five of

us when we go for my yearly birthday camping trip will help. If not, at least I get them all to myself for two full days. Next weekend can't come fast enough.

As the days get closer to my eighteenth birthday, I find myself more excited to start my new job. I really need the money. The guys and Andrhea have already spent so much on me, and it makes me feel like I'm using them. I'd like to have my own money, maybe even pay them back. Not that they would accept it. But I do plan on helping my mom out more. She'll have more money in her pocket with not having to provide as much for me. She works hard enough as it is.

But she never once complains. She tells me she loves me, and she would go to the ends of the earth to make sure I have everything I need in life. I love her so much for everything she's done for us.

The piece of garbage who helped make me did nothing but hurt us. My mother is strong, and I'm so proud of her for having the strength to leave him. We might have had to start over, but it was the best thing that ever happened to us. I met the guys and everything else is history.

"AH!" someone screams from downstairs. "A rat!"

A rat? What the fuck.

Abandoning my homework on my bed, I jump up and rush out of my room. Hunter is standing in his doorway, his eyes wild. We both race down the stairs.

"Please, stop, it's not a rat. Everything is okay," Rachel says as she tries to talk to a young girl who's standing on top of the bench by the front door. She looks to be about fourteen or fifteen. The girl is trembling as she points to the floor.

"There!" she shouts. "Kill it."

"Ah shit," Hunter says, rushing forward. He drops to his knees where the girl pointed and reaches under the decorative table. "It's okay," he says, standing back up. "Not a rat. Just Princess Fiona," Hunter brings his ferret up to look her in the eyes. "Naughty girl. You know you're not allowed to be roaming the house. Shrek must be worried sick. Daddy's gonna put you in time out. No treats for naughty girls," Hunter scolds her.

Biting my lower lip, I try not to giggle. My crazy pet loving man.

"Sorry about that. She's harmless, I swear," Hunter says, holding Princess Fiona up. The girl whimpers and ducks.

"Hunter, honey, please go put her away," Rachel says. It's only now that I realize she's holding a little baby in her arms.

"Yeah, fine," he nods, and takes off upstairs.

"New guests?" I ask Rachel as the girl takes a step down from the chair.

"Yes," Rachel says, giving me a solemn look. "This is Leah. And this little precious bean is her son, Jack."

"Hi," I say, giving Leah a friendly smile. I've just laid eyes on this girl, and already I feel a little protective toward her. You don't come into Safe Haven for just any reason. So if she's here this young with a baby, it can't be good. I can only imagine what she's already had to endure in her short life.

"Hi," she says, looking a little flustered. "Sorry about that. I really did think it was a rat. Where I'm from, they're almost the size of dogs," she says with a faint blush on her cheeks.

"Alright," Lisa says as she comes down the stairs. "Your room is all ready for you. I made sure to get a room big enough for you and the baby. His crib is in there next to your bed. Raven and the guys will go out and get anything you two need."

Leah's eyes fall, filling with tears. "Thank you," her voice cracks. "I–I don't know what we would have done if Mark didn't find me when he did."

"You're safe now. No one will ever hurt you again, not while you're under this roof," Lisa assures her. Leah let out a sob as Lisa hugs her.

The urge to find whoever hurt her is strong. Sometimes, I fucking hate people. Okay, well, most of the time, but now more than ever.

"Why don't you go take a nap?" Rachel suggests, placing a hand on her shoulder.

"I can't," she sniffs, wiping her nose on the back of her hand. "I gotta feed Jack," she starts to cry again. "But I haven't been able to make milk for hours. I feel so useless."

"What about formula? We have some here. I'm more than happy to feed this little one while you rest. You must be so tired," Rachel insists.

"He's never had it before. We didn't have any, it costs too much money. We had to breastfeed, and if we couldn't produce enough, one of the other women would feed the baby for them."

One of the other women? *Where did this girl come from?*

Lisa and Rachel give each other a look like they're wondering the same thing. But we know not to pressure anyone to tell us their stories, only asking enough information to keep them and everyone who lives here safe when it comes to why they're in need of help and a place to hide.

"Are you sure? I... I've never been away from him for long," Leah asks, looking at Jack.

"If you're not comfortable, we can make you a bottle and bring it up to you," Lisa says.

Leah starts to sway on her feet. I step forward to steady her. "Your baby is safe with us. So are you. I promise you that everything will be okay. Even if it seems like there's no light at the end of the tunnel, there is." I give her a reassuring smile.

"I could use some sleep. Just an hour," Leah concedes, her eyes closing slowly.

"I'll take you up to your room. Rachel and Raven can take care of the little one. They love babies," Lisa laughs.

Lisa helps Leah up the steps. The moment they're out of sight, I turn to Rachel. "What do we know so far?" Mine and the guys' mothers help run Safe Haven. They pretty much take care of everything but the paperwork and money. I've never met the man who owns this place, but he does make sure everyone is taken care of, no matter who walks through the doors.

Whenever I do get the chance to meet him, I'll have to thank him for letting us stay this long.

"Mark, one of Link's mechanic's, was on his way with his tow truck to pick up a car to bring to the shop when he saw Leah and Jack come out of the woods. He stopped to see what was going on. The moment he took a look at her, he knew something was wrong. He got her into the truck and brought her back to the shop to see Link. Then they brought her here. We don't know much, just that they need protection, and that's what we plan on doing," Rachel informs me, looking down at Jack.

"How old is she?" I ask.

"Fifteen," Rachel says with a sad look in her eye. "And his mama said this little guy was four months old."

"Alright. What do we have for a fifteen year old girl and a four-month-old baby boy?" I ask as I turn around and head into the kitchen, going over to one of the pantries. Opening it up, I grab a thing of formula, one for a sensitive stomach just in case, and a bottle. The can of formula is new and the bottle is washed, but I make sure to rinse it with hot water first.

"We don't get teenage girls here often. So while we have some things for the baby like diapers, wipes, cream and clothes, we don't have clothes for her," Rachel says, cooing to the baby as he starts to fuss.

"Don't worry, little one," I say, going over to him and rubbing my thumb against the peach fuzz on his cheek. He's so adorable. "I'll get you your baba."

Grabbing some distilled water and bottle warmer from

one of the walk-in pantries, I make him a bottle. "Here," I say, holding my arms out for him. "I'll feed him," I say when the bottle is done.

"You really do love babies," Rachel giggles as she hands him over to me. I take him carefully and smile down at the sweet boy.

"I do," I agree as I place the nipple into his mouth. He takes it like a champ, not even fussing as he starts to chug it down. "You must be so hungry. Your mama is exhausted, baby boy. But she's so stressed. She didn't mean not to have any milk. You're all good now."

"Do you want kids of your own someday?" Rachel asks me as she leans against the kitchen island, smiling as she watches us together.

"Oh yeah," I laugh. "At least four."

"Four," she laughs, her eyes going wide. "Well, you sure will be one busy woman."

"I'll make sure their dad helps," I counter. "Now, just gotta find a man who wants to make babies with me." *Or four.*

"I don't think you're going to have any issues finding someone to love you, Raven. You're an amazing woman. Any man would be lucky to have you," she says.

Speaking of men that I want to knock me up, Link, Travis, and Taylor walk into the room. They all stop when they see me with the baby. No joke, all of their eyes light up with something more than interest.

"Hi, boys," I say.

"Hey, Foxy Girl. Steal yourself a baby?" Taylor asks with a chuckle.

"I'm tempted," I say, looking down at Jack. He's doing so well with his bottle, and ugh, my heart at the little drinking noises as he swallows.

"You want one of those?" Link asks.

Looking up at him, his eyes aren't on me, but the baby. "Yeah, I'd like a few. I love babies."

"Good," he says, nodding before looking at Travis. "I gotta get back to work. You, Taylor and Hunter go with Raven to get anything that little boy and his mother need. Put it on Safe Haven's card."

Good? What does he mean by that? Does this mean he wants kids? Well, I guess that means good for him too because I'm gonna be his baby mama one way or another.

"Got it," Travis says.

Link looks over again, this time at me. The intensity in his eyes makes me shiver. "You look good with a baby in your arms, Little Bird," his voice is low and husky, sending a shiver down my spine.

"Doesn't she?" Rachel agrees, giving her son a look.

Link gives her a small smirk before shaking his head. "Thanks for watching out for those two."

"Of course. We love helping anyone who comes in here."

With one last look at the baby, Link turns around and leaves. I'm a little disappointed that he doesn't say goodbye to me like the others. When we hung out at his place, him cuddling with me, holding me the way he did... it was so rare, but I loved it. I want more of that. But hey, I'll settle for that sexy hand necklace he seems to love to give me.

"Ready to go, Foxy girl?" Taylor asks, stepping up to me and kissing me on the side of the head. My eyes flutter shut, and I can't help the sigh of contentment that leaves me. This is what I love.

"Yeah," I say, handing Jack back over to Rachel. "He's done, just needs to be burped," Like she hasn't already raised two kids.

She laughs. "Sounds good."

"Bye, little dude," I say before turning to the guys. "Let's go."

"Not without me," Hunter calls, popping into the room. "Where are we going anyway?"

"Going to go shopping for Leah. We don't have anything here for her," Travis tells him as we head out the front door.

"I'd offer to share my things, but I know she would want her own stuff," I tell them.

We get into the car and head to the Walmart down the street. Grabbing a cart, we start to explore every aisle. By the time we're done, I have a few outfits for her and sleep wear. I'm not sure of her bra size, so I got some sports bras for her and underwear. If something doesn't fit, we can keep it at the house for another guest and buy her something that does.

"What's that?" I ask, picking up something that Hunter put into the cart. A smile spreads across my lips. "This is so cute."

Hunter grins. "Isn't it! I thought since Halloween is

coming up, if the little dude is still here, he'll need a costume."

We don't normally go out on Halloween. We don't party, I don't drink, and sadly, we're too old for trick-or-treating. But the years we have kids in the home, we do something for them for Halloween since, for their safety, they can't go out for candy.

Even on the years we don't have kids, Hunter likes it when we dress up and watch scary movies as we put ourselves into junk food comas. I prefer that to getting trashed and hungover. Not that I know what that would feel like, but it can't be all that enjoyable.

"What do you guys know about Leah?" I ask as we bring the items to the till.

They all look at each other for a brief moment, making it obvious they know something, but they don't plan on telling me. Lovely, yet another lie. This is getting old fast.

"Not much. Just what Mark told us. We're going to wait until she gets settled in before talking to her."

"Isn't that your moms' job?" I question as the lady scans each item.

"What?" he asks, brows furrowed.

"To find out all the information for each person staying at Safe Haven. Why would you guys need to know anything about her? I mean, sure, I know you must be curious because someone who works for Link found her, but why would you need her whole life story."

"What's with the third degree?" Taylor asks, trying to

brush my question off. He hands his card to the cashier to pay. They each grab bags before heading toward the exit.

I stay a few steps back, my eyes watching them. It's like I'm starting to notice things I've never bothered to allow myself to see.

These guys are keeping things from me, that much I know. The question is how much?

We pack everything away into the trunk before getting into the car. As we're driving back home, Travis gets a call. "What's up?" he answers.

"You know what sucks, half the stupid clubs we signed up for don't even start until the new year," Hunter sighs. "I was all excited to just sit and game for a few hours."

"I mean, reading club starts next week. Come read with me. I got books about a girl getting railed by a harem of men." I grin over at him.

"You and your reverse harems," Hunter chuckles. "I'm starting to think you want to be the one fucked by a bunch of guys."

"I do," I say without hesitation.

He blinks at me in shock. "Really?"

"Why not? To be worshipped by a bunch of men who love me. Who want to bring me so much pleasure that I can't stand anymore? To be stuffed full of dicks until I can't breathe. Yeah, sign me up, thanks." I raise a brow, giving him a smirk. His eyes dart to Taylor, who's watching over his shoulder with interest, then to Travis who's still talking on the phone but watching me through the rearview mirror.

Hunter blows out a breath. "I–ah–wow," is all he can say. *Oh, look at that, I've made him speechless.*

We pull up to the house, and the guys help me unload everything, bringing it all inside.

"That was Link on the phone earlier. He wants us all at the shop. Big job tonight. He needs all hands on deck," Travis says to Taylor and Hunter.

I don't miss the way Hunter's eyes light up with glee. "Nice. Gotta love overtime hours."

"So I'm going to be alone. Again," I huff out. I know it sounds needy of me, but I hate being alone, and we haven't spent much time together the past week. I need my guy time.

"You're not alone, Little Dove," Travis says. "Our moms are home. You could get to know Leah better. Maybe get some more baby time."

"Also, I'm pretty sure you were doing homework before Leah and the baby arrived. Could always finish that." Hunter grins. *Asshole.*

"Thanks for reminding me. Because I just love math," I sass sarcastically.

"No problem, babe," Hunter says, smacking a kiss on my cheek before slapping me on the ass. I jump in surprise.

He's been extra handsy since the whole Jeff thing. I'm not complaining. I love it. But it's not what I wanted, I want more.

"Be good, Foxy Girl," Taylor warns. He smirks down at me, his shaggy black hair falling over one of his eyes.

"Aren't I always?" I ask, batting my eyelashes.

He lets out a deep chuckle that has my body coming alive. "Whatever you say, babe," he says, kissing me on the forehead, so his brother can take his place.

That's two for two with the 'babe.' This is new.

"We'll be back. We always are. Just keep yourself busy. If you're sleeping when we get home, we'll come snuggle," Travis says. He doesn't call me babe, but he cups my face, his finger brushing against my cheek. His blue eyes search mine for a moment before leaning forward to kiss my temple.

Standing in the doorway, I watch three of the four parts of my heart get into Travis' car and take off again. Back to the fucking shop. At this point, they're there more than they are home.

Letting out a sigh, I grab all the bags and bring them up to Leah.

She's grateful for what we got her, insisting we didn't need to. I end up leaving after having a few snuggles with Jack, seeing she's scared, nervous, and overwhelmed. She's going to need a few days to adjust to everything before she can allow herself to realize she's in a safe place. If she can't, I'll try my best to help her see that she is.

Going to my room, I try to use my alone time to do school work. After skipping three questions I couldn't figure out the answers to, I give up.

For little while, I read, watch a TV show, and scroll on TikTok. By the time I take a look at a clock, I see that it's one in the morning.

"What the fuck?" I say, not realizing how late it is.

Texting the group chat the guys and I have, I ask where they are. While I wait for one of them to answer, I get ready for bed. After brushing my teeth, I slip into a pair of PJ pants and Travis' hoodie.

Grabbing my phone, I see no one has answered me. I could try calling them, but now I'm annoyed. They work at an auto body shop. Along with a crap ton of other guys. What the fuck would they be doing this late?

Well, I'm about to find out because I know this isn't about fixing someone's vehicle. They've been slipping out of the house more than once at crazy hours, and I'm going to find out why tonight. I'm done being left in the dark.

Slipping on some flip-flops, I grab my phone and head to my mom's room. One of the things we have in common is that we both sleep like the dead, so I don't wake her up when I steal her car keys.

Being as quiet as I can, I sneak downstairs and out the door, making sure to lock it behind me before getting into my mom's car.

I've had my license since I was sixteen, I've just never really driven because I don't have a car, and the guys take me everywhere I need to go.

Pulling out of the driveway, I start heading toward the shop.

I'm not sure what Link and the guys are going to say or do if they find me there, but I don't care at this point. I'll deal with the consequences later.

Right now, I wanna see what they've been keeping from me.

CHAPTER 14

QUINTON

I am not at all surprised to see Raven walking down the front steps of her house. The guys are at the warehouse, doing what they do best. And I'm here, doing what I do best. Watching Raven while the guys are working. Not that I mind. Knowing that I can keep her safe when they can't gives me as much peace of mind as it does for them.

Raven looks around, as if she's checking to see if anyone is watching before slipping into her mom's car. I take this as my cue to leave my watch post from the shadows of the backyard where her bedroom window faces and get into my car that's parked in the back alley.

Quickly, with my headlights off, I drive to the end of the road and wait until Raven passes me. Once she does, I wait a few seconds before pulling out to follow her. I already know where she's going. The guys should have been home hours ago, but this job was bigger than we expected. Lincoln texted me to tell me that they had a squealer, and it was going to be a long night.

I've noticed Raven has been starting to be more curious about what's going on around her, more than she used to be. I knew it wouldn't be long until she decided to take matters into her own hands and get the answers she needed.

That's why instead of stopping her as she heads toward the warehouse while the guys are knee-deep into they're work, I'm following to make sure she stays safe until she sees the truth with her own eyes.

The guys have their reasons for not telling her what they really do, and I understand why they would want to protect her for as long as they can. The life we live isn't for everyone. It's dangerous and messy. But they're seeing her through the eyes of the boys who fell in love with her at first sight.

I'm seeing things through the eyes of someone who fell over time, from a distance. There's a lot I see that they don't. They're afraid that once she sees the monsters that lurk within each of them that she'll run and hide.

But I know better. Raven is hiding her own demons, making her the best fit for them. I don't think Raven will hide. Instead, she'll embrace this new life she's about to walk into.

She parks the car on the side of the road, just before reaching the warehouse. I watch as she takes off running in its direction. I pull up a little further, parking as close to the trees as I can.

Getting out, I watch her looking around, trying to find the best way to get inside.

Funny thing is, it won't be all that hard because this place isn't heavily guarded. No one has ever had the balls to step foot on any of our properties. Not when the end result is going face to face with Lincoln.

She just needs to get through the shop to get to the warehouse.

There's someone on the main door, but Raven doesn't even bother trying to go that way. Raven climbs the fence, jumping over the other side. "Shit," I mutter as I take off running after her. Climbing the fence, I check to see where she went. She's hiding behind a tree, taking in the warehouse. There's no way she can just walk through the front door, she would be caught by someone in seconds.

When my feet hit the ground on the other side, I pull my hood up so my face is hidden and start walking out in the open.

Through the corner of my eye, I can see Raven watching me, slinking back into the darkness behind the tree.

Looking around, I make sure no one else is around before pointing to the window she's going to need to crawl into to get inside the warehouse. I don't say anything, don't turn her way. I wait a moment before lowering my hand, giving her time to look in the direction to where I'm pointing to before I walk toward the warehouse entrance.

Only, I don't go inside, just getting out of her view so she thinks the coast is clear. Now, will she take my help or turn and run back, thinking she's caught?

Something tells me Raven is willing to deal with being caught if it means getting answers.

As for me? I don't know what Lincoln will do to me when he finds out I not only let her leave, but showed her a way in to see the very thing they've been hiding from her for years.

Unlike them, I'm not going to sit back. She deserves to know everything. And if they won't be the ones to tell her, then I'll assist her in finding it out on her own.

I am just hoping I didn't make a big mistake.

RAVEN

I'm seeing things, right? Is there really a guy standing out in the open as I search for a way into the warehouse, pointing to a window above a fire escape?

Blinking in surprise, I watch as he lowers his hand and walks away. *Why is this man helping me? Who the fuck is this guy anyways?*

Also, why are there not more people watching this warehouse? I can hear the music inside, so I know there must be people in there.

Is this some kind of underground club? If so, I'm going to be so fucking pissed at the guys. Why wouldn't they tell me about a club? I'm not of age, but something tells me they don't give two shits about the law, and neither does this place.

Fuck it. I know none of these people will hurt me, they all work for Link. The guys would lose their shit. I'm gonna risk it because I made it this far already. Not that it was very hard to do so. This is almost way too easy.

I really don't care because I'm ducking out from behind the tree and running toward the fire escape.

"You really need to work out more," I mutter to myself as I climb the ladder, my knees already burning.

When I get to the top, I have to be careful as I try to open the window. There's no ledge to get up on, just the ladder under my feet holding me up right.

With a little bit of effort, I manage to push the window in. Climbing up the last few steps, I swing myself inside.

Once my feet touch the ground, I look around at my surroundings. It's dark, so I take out my phone to turn on the flash light.

Seeing no one else around me, I search the level I'm on, but there's nothing other than empty rooms filled with dust. A few rooms filled with boxes. Whatever this warehouse is used for, it's not being done on this level.

Voices from below have my head snapping in that direction. Creeping over to the railing, I look down to the next level. There's lights on down there, a few guys walking around. I note what direction they go in and decide to go the other way. There's two sets of stairs to the next level. One that will lead me right where those guys were and another through a door. I take the back steps. As soon as the door is closed behind me, I take a deep breath.

My nerves are all over the place with not knowing what's going to happen, who I might run into. But there's no real fear. I know that no one here would hurt me, I've seen the way some of Link's men look at him, like he's the reaper just looking for an excuse to end their lives. *So fucking hot.*

Excitement fills me as I go down the first set of stairs. Looking out the window of the door, I see the level I just saw the guys on. There's not much from what I can see. It looks a lot like the garage does, a large open space with a few cars and some tools alongside the wall.

Huh. Maybe all they do is fix cars?

The curiosity in me has me going down the next flight of stairs. This must be the level the music is coming from because it gets louder the lower I go.

Getting to the next level, my suspicions are confirmed. I lower my phone light to my side so that no one can see it as I look through the little window on the door to see what looks like some kind of underground club.

Well, fuck right off! That's bullshit. You're meaning to tell me this is where they've been spending all their time. Why the fuck haven't I been allowed to come here? I highly doubt they give two fucks about legal age. This is bullshit. So they have this whole other life that I don't know about.

I'm pissed, so fucking pissed right now. I'm seconds away from barging in there, finding them and giving them a piece of my mind.

That is until I hear screaming. And I'm not talking about the *I'm having a good time* kind, but the *I'm being tortured and murdered* kind.

Okay, we got a plot twist. I'm gonna go with that and say that maybe there is more going on here. And I'm also going to be the dumb white girl who goes toward the sounds that would have anyone else shitting their pants and running for their life.

This time, I head down the next set of stairs with more caution. If someone is getting murdered, the last thing I wanna do is come up behind the killer and scare them, making me their next victim. *I'd like to get dicked down at least once by each of my guys before I die, thanks.*

Getting to the end of the stairs, I turn the corner and come face to face with a door. With each step closer, the screams get louder. Then I hear it... a voice I know all too well.

"Fuck yeah! Did you see the way my knife sliced through his skin? Like fucking butter." It's Hunter. It has to be. I know that voice, that excited laugh.

I don't think, only walk closer to the door, needing to see this with my own two eyes.

Peering into the window, my heart starts to pound in my chest, my belly a tornado of nerves as I take in the sight before me.

Link, Hunter, Travis, and Taylor are all standing there, no shirts on, their tattooed skin splattered in blood.

Sitting tied to chairs before them are three bloody and beaten men.

Well, this is not what I expected to find. Why does this make so much sense? So... do they work for Black Venom Crew then?

No. No, because Link owns this place. This shop and warehouse. That means... *Link runs Black Venom Crew. They are Black Venom Crew.*

Holy shit. *Holy shit.* HOLY SHIT! My guys are fucking killers! Like ruthless murderers.

And now I understand why they didn't tell me. I should run. I should go to the cops and tell them what I'm seeing, who's really behind all these people going missing over the past few years.

. But I'm not going to. The idea of anyone finding out who they are terrifies me. I don't care what they do or who they are. They're mine. And I love them no matter what.

Knowing they are so powerful and ruthless sends a delightful shiver through my body.

Like a fucking creeper, I watch in the shadows as they do their thing. I don't know what the guys on the chairs did to deserve this fate. But I know one thing for sure, they did deserve it.

My guys would never hurt someone who's innocent. We live in a house meant for women and children to get away from sick and evil monsters.

They're a whole different breed of monsters.

I'm in awe as Hunter laughs like a mad man, striking his knife at one of the men, making him scream.

The twins have wicked grins as they taunt their guy, poking and prodding at him.

And then there's Link. He stands there like a statue, looking at the three guys, his face blank. One guy is pleading, begging, but Link just stands there.

Hunter takes out his guy first, stabbing him in the carotid artery. Blood starts to spurt and run down the dude's neck as he chokes on his own blood. "It's like if splatter paint and a fountain made a baby," Hunter cackles.

"What the fuck does that even mean?" Taylor asks with a snort.

"Please! I'll tell you everything you need to know," dude number two begs.

"No one is fucking talking to you," Taylor snaps, punching him in the face with what looks like a set of brass knuckles. Dude cries out, his head snapping to the side.

"Look, it's not my fault you don't see the beauty in blood," Hunter says.

I just saw my best friend, the man who's been glued to my side since I was eight, -someone who helps me through my fucking period cramps- kill a man. And laugh about it.

And you know how I feel? Not shocked, scared, or upset. Nope, I thought it was hot. I mean, the way his arm bulged as he used his muscles to sink that knife in there... *swoon.*

Okay, so I'm fucked in the head. I kind of had that suspicion all along. But hey, looks like the men I wanna spend the rest of my life with are too, so at least I don't have to worry about scaring away a man.

"Please," dude number two says again. "We had to. He told us we had to!"

"Shut up!" dude number three hisses through his swollen and cut lips.

"I'll do whatever you want, just please don't kill me," number two wails.

"You *had* to?" Travis repeats with a scoff before looking

up at the others. "You hear that, guys? He said he *had* to team up with these two fuckers to rape a teenage girl. Sounds legit if you ask me."

"We didn't want to. I swear," number two says.

"Pretty sure the video you guys took to give to the guy who hired you as proof showed that you very much *wanted* to. You're fucking sick and depraved, all of you. And you're going to hell and we get to be the ones who hand-deliver you to the Devil himself," Hunter gloats, getting into his face with a sadistic grin.

"Can we get this over with?" Link grunts. "Normally, I love to have some fun beforehand, but Raven was expecting you guys home hours ago. I don't want her to wake up alone."

Awe, that's kind of sweet coming from the big man dripping in blood.

"Fine," Hunter says. "I'll take care of this guy with the cleanup crew while you guys take care of these two."

I suck in a breath when I get a full view of the front of him. Hunter has blood splattered all over his tattoos, dripping down his abs. He takes his bloody hand and runs it through his hair, the blue and red mixes to make a purple. He uses the back of his other hand to wipe some blood off his face only to smear it more.

What a time to be turned on. But here I am, seconds away from bursting into the room and jumping one of them, and demanding they let me ride them like a pony.

Hunter grabs a bottle of water off the ground and takes a big drink before dumping the rest of it over his face. It's like my own fucked up strip show or something. This night is turning out to be amazing. I do not regret leaving the house to come here.

Hunter shakes the water out of his hair, just adding to the whole scene of looking like a killer stripper.

I pout as Hunter takes the dude on the chair out of the room, leaving my line of vision. Thankfully, I have three other gorgeous men to look at.

"I really don't want to have to listen to this man blubbering like a fucking baby anymore," Travis sighs, grabbing a gun from his back pocket and pointing it at his head.

"Wait!" Taylor says. I almost laugh at the look of relief on the dude's face like he just might have another chance. But Taylor takes his own gun out and points it at the dudes junk. "Thought he should feel what it's like losing his dick first," Taylor explains with a shrug, before firing off a shot. My hands shoot up to cover my ears as I wince from the sound.

The dude screams, but they're cut off when Travis shoots him in the head. "Much better. He was giving me a fucking headache," Travis says.

"Now. Do you wanna tell us who you're working for and we can shoot you in the head. Swift and painless. Or, do you wanna keep being a stubborn fucker when you know you're going to die anyways and be in agonizing pain for a good ten minutes before I end you. Up to you, but it's gonna feel like a lifetime," Link says.

"Fuck you," number three spits, but he's too scared to have any heat behind it. "I'm not telling you shit."

"Can we just kill him? I wanna go home and cuddle with Ray," Taylor pouts.

"You can kill me. You can kill anyone you want, but he's gonna send more. There's going to be more girls. There always is. That pretty little blonde I've seen you guys around town with might even be next."

Uh-Oh, that's not good. He said stupid shit. Well, I guess it's the slow and painful route for him.

Link's body goes stiff as stone. "Don't you fucking talk about her. Don't you even think about her!"

"I bet he might even be nice enough to send you the video after it's done," the guy smirks.

Like a snake striking, Link has his hand around the guy's neck in less than a second. The man gags, his eyes bugging out as Link squeezes with all his strength. "No one speaks about our girl like that. If you weren't going to die already, that would have just sealed your fate." Link looks up at Travis. "Hold his mouth open."

Travis grins, stepping up to pry open the guy's mouth. His muffled screams fill the room as Link lets go of his throat, reaches into the guy's mouth to pull out his tongue while bringing up a silver blade. "I'd like to hear you talk now," Link sneers, his voice low and taunting. With one swift flick of his wrist, Link cuts off his tongue. Blood is dripping down his face as his screams turn garbled. Link takes the severed tongue and shoves it in the guy's mouth, and forces it closed.

Link says nothing, his jaw clenched with a look of pure

rage on his face as he holds the guy's mouth shut, making him choke on his own tongue and drown in his blood.

Part of me wants to puke, because this shit is gross. All of it. I don't like blood. But it does happen to look so good on them.

And the other part is wondering how fucked up would it be if I slipped my hand into my pants and rubbed one out because, fuck me, the way Link ended this man for talking about me like that is what my dirty dreams are made of.

Is it too soon to book a wedding venue? Maybe we should kiss first.

He stops fighting, his body going still. "Fucking waste of space," Link hisses and spits on the guy's face. "I'm too fucking wound up, I need to go spend some time with the punching bag or I'm going to need to find someone else to kill. I'll get the crew to clean this up. You guys go shower and get back to Raven."

Oh shit, that's me. Fuck. I need to get back home now, or I'm screwed.

Taking one last look, seeing my guys through new eyes, I take off up the stairs, two at a time until I'm back to the top level.

Finding the window, I open it up and my head spins. Fuck, that's high. Sucking it up, I climb down. Once I'm on solid ground, I take off running the way I came from.

It's only when I'm in my car, driving back to the house that I realize I left my phone at the warehouse.

"Fuck!" I shout, hitting the steering wheel. There's no

way they're not going to find my phone and when they do, I'm fucked.

The buzz of the moment starts to fade as I park the car back in our driveway. Walking up the steps and into the house, the realization that my best friends are a group of murderers really sinks in.

After putting my mom's keys back, I race up to my room. I'm rushing to get into my PJ's and I climb into bed when I notice my phone is plugged in and charging. "What the fuck?" I whisper, brows furrowed as I pick it up, revealing a note. Grabbing the note, I read it.

> *Thought you might be needing this back. I don't think your guys would be all too happy if you lost this. Might raise some questions.*

A smile finds my lips. "Thanks, mystery man." I say, crumbling the note up and tossing it into the trash can. I have no idea who that person was tonight, but they were a massive help. Snuggling into my blankets, I close my eyes. But I can't sleep, my mind racing.

They've lied to me for who knows how long. I can kind of understand why, it's a big fucking deal, but it hurts to think that that they didn't trust me enough with this information. Or that they didn't think I could handle what they really do.

Well, fuck them all because I didn't take off screaming, I didn't run for the hills. I'm still here, and if anything, I'm more in love with these guys than before. I've heard the rumors about what Black Venom Crew does. And while it's fucked up, in my opinion, they're doing God's work. Because I believe there's no room on this earth for people who hurt or beat women and children, who take advantage and rape another human. People like my dear old pops, wherever the fuck he is.

My door opens not too long after, and I close my eyes, pretending to be asleep.

"Shhh," Travis says as they all make their way into my room.

"Why? This girl sleeps like the fucking dead. We could play poker and use her body as the table and she wouldn't wake up," Hunter chuckles.

"I guess that's true. She's never woken up while Link's been in here jacking off," Taylor says.

Wait. Hold the fuck up. He does what? And why the fuck is my body flushing with need at the thought of it.

You love all the dirty fucked up things you hope they do to you some day, don't even deny it.

"I'm taking this side, you can go on the other," Travis says.

"And where the fuck do I go?" Hunter huffs. I bite the inside of my cheek to keep myself from smiling. Good thing the room is dark.

"I don't know, the end of the bed?" Taylor snickers.

"Fuck you," Hunter mutters. I feel the bed dip as all three of them get on. The twins get under the covers with me while Hunter takes the end of the bed. I wanna tell him to sleep between my legs and rest his head on my belly, but I can't let them know I'm awake. They only do this when they think I'm sleeping. This isn't the first time I've faked sleeping before.

I'm not sure what twin, but one of them pulls me partly onto their chest while the other spoons me from behind. I can't tell who is who because everyone smells fresh out of the shower.

I have to hold back a whimper as I feel a hard cock press into my ass. They're killing me.

My once racing mind slows, coming to a conclusion I knew all along. It doesn't matter to me what they do, they're mine, and I'll love them until the day I die.

CHAPTER 15

RAVEN

"**Y**ou got everything?" Hunter asks as he walks into my room.

"I think so," I say, looking over my shoulder.

Every time I look at one of them, I get a rush of excitement. Now that I know who they really are and what they're capable of, I see them in a whole new light, but in a good way. They're still my best friends, my family, my everything; but now, they're so much more.

I'm not as pissed that they've been keeping how they feel about me to themselves now that I know the truth. They probably think they'd lose me if I ever found out, waiting to find the right time to tell me.

But now I want them more than ever, and I have to keep this to myself. It sucks.

"Ah, Ray. We're going camping..." Hunter says, grabbing

my swimsuit out of my bag. "In the middle of October. In the mountains. I don't think you're going to be needing this."

"That's where you're wrong," I sass, snatching it from him and shoving it in my bag. "Remember when we went quading last year right before we had to leave to come home. We found that hot spring? Yeah, I wanna go to that."

"I'm down for that. I'll tell the guys to pack their trunks," he says, kissing the side of my head before leaving my room.

I'm momentarily shocked as I stare blinking at my bed. Hunter became more affectionate and not in a friendly way since the whole Jeff thing. I both love and hate it because I feel like I'm getting mixed signals. Is he only acting like this out of jealousy? How long will it last before he goes back to the way he was? He's always been the touchy feely type but this feels... different. I don't want to get my hopes up, to start loving the attention, only to have it ripped away from me later on.

I hate feeling so insecure, but these guys are giving me fucking whiplash at this point.

When I make sure I have everything packed, I head downstairs to meet the guys outside. A smile finds my lips when I see them all joking around. Link borrowed a truck with a trailer attached to the back for the quads. We plan on sleeping in tents, me with Hunter, the twins together and Link by himself.

"Hunter, catch!" Taylor shouts. Hunter is bent over, arranging things in the back.

"What?" Hunter asks, standing up. His eyes widen as

Taylor tosses a sleeping bag his way. It happens so fast that Hunter doesn't have time to react. The bag hits him with force, making him lose his balance and trip over something in the back. "Fuck!" he screams as he falls over the side of the truck.

The twins burst out laughing, giving each other a high five. I start giggling as Hunter runs around the front of the truck, tackling Taylor to the ground. The two of them start rolling around on the front lawn like a couple of kids.

"That's enough," Link barks as he jumps off the trailer. "Grow the fuck up."

"I think it's cute. Who wants to grow up? It's one step closer to death," I say, jogging down the steps.

"I'm not afraid of death, Little Bird," Link says as he walks towards me. I bet you're fucking not. Death should be afraid of you.

I try not to drool as I remember him covered in blood, the way he took that man's life for daring to talk about me sends a shiver down my spine.

"I am," I admit. "Dying means leaving you guys. And that just won't fly with me," I say, shrugging as I move to step past him. He grabs my arm to stop me and bends over to whisper in my ear.

"Don't be. As long as we're around, nothing will ever happen to you. And none of us plan on ever going anywhere."

My heart rate picks up as I feel my body flush.

The guys get off the ground and dust themselves off. I

giggle as I step towards Taylor, picking some grass out of his shaggy midnight hair. "Crazy boys," I tease.

"Yes, but we're *your* crazy boys." Hunter grins.

"And your crazy boys are about to take you on your last birthday camping trip before you're an adult," Travis says, stepping up to kiss me on the side of the head. His lips linger, and when he pulls away, I have to stop myself from reaching out to pull him closer.

"Getting old, Ray-Ray," Taylor jokes. "Soon you're going to be sixty with tits hanging down to your knees."

"Fuck off," I laugh, unzipping my hoodie to show off my boobs that are practically spilling out of my tank top. "No sagging here." I'm not wearing a bra, my nipples and piercings pressing against my shirt. All of their eyes drop to my tits. Biting my lip, I hold back a giggle.

"Little Bird," Link says, his voice a warning tone.

Sighing, I roll my eyes and zip up my hoodie, getting disappointed groans from the guys.

"Sorry, Daddy," I tease, loving how his eyes light up with a fire and his jaw clenches. "I promise to be a good girl on this trip. If not, you can punish me."

I said I'd stop fucking with him to get a rise, I said nothing about flirting and teasing. It's fun, getting a reaction out of him.

"Get in the truck," he says, taking my bag from me.

"Yes, Daddy." I wink, snickering at the growl I get from him.

We all pile into the truck. The moms come out onto the front steps to wave goodbye, telling us to have a good time.

Leah seems to be settling in well. She's still shy, not talking much, but both her and the baby are safe, so that's all that matters for right now. I'll be there for her when she's ready.

"Let's get some music going on in here," Hunter says as we pull out onto the highway. I'm sandwiched between the twins, drowning in their scent. I'm trying really hard not to turn my head, shove my face into one of their shirts and inhale deeply like a creeper.

"Let's not." Link grunts.

"Windows down, please," I ask, smiling as all of them roll their windows all the way down at the same time. They know I get car sick pretty easily, and the only way I can ride is if I can feel the cool breeze on my face.

Normally, I sit up front so I can stick my head out the window if needed, but I wanted to spend time with the twins like this.

Closing my eyes, I rest my head on the back of the seat and enjoy the breeze.

One after the other, the twins take each of my hands, entwining their fingers with mine. I smile again, excited for this weekend. Maybe this is exactly what I need with them.

Everywhere I go by Hollywood Undead starts to play and Hunter immediately starts to sing along. A few seconds later, the twins join in. By the time we get to the main chorus, I'm singing at the top of my lungs along with them.

Link shakes his head, a small smirk twitching on his lips. He loves this, he just won't admit it.

"Fuck," I groan as we bump along the back road as we drive toward our camping spot.

"You okay, Little Mouse?" Hunter asks, turning in his seat with a concerned face.

"No," I mutter, trying to take deep breaths. "No air flow, and all the bumping around is making me feel sick."

"Want me to turn the air conditioning on?" Link asks, looking at me in the rearview mirror.

"No. It doesn't do anything for me," I sigh, really hoping I don't puke. Not that they haven't seen me get sick before. At some point, each of them have been there for me while I had the flu, holding my hair back as I got sick. I love them.

"Here, Foxy Girl," Taylor says, leaning over to unbuckle me. His stubble jaw grazing my lips. As he pulls back, he side eyes me and smirks. He's so damn handsome. And I get two of them.

"What are you doing?" Link asks.

"She needs to stick her head out the window, you know the drill," Taylor says, pulling me into his lap.

"Thanks." I smile.

"Anything for you, Foxy Girl," he says, kissing me on the cheek.

This time, the feeling of his lips on my skin lingers as I move around in his lap so that I'm kneeling between his legs sideways as I practically hang out the window.

"You better not let her fall," Link snaps.

"No fucking shit." Taylor chuckles, grabbing a hold of my hips.

As I take in a big lungful of air, I start to feel better. Taylor rubs his thumbs on the exposed skin where my shirt rises above the waistband of my leggings. My skin warms where he touches, sending a shiver through my body.

We bump along the road, the movement no longer bothering me. Not wanting to risk it, I shift back enough so that I can lay my head on my arms as they rest on the window.

The new position makes my ass stick out, and I try not to laugh as Travis curses, getting a good view of my ass.

Taylor keeps hold of my hips, making sure I'm safely inside until we reach our camping spot.

"Thank god," I say in a rush. Maneuvering myself around, I climb out the open window, desperate to get out of the truck. The guys chuckle, while Link mutters under his breath that I'm crazy. As if he isn't fucking psychotic. He hasn't seen my crazy yet.

All the guys get out of the truck, and we check out the camping spot. "I love it here," I sigh as I take in the little lake.

"Our own little home away from home," Taylor says, slinging his arm around my shoulder.

"So, what do we do first?" I ask, turning around to look at the others.

"Unpack the truck. Then, once everything is set up, we can unload the quads," Link says.

We only have a few hours before sundown and by the time we're done setting everything up, it will be pretty much dark. They wanted me to skip school so we could get here early, but I turned them down. Thankfully, they didn't fight me on it.

We all work together to get our tents set up. While the guys work on the quads, I start on supper. Hot dogs tonight, but we plan on catching some fish tomorrow.

"I'm starving," Hunter whines, taking a seat in the chair next to me as he starts to put together his own hot dog.

"Same," Travis says, doing the same on my other side.

"I'm going to set up a few snares over there," Link starts. "So stay away. Gotta piss or take a shit, go the other way," Link finishes as he starts to walk away.

"Talk dirty to me, Big Daddy!" I shout after him, earning me the middle finger. I laugh as I take a bite of my food.

"You sure do like calling him Daddy," Taylor comments, taking a spot on the other side of the fire.

"Aww. Do you feel left out? I can start calling you Daddy too." I grin.

His eyes light up briefly. "Nah. I'm more of a Sir kind of guy." He winks. *Noted.*

Rolling my eyes, I try to ignore how much I'd love to call him Sir.

"I'd have to agree. Link is more Daddy, I'm with Taylor

on the Sir thing," Travis says, giving me a smirk. *Yes, fucking please.*

"What about you?" I ask Hunter.

"I'll be anything you want me to be, baby," he says teasingly, but his eyes are full of heat.

"What would you wanna be called in bed?" Taylor asks me. Okay, so we're doing this right now.

I shrug. "Not really sure. Never had sex before."

"Good," Hunter mutters as he takes a bite of his hot dog.

"But from the books I've read, I think I know a few things that would work for me, things I think I'd enjoy."

"Like what?" Travis asks me with interest.

"Well," I start. How far is too far with these guys? Am I just going to casually tell them my kinks? I mean, isn't this kind of what best friends talk about? "So far I've found out I have a praise kink."

"You like being a good girl, Little Dove?" Travis asks, his voice low and husky.

"For the right man, yes," I say back.

"What else?" Taylor asks.

"I'm not sure if I'd like it done to me, but I enjoy reading about primal play, breeding kinks, and other stuff like that. I don't think I've read anything that's turned me off. And I've read everything from super sweet and fluffy to down right fucked up."

"Fuck me. Every man's dream girl," Hunter groans.

If that's true, then man the fuck up and tell me.

Link comes back not too long after we're done eating, taking his plate to sit down and eat.

"Little Bird," Link's voice pulls me from my sleep. I must have dozed off while we all sat around talking. "Bed time."

"Okay," I say with a yawn. "You coming?" I ask Hunter. He gives me a wicked grin.

"Are you offering?" he wiggles his brows.

"Hunt!" Link barks.

Hunter shoots his brother a glare before looking back at me. "Yeah, Little Mouse, I can come to bed if you don't wanna be alone."

I'm not afraid of being out here, I know the guys wouldn't let anything happen to me. But I'm here this weekend to spend time with them.

He gets up and steps over to me. I think he's about to offer me a hand to help me up, but instead he scoops me up into his arms. "Later, fuckers. I'm getting cuddles with our girl," Hunter calls to the guys.

"I can walk, you know," I laugh, the tent's not too far from the fire pit.

"I know," is all he says, only putting me down when we get to the tent door. He unzips it, and we both walk in. This tent only fits two people, but I love that it has height. It makes it easier to get changed.

Hunter turns on the light that we attached to the top of the tent so that I'm able to see my bags.

Grabbing my PJ pants, I take off my jeans, not caring that Hunter is watching. Once I'm dressed and more comfortable, I turn to Hunter. "Take it off."

"What?" he asks, his brows shooting up.

"Your hoodie, dummy," I laugh. "I'm cold."

He grins, not bothering to ask me why I don't just use one of the ones I brought with me. I watch as he grabs the bottom of the hoodie and starts to pull it up over his body. His shirt lifts a little with it, giving me a nice view of his V.

Would it be weird if I licked it? Maybe just a little.

"Thanks," I say, taking it from him. He watches as I put it on, getting a possessive gleam in his eyes at the sight of me wearing his clothes.

"Come on, Little Mouse, let's get your adorable ass to bed," he says as I snuggle into his hoodie.

We zipped the sleeping bags together, choosing to share, and after we get under the covers, Hunter pulls me to his side, spooning me. We lay like that for a while, not speaking. The only sounds are the night life around us and the others at the fire pit. I can hear their soft murmurs as the fire crackles.

That mixed with the way Hunter is playing with my hair, has me drifting off to sleep.

When I wake up the next morning, I really gotta pee. But I don't wanna crawl out from under the sleeping bag for two reasons. One, it's fucking freezing out there– my nose is an icicle right now.

And two, Hunter's morning wood is pressed into my ass. How bad is it that I'm very tempted to pull down his boxers and just back my way onto his dick right now?

I'll keep that in mind for the future.

Laying here for as long as I can, I enjoy the heat he's radiating as his body is pressed up against mine. But my bladder wins, and I really need to get dressed and go outside to piss or things are about to get real embarrassing.

Of course, I can't resist pretending to stretch as I arch my ass back against his cock.

"Little Mouse," his sleep-filled voice croaks. "Keep doing that, and I'm gonna be cumming in my boxers really fast."

"Wouldn't want that," I say with a smile on my face that he can't see. "Sorry." Not sorry.

"Where are you going?" he asks, reaching for me as I climb out of the sleeping bag.

"Gotta pee," I say, shivering as I quickly look for my shoes. "Fuck, it's cold. My nipples are like stone right now."

"Ray," Hunter groans. I look down at him as he wipes a hand over his face. "Don't talk about your tits right now."

I snort out a laugh as he adjusts himself under the sleeping bag. Slipping on my sneakers, I grab Hunter's jacket. "Be right back."

Unzipping the tent, I step outside. I'm surprised to see that Link is up. He's over by the fire with a whole breakfast set up.

"How did you sleep?" his low, husky voice makes me shiver for a whole new reason.

"Not bad," I answer. "A little stiff, and it's fucking freezing. Thankfully, Hunter helped me keep warm."

"Good." He nods, looking back down at the pan as he flips the sausage. "Where are you going?"

"Pee. Where's the TP?"

"Over there," he says, nodding his head towards the picnic table we brought.

Rushing over, I grab it out of the bag before racing off toward where Link told us to use the bathroom.

"There better not be any fucking poison ivy," I mutter as I look around for a spot to pop a squat. They brought a portable toilet, but I'm camping with four men, no way I'm going anywhere near that thing.

Finding a spot by a tree, I look around and find it well hidden. Gathering the jacket, I move it out of the way with one hand so I don't get any pee on it and use my other to pull down my pants. After squatting down it takes me a moment, but finally I get some relief.

"God, that feels good," I sigh, making sure I don't piss on my feet.

When I'm done, I step to the side and out of the way to wipe. Just as I'm done and am about to pull up my pants, Taylor pops out the bush.

"Boo!" he shouts.

I scream, trip over my foot and fall bare ass into the bush.

"Taylor!" I shout as he bursts out laughing and runs away. "I'm gonna kill you!"

Fucking asshole.

Once I manage to get to my feet, I pull my pants up and start running back to camp. When I get there, I'm fuming as I search for the fucker.

"You!" I shout as I storm over to where he's now sitting by the fire.

"Me?" he says, pointing to himself. "What did I do?"

"Oh, fuck off," I huff. "You're lucky I didn't land on any sticks. What a way to lose my ass virginity," I grumble.

"I have no idea what you're talking about," he says, but the grin on his face says otherwise.

"You suck." I glare at him.

"Nah, baby, but I can lick," he says, his grin widening. I bet he can. Wait, I don't wanna know how good he is. He's been with other women and the idea of his mouth on them makes me wanna find all the bitches he's fucked and kill them all.

The thought has me remembering the fact that I'm alone, in the woods in the middle of nowhere, with four killers. And I'm not at all scared by the fact.

"Why are we talking about your ass virginity?" Hunter asks as he comes out of the tent.

"This fucker popped out of the bush as I was peeing and scared me!" I say waving my hand toward Taylor.

"Was he trying to fuck your ass or something?" Hunter questions, looking confused.

"Never mind," I sigh, shaking my head.

"You know, Dove," Travis says, handing me a cup of coffee he made me. "You really shouldn't go too far alone. You never know what's out there. Could be a murderer lurking." He kisses the side of my head before joining the others.

I take a sip and sigh happily. "I have nothing to worry about," I state.

"Oh yeah, and why's that?" Link asks, handing me a plate of food.

"Because I have you four. And I know you would never let anyone hurt me." They all look at me with fire in their eyes, like the idea of someone laying a hand on me makes them murderous. And after what I saw and how Link acted when that man mentioned me, I know they would kill for me. In a way, they already did.

"Never, Little Bird. I'd love to see anyone try," Link growls.

Standing here, sipping my coffee, I watch my guys talk about all the things we have planned for today.

I have no idea what's going to happen in regards to my life, but as long as I have these four, I don't care what happens. They just need to be with me, by my side.

CHAPTER 16

RAVEN

"Where's Link?" I ask as I come back from my random little walk around the campsite. We got back from quading a half hour ago and have just been hanging out around camp since. It was a lot of fun. The trails haven't been used by anyone but us, so they're not as worn down as they should be. We got stuck a few times, but overall, it was fun to speed through the woods.

We ended up stopping at the top of a smaller mountain and the sight was breathtaking. I made sure to get photos with the guys. I'll be adding those to my album for sure.

It's noon now and we came back for lunch before we head out to do some fishing. Link wants to catch a few fish for supper but we have food just in case.

"He's around here somewhere," Hunter says from his

seat by the fire pit. "He said something about checking the snares."

"Kay." I nod. "I'm gonna go take a dip in the lake, see if I can wash some of this mud off me before we head out again."

There were a few muddy trails we went on. The guys went around on the sides, but it was so slanted and I didn't want to risk the quad tipping, so I went right through, and in return I got pretty much covered in mud head to toe. I don't care, I loved every moment of it.

"The twins went down to do the same. Stick with them," Hunter tells me, closing his eyes as he relaxes back into the chair.

"Why?" I ask.

"Because I don't want anything happening to you, Little Mouse. Be a good girl and listen for once please," he says, all while keeping his eyes closed.

"You're no fun," I tease.

"Lies, and you know it." He grins.

Rolling my eyes, I start heading down to the water. I hear laughing as I reach the edge of the trail. Our campsite is set up near a small waterfall and river, and that's where I find my boys. Their clothes are laying on the beach, but I don't see them in the water.

And then, fuck me, they both emerge from behind the waterfall. They stand under the beating water, heads tipped back as they clean themselves. And they are very much naked.

My eyes widen as I take my time, enjoying every inch

I'm able to see from here. *Why do they have to be so far away?* I can't appreciate them as much as I want to.

But there's no mistaking the fucking tree trunks just hanging between their legs.

As if they can feel my eyes on them, Travis lowers his head and opens his eyes, finding me standing on the river's edge.

I could do one of two things right now. I could turn around and give them privacy by heading back to camp, or I can give them a show of my own.

Of course, I'm going with option number two.

Dropping the change of clothes and towel, I grab the edge of my shirt, pulling it up and over my head. The cool air makes my skin prickle as I make quick work of my pants next.

Once I'm standing there in just my bra and underwear, I look back up at the guys.

Their once limp cocks are now standing at full attention as they watch me intensely. I'm crazy because this water is ice-cold, and I'm about to go in fully naked when all I needed to do was change and wash the mud off my arms, hair, and face.

But I just can't resist teasing the guys by showing what they can have but are too stupid to take. Finding the clasp of my bra, I unclip it and let it fall to the ground. My nipples harden as my breasts fall, feeling heavy.

For the fun of it, I spin around to pull down my panties, giving them a new view of my ass as I bend over to take them off.

I turn towards the water and curse myself for doing this. "Just jump in, quickly wash off, then get out," I mumble to myself.

Taking a deep breath, I jump in before I give myself the time to chicken out. I'm close enough to the waterfall that the water is deep enough to bring me down far. I scream underwater at how cold it is, like fucking ice. *The things I do to get their attention.*

When I break the surface, I start to scrub my arms and face free of the mud before working on my hair.

It's going to have to be enough because I'm about to get hypothermia if I don't get out soon.

As I swim toward the shore, I look around, but don't see the twins anywhere. Assholes couldn't even stay to finish the show. But they sure as hell can't fake the hard dicks they had, so I'll take the win.

Pulling myself out of the water, I go to grab my towel but Hunter is standing there with it in his hand, holding it out to me.

"Thanks." I grin as he stares at me with a look that says he's on the verge of breaking.

Just break then! Do what you're dying to do, it's not that hard.

"I got worried when the twins came back and you weren't with them," he states, his voice thick with need. "I– I need to go, ah, use the washroom," he says, turning around, but I don't miss the way he adjusts himself in his pants.

Washroom? In the woods? He's so flustered he doesn't even realize what he's saying.

I giggle, drying myself off. When I'm done changing into my clean clothes, I put my sneakers on and turn to go back to camp when I hear a loud wack.

Turning my head in the direction of the sound, I freeze. Link is on the beach, down the river in the opposite direction of the waterfall.

His shirt is off, and he's covered in blood. For a moment I get worried. Did someone follow us up here? Was there really someone lurking in the woods, and Link just took care of them?

But then I see him raising a hatchet in the air, bringing it down onto the rock in front of him. Guess he caught some rabbits because the head of one just got chopped off.

I don't know if I should feel sick, sad, or turned on. Maybe a little of everything?

Like a creeper, I stand and watch him skin the rabbit. Trying to ignore the blood and everything, I focus on how his muscles flex with each movement. How he glides the blade smoothly as he works.

I wonder how he got so skilled at using his knife. Has he done something similar to a person before? Because we only come out here once a year, so I know it's not from hunting. At least not this kind.

When he's done, he walks over to the water to wash the blood off his hands and arms before grabbing the rabbit and heading back up toward the camp.

"Well, that's one way to attract bears," I say as I look back at all the leftover rabbit. "I wonder if he could take a bear?" I muse. *Okay, that would be terrifying but also hot as fuck.*

But he would totally lose unless he had a gun. I'm sure he's good, but is he that good? I don't wanna find out.

Feeling my belly rumble, I head back up to the campsite too.

He already has it on the fire by the time I get there. "I see you had some luck," I comment as I stop next to Hunter.

"Yeah, caught three. Should be enough for lunch. But we're going to need to catch something for supper," Link replies. I didn't see the others he caught. He must have been working on them while I did my strip tease for the twins. "Also, never go swimming naked around anyone but us, understand?" he says, looking up at me from his kneeled position by the fire.

Well, that answered my question. I hope he watched too. "Whatever you say." I grin. The urge to call him *Daddy* is right on the tip of my tongue. Turning to the twins, I grin harder. "Where were you two?" I ask.

They both narrow their eyes at me. Freaky twin shit. "Like you don't know," Taylor says.

"I have no idea what you're talking about." I shrug. "I went down to the river and washed off."

"Mhhmm, must have been a good swim," Travis says.

"It was," I say. "It took a *long* and *hard* time to get the mud off, though." My eyes flick down to their crotches.

"Sit," Hunter interrupts, pulling me down into his lap. He wraps his arms around me, bringing his lips to my ear.

"It's not nice to tease, Little Mouse." The breath against my ear makes me shiver.

"I'm not teasing," I pause before finishing my whispered response. "Teasing implies showing off something someone can't have."

He growls, his grip tightening around me, but he says nothing.

We eat lunch and clean up before hopping back on the ATVs. As we ride through the woods, I have a massive smile on my face. I love riding. I'm going to have to see if the guys can take me to a campground with more trails some day. The ride would be a lot smoother than these overgrown ones.

Breaking out into a clearing, we come to the lake that we're fishing at for the day. Parking the ATVs on the shore, we unpack everything we brought from the packs.

"Who's going with whom?" Hunter asks as we finish setting up the boats.

"You three can go together. Raven's with me," Link says, loading up the boat.

"What? Why do you get her?" Hunter protests.

"Because I fucking said so," Link retorts, raising a brow at his brother.

"You fucking suck."

"Ahh, boys don't fight over me. There's enough of me to go around." I'm not at all joking, either.

"That's what we're counting on," I hear Taylor mutter.

"What was that?" I ask.

"Nothing, Foxy Girl. You go have fun with Daddy

Link," he says, pulling me into his arms. "But don't have too much fun," he mumbles into my ear before kissing the side of my head.

"I'll try not to." I giggle. "Although it might be hard, I mean, how can I not have the time of my life with Mr. Dark-and-Broody over there. He screams 'life of the party'."

"Be good," Travis says, stepping up next to us. "You've been pushing him a little too much lately. Know when to stop."

"Fine." I stick my tongue out at him. "When did you all grow up to be boring adults?"

"Just wait. In two weeks, you're gonna be an adult too." Taylor laughs.

"Never," I say, lifting my chin. "I'll forever be a child at heart. Adults are boring as fuck." No offense to our mothers, but they really don't have lives outside work.

"Trust me, Dove. There's nothing boring about us." Travis smirks, kissing my temple before smacking my ass on his way over to his boat. That I can believe.

"This is boring," I sigh dramatically. We've been out here for two hours. I'm not allowed to talk because *I might*

scare the fish Link says. Yet I can hear the others way over there laughing up a storm, and they caught a few already. *This is bullshit.*

"It's fishing. It's not meant to be fun and exciting," Link snaps. He's getting frustrated because he hasn't even gotten a bite.

You wouldn't guess at first glance that these guys are the real outdoorsy type. They love to hunt, fish, and camp. So seeing this big tattooed killer with a fishing rod in his hand, getting pissed because he can't catch a fish, is kind of funny.

"Whatever," I mutter, looking over at the other guys. They cheer as Taylor catches another fish. "Thank god for the others or we would be starving tonight."

Link shoots me a glare as he lets out a low growl. "No one asked for your opinion. Sit down and shut the fuck up."

My eyes widen. "Excuse me?! Don't fucking talk to me like that."

There's a difference from Link's normal bossy controlling way with me and this. This makes me feel belittled and stupid.

He lets out a frustrated sigh. "I'm sorry. Just, please."

I don't say anything back, but give him my best resting bitch face.

He shoots to his feet, the boat rocking from the movement. "I got one!" he says with excitement. It's kinda cute. "Grab the net."

Grabbing the net quickly, he starts to reel the fish in. Wanting to have the net ready, I make the mistake of standing next to him, causing the boat to tip more. I end up knocking into his arm and the rod flies out of his hand into the lake.

"Fuck!" he shouts, grabbing handfuls of his hair.

"I'm sorry," I say. "I didn't mean to."

"Just, god... just—" I make another mistake as I reach out to touch him, hating to see him all worked up. He shrugs me off, making me lose my balance, and I fall into the fucking lake.

The water is cold as I go under. *Stupid fucking fishing!* I don't even like doing it.

Rising to the surface, I start to curse. "What the fuck! Are you crazy?" Wiping the water from my eyes, I see Link bending over the edge of the boat with his arm extended to me.

"I'm sorry," he says. "Take my hand."

"Fuck you!" I spit. "This was supposed to be fun. Something we do every year for my birthday. Why the fuck did you want me on the boat with you if you were going to make me sit there and shut up for two hours? This is me, for fuck sakes, I like to talk!"

"Take my hand, Little Bird," he says, his jaw grinding.

"No," I argue, turning around and swimming toward shore.

"Raven!" he shouts. "You fucking brat!"

"And you're a fucking asshole!"

I'm pissed off, cold, and just so fucking over fishing. I want to go back to camp, get in warm clothes, and sit by the fire.

When I reach the shore, the others are waiting for me. "What the hell happened?" Hunter asks, worry in his eyes.

"Your big gorilla of a brother got pissy because I caused him to lose a fish by accident. He shrugged me off when I tried to comfort him, and I went overboard," I explain, panting as I stand there like a drowned rat.

"He can be a dick sometimes," Hunter sighs. "Are you okay?"

"Sometimes?" I scoff. "Try all the time. And yeah, I'm fine. But I want to go back to camp. I'm over this shit."

Hunter looks over at the twins. "I'm going to go back with Raven. Do you guys mind staying here and helping put everything away?"

"Yeah, go, it's fine." Travis nods, then looks at me. "You sure you're okay, Dove?"

"Yeah," I say. He pulls me in for a hug, not caring that he's getting wet.

"At least we got something to eat for the night," Travis says with a cocky smirk when we pull apart.

"He's just gonna love that." Taylor chuckles. "Be prepared for him to be a broody fucker because he didn't get anything and Ray is mad at him."

"He deserves it," I mutter.

"He does," Taylor agrees. "Go get changed and warmed up. Take the fish. By the time the two of you get them prepped and cooked, we should be back."

"Fine," I sigh, heading toward my ATV.

The ride back wasn't fun like it normally is. As much fun as I had today, it's all been ruined. I get it, this is who

Link is, but does he always have to be so fucking serious? Would it kill him to let loose and have a little fun sometimes? He needs to remove the stick up his ass before I say something and really get myself in trouble.

Hunter and I work together to gut and cook the fish. Taylor was right, by the time it's ready to eat, I hear the guys' engines.

"Little Mouse," Hunter says. We've been quiet since we got back, Hunter knowing I'm not in the mood right now.

"Yeah?" I ask.

"Don't be too pissed for too long, okay? I don't want this to ruin your trip."

"We still have tomorrow," I say. "But I'm tired, hungry, and so over today."

"Come here," Hunter coaxes, sitting back in his chair. I get up and out of mine to sit in his lap. He gathers me up in his arms, holding me close. I sigh and snuggle into him, enjoying being this close. I love this man, and more than ever, I just want to tell him I love him. I really wanna kiss him again. I want to say something, to tell all of them how I feel, but something tells me that at this point, it's not going to be enough.

Maybe I should just tell them I know they're Black Venom Crew. If that's what is keeping them quiet, I should let them know that it doesn't bother me. That I don't care and want them no matter what.

The rest of the night is depressing. The guys come over to the fire and eat, no one says anything.

Hunter is a fucking sweetheart and feeds me. It's cute

and corny but I love it. After we're done, I get passed over to Travis while Hunter goes to pee.

I end up falling asleep in Travis' arms. The next time I wake up, it's to the sound of my name being moaned in a very sexual way.

Oh my god. Is... Hunter... is Hunter jacking off next to me?

My eyes crack open, but it's too hard to see anything. "Fuck," Hunter grunts as I hear the sleeping bag moving. "That's it, Little Mouse. Wrap your pretty pink lips around my cock. Swallow me whole like the good girl you are."

My body flushes with need, a fire in my lower belly roaring to life. My breathing starts to pick up with each passing second. The sounds coming from him have my clit aching.

Biting my lip, I carefully move my hand down into my panties. My fingers find my clit, and I start to rub it, slow and steady, as Hunter continues with his dirty talk.

"So fucking perfect," he groans. "That's it, baby girl, choke on me. Gag on it."

Fuck, fuck, fuck. I'm so turned on right now, my panties are soaked. Needing more, I slowly adjust my body so that I can thrust my fingers inside.

"I'm gonna cum, Little Mouse. You better swallow every last drop," he pants out. My slick coated fingers find my clit again. I rub faster, chasing the burning need inside me. *God, I wish I was doing everything he's saying.*

"Fuck!" he grunts out a long groan. The sound of him cumming has a whimper slipping from my mouth. And from the way everything goes very still and very silent, he heard it.

"Raven?" he whispers.

Shit. Do I answer him? Or do I pretend I'm sleeping. I mean, he's the one jacking off next to me, just should I act like I didn't hear anything.

"Yeah," I squeak, my clit throbbing. I need my release so bad, that if I don't get it, I might cry. I'm desperate enough to say I need to pee and try to masturbate in the bushes, but it's not that easy for girls.

He curses. "By any chance, did you hear all of that?"

"Maybe?" I say, my body shifting as my hips thrust against my hand.

"Little Mouse?" he says my nickname like it's a dirty question, and fuck me his voice is deep and husky. And god, it's not helping anything.

"Yes," I breathe out.

"What are you doing under there?" He shifts his body so that he's laying down next to me, his face inches away from mine.

"Ummmm." What do I tell him? *Hey, sorry, I was finger fucking myself to the sound of you jacking off as you imagine me choking on your dick?*

His hand touches the arm of the hand that's in my panties right now, and I suck in a breath as he slowly slides his hand down my arm. "Naughty girl," he groans as he stops where my hand disappears under the fabric of my bottoms. "Were you touching yourself to the sounds of me?"

"You started it," I shoot back, a very weak comeback if I must say.

He chuckles, his breath puffing out against my lips. We're quiet for a few moments, and even though we can't see anything, I know we're both staring at each other.

"Do you need help with that?" he asks me, his hand dipping lower until it's covering mine.

"Yes," I say so fast I don't even think about it. My heart is doing really funny things in my chest right now. *Is this really happening?* I know we kissed. And it was an amazing kiss at that. But this? This is so much more than a kiss.

If we cross this line, does that mean he's finally admitting he wants more than just friendship with me? I can't help but get a rush of excitement.

Hunter grabs my hand, pulling it out of my panties. When he doesn't let go to replace mine with his, I open my mouth to ask him what he's doing. But then he raises my hand, and I feel wet lips wrap around my fingers. Hunter sucks them into his mouth, his tongue lapping at my juices.

I whimper, my body flushing with need as he lets out a feral growl. His lips collide with mine as he kisses me with a desperate need.

I moan, the hand that was once inside me tangles into his hair, grabbing a handful, pulling him closer.

Hunter slips his hand in my underwear and cups my pussy. "You're so fucking wet, Little Mouse. Is this because of me?" he whispers against my lips.

"Yes," I moan as he kisses me again.

Taking two fingers, he thrusts them inside me. I cry out

into his mouth, arching my back as I press myself closer to him.

"You're so fucking tight," Hunter growls. "I can tell you're untouched. My sexy little virgin. Are you saving yourself, Little Mouse?" he asks.

"Yes," I whimper, pleasure filling my body as he works me over.

"Who for?" he asks. *Fuck, this is a loaded question.* No matter how I answer it, lie or truth, I could get hurt. So, I do what I wish they would do and tell the truth.

"You."

"Fuck!" he hisses. Hunter pushes on my back, draping himself half over me as he uses his other arm to hold himself up. "You drive me crazy, Little Mouse. So fucking mad. Temptation wrapped in a pretty little bow."

"Then unwrap me," I challenge.

His tongue thrusts into my mouth, matching the magic his fingers are doing.

My head is fuzzy as so many feelings rush through me. Love, joy, fear, and relief dance inside my chest along with the mind-blowing pleasure he's bringing me as his fingers rub against my sweet spot and his thumb plays with my clit.

We kiss like lovers who only have today. Why does my heart scream at me that it's because we do? I'm stupid enough to believe this will be it, that after he brings me to my peak and I shatter in his arms, that we'll magically be together like I so desperately want.

My core quivers around his fingers as I feel my orgasm creeping in on me. We break the kiss, both of us panting as he puts his forehead to mine. "Cum for me, Raven. Shatter around my fingers."

His thumb presses down on my nub as he hooks his fingers deeper in, hitting me in just the right spot.

"Don't stop. Please, please, don't stop," I sob as I reach out to cling to his arms.

"Never," he growls. "That's it, Little Mouse. You're doing so fucking good. Cum for me."

And I do. "Hunter," I gasp, my eyes rolling back as I arch off the ground. My pussy clamps around his fingers as my body writhes beneath him. He continues to work me over through my release, giving me delicious aftershocks as he prolongs my orgasm.

We go still, the only noise is my heavy breathing as I come down from my high.

Hunter removes his hand from my panties, but leaves his forehead connected to mine. I'm starting to panic. Fuck, he's not saying anything. I knew it. I knew the moment it was over he would pull away, act like nothing happened.

And he confirms my thoughts with his next words. "We should get some sleep," he says, kissing me on the forehead before rolling away from me.

I hate this, I fucking hate this. I don't cry, and not over stupid boys. But as I lay here, staring up into the black nothing, my eyes sting with tears as they well up and spill over.

Biting the inside of my cheek, I try to steady my breathing. Rolling over onto my side, with my back to him, I wait for what feels like forever.

Once I know he's asleep, I quietly get dressed and slip

out of the tent. I don't wanna be here when he wakes up. I don't want to look him in the face after we shared something that meant the world to me, and he just rolled over like I was some cheap fuck.

My soul hurts, and my heart is shattered. I can't believe he would do this to me. Maybe I was wrong. Maybe they don't want me the way I want them. They're probably just afraid to tell me that because they want to stay friends, thinking I'd leave them if they told me the truth.

Needing to leave because I'm unable to be around them right now, I creep over to the ATVs.

Mine is thankfully the furthest away from the tents and the closest to the road out of here. And luck must be on my side because the key is still in the ignition where I left it. Putting it neutral, I put all my strength into pushing it as far away as I can get it.

It takes me a good half hour but once I get it to where they can't hear me, I start the engine and get the fuck out of there.

It's still the middle of the night, but the ATV has head-lights to guide my way. Once I make it to the highway, I gun it, going as fast as I can. The wind is cold against my skin as I speed down the road. This is in no way safe, but I'm too pissed off to care.

I'm fucking done. I'm so fucking done with all of them. They want to act like I'm just their bestie? Fine, that's what I'll be. I've all but told them how I felt, and they still do nothing.

I'm glad I said nothing because they would have just

fucking rejected me and made me look like a fool. Like Hunter did tonight. I'm done throwing myself at them. *God, I'm so pathetic.*

It hurts so fucking much. I love them more than my own fucking life and the thought of never having them as more than a friend is not something I can deal with at the moment.

It was too good to be true. You really think four guys are going to want to share you? I know mom always told me to dream big, but maybe I should lower my expectations. At least it will save me from a broken heart.

CHAPTER 17

TAYLOR

"Raven!" someone screams, causing me to jolt out of my sleep.

"What the fuck?" I grumble, my mind hazy with sleep.

"What's going on?" Travis asks, sitting up next to me.

"Raven!" they scream again. It's Hunter.

Travis and I look at each other with wide eyes. "Fuck." We scramble to unzip the tent, practically tripping over each other to get out.

"What the fuck is going on?" Link barks as he exits his own tent.

Hunter swings his gaze over to us. "I woke up to an empty tent. I thought maybe she went to take a piss, so I waited. But after a while, she didn't come back. I looked everywhere around here, she's not here," he says in a panicked voice.

My eyes swing back to Link. His face turns to fury as he storms away, no shirt or shoes.

Come on, Foxy Girl, where are you?

We all follow Link as he goes over to where we parked the ATVs only to find hers gone. "What the fuck?" I say, waving my hand to where hers should be, a rush of confusion mixing with my own panic. "Where did she go?" I ask Hunter.

His face falls, going pale. "Fuck. Fuck, fuck, fuck!" he yells, grabbing handfuls of his hair. "It just happened, I didn't mean for it to happen. Fuck, I really fucked up."

"Hunter!" Link shouts. "What are you rambling about. What did you fucking do?"

He looks up at us with stricken eyes, and my heart starts to pound in my chest. "She sleeps like the dead. I didn't think she would hear me. God, all I could think about all day was her naked from her dip in the river. I couldn't keep my damn dick down. So, when she was sleeping, I jerked off!"

"And what? Scared her off?" I ask, brows furrowing. There's no way Raven would have been freaked out or have gotten uncomfortable about something like that. Our girl has made it known on more than one occasion that she wants us. Today being one of those days.

When she gave us that little strip tease on the beach, it took everything in me and my brother to not swim over to her and take her right there in the water. She's so fucking gorgeous, just thinking about her always has us hard and ready.

That's why we left before we did something stupid. Something stupid that I have a feeling Hunter did.

"No." Hunter lets out a long, deep sigh. "She fucking touched herself to it! There was no way in hell I could have stopped myself. There's only so much restraint I have, and I've already been slipping these past few months. I love her, so fucking much. It hurts not being able to touch her like I wanted to. So I broke."

"What did you do?!" Link barks, taking a step forward and visibly vibrating. "Did you fuck her?"

"No! I– fuck. We made out as I touched her okay. I helped her take the edge off."

"Did you at least make her cum?" I question. Bad time for jokes, but fuck, if this wasn't a serious situation right now, I'd be sulking like a little bitch that he got to touch her.

He shoots me a death glare. "Yes, I fucking made her cum!"

"What happened after?" Link asks, his voice low and dangerous.

"That's where I fucked up." Hunter spins around to punch a nearby tree. Cursing, he shakes out his hand. "I'm so fucking stupid. I didn't know what to say after. I wanted to tell her the truth, tell her that I'm not just in love with her, but fucking obsessed with her. I wanted to demand her to be mine once and for all." Hunter sneers at his brother. "But I couldn't because you're so fucking insistent on keeping that damn deal we made a long time ago. I can't wait until she graduates. It's fucking ridiculous."

"So what did you say, Hunter?" Link steps closer to him.

These two look ready to explode. Looking at Travis, I silently ask him if we intervene. He shakes his head, and I sigh. *Fuck.*

"I told her we should get some sleep, and then I rolled over." He cringes.

"No, no, you fucking dick head!" I groan. "Are you fucking stupid?! God, Hunter!"

"I know, I know, okay! I hate myself. It was so fucking mind-blowing, everything I've ever wanted with her and more. To finally touch her. And I fucked it all up."

"I swear to god, Hunter, if that's true, I'll kill you," Link grabs Hunter by the shirt. "This is what I wanted to avoid. I wanted to bring her into this as smoothly as we could. We don't know how she's going to react to us being Black Venom Crew. If she tries to run, to push us away, I will fucking lock her up. I'm not losing her. She's mine Hunter, fucking MINE!" Link's chest heaves, and his eyes show off the crazed killer he really is.

"Ours!" Hunter barks back.

"You better fucking fix this. I swear, Hunter, you better not have fucked this all up. She wants us. If she can get past what we do, this will work. I don't want her hating us." Link growls.

"She doesn't hate us," Travis says. "She's hurt. She wants us to give in, to tell her how we feel. She's not stupid. Raven's been pushing our limits because she knows we want her. And she's made it clear she wants us. She's probably just hurt that you guys crossed that line and you still didn't tell her," Travis says.

"Maybe we should move up the timeline of telling her," I suggest.

Link shoots me a glare that has me wanting to step back. "No. We stick to the plan. I want her to have as much of a normal life as she can before I make her my everything. I'm not kidding. She will always be by my side, or one of yours. She won't have the freedom to go out with her friend. To go shopping or do whatever the fuck girls do together. Her life is going to change in a way I don't think she's ready for. Once I open the locked door that I have when it comes to her, I won't be able to hold back."

As much as I think this whole fucking thing is stupid, and has always been stupid, he's got a point. He's way more fucking intense compared to the rest of us. I mean, we've each got our own loose screws; I'd like to thank our dear old dads for fucking us all up nice and young, but Link is the one everyone has to worry about. He would never hurt Raven, at least not in a way that would cause her serious harm. And it would take a lot for him to do something to one of us, but everyone else? In his eyes, they're fair game. He's the monster in the stories that parents tell their kids at night. The one under your bed or in your closets.

Sometimes I wonder if the little bit of humanity he shows is an act, but then I see the way he looks at Raven when he thinks no one is watching, and I see a glimpse of a soul. It's heavily darkened but it's there.

Link lets go of Hunter, giving him a good shove that makes Hunter stumble back. "I'm going to check in with Q. Service up here is fucking shit. Have this place packed and ready to go by the time I get back," he orders, hopping onto his ATV, starting it up and racing down the road.

"Seriously, dude?" Travis and I say at the same time. We don't do the freaky twin shit often but when we do, we can't help but grin and give each other a high five.

"Fuck you," he sneers. "She had her fucking fingers in her cunt while she listened to me. You're lucky, all I did was finger fuck her when I really wanted to pin her down and fuck her pussy until it was weeping around my cock as she begged me for more."

"Yeah, you got a point. I don't think we would have done anything differently," Travis sighs, running his hand through his shaggy black hair that mirrors mine.

"Well." I give him a savage grin. "How does she taste?" Travis chuckles as Hunter groans like he's ready to cum in his pants just thinking about it.

"I don't have the words to describe it. Incredible, delicious, amazing, mind-blowing... fuck, she's everything I've imagined and more. And that's just from tasting her juices from her fingers and mine. I can't wait to bury my face between her thick thighs and smother myself as I feast on her cunt."

"Same, brother, same," Travis mutters, adjusting his cock in his sweats. "I'm not gonna lie, I'm so damn jealous."

"You better not be planning on fucking some bitch to get rid of that," Hunter says, narrowing his eyes as he nods at Travis' cock. "It's time that shit ends."

"It has ended," Travis says defectively. "I haven't touched anyone since the summer."

"What about you?" Hunter asks, narrowing his eyes at me.

"To be honest, it's been so long I can't tell you who the last person I fucked was. Even if it was yesterday, they're not important enough for me to remember their names. Now, before you get all pissed off at me, any girl me or Travis fucked, they knew what they were getting into. This whole fucking town knows how madly in love we are with Raven. They knew what to expect if they chose to go behind closed doors with us. But they did it anyway. Some loved being degraded and shit, and others just wanted to be able to say they fucked me or my brother."

Whatever the reason, to us, they were a hole to fuck, something to get our sexual energy out with. And we made sure they knew that was all they were to us because the only person to get us completely will be our queen.

Over the years, some of the girls thought they could be the ones to make us change our minds, to steer us away from claiming Raven one day. But it was all a waste of their time. As time went on, they gave up and just settled to be fucked by one of us.

Now, I know what you're thinking, why didn't we just wait until we got to be with Raven? Well, I can't give you a good enough answer. With what we do, we need a release. The stupid plan in place meant Raven wasn't an option yet. She wouldn't have been ready anyway.

You can say it's fucked up, you can call us disgusting. But remember, we're not the heroes in this story. We love our girl, in our own fucked up way.

"Come on. We better get this place packed up. I want to go home and make sure Raven is okay," Hunter says sadly. I feel bad for the guy. Sure, he fucked up, but he wants his girl. We all do.

Sometimes I can't stop thinking that there's a good chance Link is wrong. I don't think Raven would care about what we do, or how we act. We've spent pretty much every day of the past ten years together. She wouldn't leave us because we weren't exactly who she thought we were.

Not that we would let her leave anyway. Link was serious. He would lock her up until she came around to the idea. As much as the fucker would love it, we don't want it to have to come to that. But if it meant her being ours forever, we'd do it. She's my Foxy Girl, and I'd do anything to keep her.

RAVEN

These past two weeks have fucking sucked. I've never been in this bad of a funk for this long, if ever. I hate it. Hunter and I haven't talked since that night and not for his lack of trying. He's camped outside my room, begging me to hear him out. He has snuck into my room while I was sleeping, leaving his scent behind when he leaves in the morning.

As much as I wish I could pretend nothing happened, I don't want to. What happened between us, that meant the fucking world to me. I've never felt so wanted, so adored in that moment from one of the men who are my whole damn world.

I thought I was tough, that it would take a lot for me to break, but him rolling over and going to sleep like I was some random hookup at a party... yeah, that was a knife to the heart.

I've never questioned myself before, but that's all I've been doing these past two weeks.

At school, I'm with Andy. Hunter is always nearby, watching like a kicked puppy, and it kills me. I want things to go back to the way they used to be before he touched me. Before he touched me in a way no one else ever has. I gave him my body to do with as he pleased, and all he did was hurt me.

I know he's sorry, I can see the devastation on his face for causing me pain, but it doesn't erase it. All he has to do to fix it, is tell me he loves me and that I'm his.

As for the others... nothing has changed with Link. He's still there to check in on me, the grumpy asshole. But the twins have become more... affectionate. Always touching me, holding me, loving on me. Like they always have but more frequent.

It's another tease to my already aching heart, but one that I need to forget.

Today is my birthday. I'm officially eighteen. I woke up to my mom hovering over my bed with breakfast and a cup of coffee for me, so the day started out amazing. We hung out in my bed and talked about random things. I loved that time with her. That's one thing I love the most about my mom, no matter how hard she works, she's always made sure to make time for me. She's one of my best friends, and I'm so glad I got her as a mom.

But after the buzz of my birthday morning wore off, the rest of the day was depressing as fuck. The twins took me out for lunch and spoiled me with gifts, but it got cut short because Link called them into work.

Now, was that work fixing cars or killing people? Who fucking knows. I wanted to tell them at that moment that I knew who they were, what they did and ask them to take me with them. If they just told me, I wouldn't have to be dropped off at home all the time, so they can do whatever the fuck they do. I mean, I don't wanna sit in the room as they gut people, but that little club they have going on looked nice. I could always hang out in there.

But nope, here I am, sitting in my room, on my bed, scrolling through my phone mindlessly. I didn't ask Andy if she wanted to do anything because I'm so used to just spending my birthday with the guys, I didn't even think to ask.

"Ray?" Hunter's soft voice has me looking up. "I gotta head out soon. I just wanted to see you on your birthday. Can I come in?"

My belly flips and tears fill my eyes. I hold them back as I get off the bed and walk over to the door. He watches me with rapt attention, his pupils dilating the closer I get. Grabbing a hold of the door handle, I give him a cruel smirk. "Sorry, I think I need to get some sleep," I sneer before slamming the door in his face.

My back meets the door as I close my eyes, tipping my

head back. "Fuck!" Hunter shouts, before there's a bang on my door, making me flinch. I hear his feet pounding down the stairs.

Rushing over to my window, I hear the front door slam shut and a second later Hunter is stomping over to his car. He angrily gets in and peels out of the driveway before speeding down the road.

"I fucking hate this," I say to myself, my voice cracking. Wiping the tears that slipped free with the sleeve of my hoodie, I grab my phone and call Andy. "Hey. What are you up to?" I ask when she picks up.

"Was gonna watch some Halloween movies at home. Maybe go to a party. Why, what's up?" she asks. "Also, Happy eighteenth birthday, bitch! I wish we could do something. But noooo, always them boys," she jokes. I told her what happened with Hunter after a few days of freezing Hunter out. She's just as pissed as I am at him, but she keeps it to herself.

It makes sense why she seemed to know who Hunter was when we first met. She knew they were Black Venom Crew, and I'm starting to think this whole fucking town knew but me, the more I think about it. So much has started to make sense when it came to the guys and how people treated them.

I'm not mad at her for not telling me. I'm almost positive they made her agree to keep her mouth shut. Something I'll be talking to them about when they know that I know.

I do plan on telling her what I saw. She might be okay

with keeping things quiet, but I need someone to talk to about this. It's driving me crazy.

"Actually, they all ditched me for work. Wanna do something?" I ask.

"Hell yeah!" she says. "Wanna come over and have a girls' night?"

"What about that party you were talking about?" I ask. I've never been to one, but this is my year of trying new things. And as much as I haven't had an interest in drinking, I could really use something to take my mind off everything.

"Yeah, okay. But are you sure?" she asks.

"I mean, I'm not going to get dressed up or anything but I could use an hour or two out of the house."

"Kay. I'll be there in twenty to pick you up."

"See you then." Hanging up, I leave my room to go wait for Andy downstairs. Walking into the kitchen, I see Leah with a crying Jack in her arms. She looks like she's struggling to make a bottle. "I can hold him... if you want," I tell her.

She startles, spinning around. She looks like she was crying, and I feel so bad. "Would you?" she asks, sounding defeated.

"Of course," I say, taking Jack from her. "Hi, sweet boy," I coo as he continues to cry.

She turns around to make the bottle as she talks to me. "We were out for a walk. I thought he would nap but he was so alert, looking around at everything," she laughs. "I got caught up and time got away from me. We missed his nap, and now he's not a happy boy."

"I'm sure once he gets his baba, he'll be right as rain.

Won't you, baby?" I kiss his forehead.

When the twins aren't home or kidnapping me for themselves, I'm hanging out with Leah and Jack. She still hasn't said anything about where she comes from or how she ended up on the side of the road, but she looks a lot more at ease. Like she finally feels safe. I'm glad.

"The guys actually let you walk around?" I laugh as she shakes up the bottle.

"No." She gives me a small smile. "Mark was always close by."

I've seen how that man looks at her. She doesn't know it, but he's smitten with her and with Jack. I don't know him well, but if Link trusts him, he must be good enough.

"You know they're only worried about you right? We kind of take it upon ourselves to look out for the people who come to stay here," I tell her.

"I know. And I'm so thankful for everything you've all done for us. I don't know what I would have done without you."

"It's no trouble." At that moment, a car horn blares from outside, telling me my ride is here. "I gotta go. Are you going to be okay?"

"Yeah." She smiles. "Thanks for holding him. I think we're both going to have an early night tonight."

"Any time. And I mean that," I tell her, giving her a wave before jogging out to Andy.

"So, you ready to party?" Andy asks me as we pull out of the driveway.

"No, but I'm ready to forget for a while."

CHAPTER 18

RAVEN

This party isn't like the ones I've seen in movies. It's in some abandoned house with gross old couches and coolers filled with beer. And it's full of people who hate me, so this is going to be fun.

"Want something to drink?" Andy asks as I stick my middle finger up at some dudes giving me the stink eye.

"Is it even safe?" I ask, looking around. "I guess, if it's unopened."

"Good idea," she says with a laugh. "I'll go find us something."

I stand there, not wanting to move from my spot. There's music playing, but it's kind of just a low hum in the background. I play on my phone for a few minutes before Andy comes back, handing me a can. "Here, found these. Managed to grab the last few. You can have these, I'm good with beer. And because I'm driving, I won't drink much."

"Thanks," I say, looking at the can. It's a cooler. Shrugging my shoulder, I crack it open and take a drink. The carbonation fizzes on my tongue as I swallow. "This is good," I tell her, loving the strawberry taste. "It's like drinking pop."

"Be careful with that. It's easy to get lost in how many you drink because you can hardly taste the alcohol."

Nodding, I look around the room again. "Banging party," I tease.

She snorts a laugh. "This is actually really fucking sad. I was expecting there to be at least one decent party, it's Halloween for fuck's sake. But I guess everyone went to the next town over to party with the rich fuckers."

"Whatever. I just want to drink and forget," I tell her.

"Then that's what we're going to do." Andy and I manage to find some plastic chairs that are fairly clean and take a seat away from the other party goers.

"So, I wanted to let you know something," I start once I finish my first drink and open another.

"Okay? Should I be worried? Are you breaking up with me?" She gasps and I laugh.

"No," I sigh.

"Then what? You can tell me anything. I'm going to come out and say it, you're my best friend. And I know the guys are your number ones, but I'm making myself your number two," she says, then cringes. "That sounds wrong." We both burst out laughing.

"Okay, so you know I've always had a suspicion that the guys are hiding something from me right?"

"Yeah..." she says slowly.

"One day, they left me at home to run off to the shop, like they always fucking do," I snark, taking a swig of my drink.

"And?" she asks, looking a little more interested in what I have to say.

"They didn't come home when they said they were going to. They weren't answering their phones. So, I thought I'd go see what was keeping them."

"Did you go to the shop?" she asks, her eyes slowly growing.

I can't help but smirk. "I did."

"Raven... did you go into the warehouse? Please tell me you didn't," she pleads, her voice growing panicked.

"I did," I say again.

Her face falls into her hands. "Oh god," she groans. "Do you know?" She doesn't look up as she asks that.

"Well, if you're asking if I know that my four boyfriends are part of Black Venom Crew, then yes, I know."

She lifts her face from her hands. "So..."

"I wish they didn't keep it from me. It's a big fucking deal. Like one of the biggest things you can keep from someone. But I also get it. They probably think I'd be running for the hills if I ever found out."

"But you didn't," Andy points out.

"No. Did what I see surprise me? Sure, but it didn't bother me." I snort a laugh. "Okay, that's a lie, the blood was not for me. But to see them so powerful, to hold someone's life in their hands and have the power to take it away... God, maybe I'm fucked, but it's so damn hot." I groan as I take another drink.

Andy bursts out laughing. "Never tell them I said this, but they are so stupid to ever think you wouldn't want them. Girl, you're practically creaming your panties thinking about it."

"I am," I sigh. "And they are stupid, stupid boys who need to tell me the truth. They're my everything, my world, and I hate that I'm the only one who didn't know."

"Are you mad at me?" she asks, her face filling with sadness.

"Nah. Link is a scary motherfucker. I wouldn't want to risk getting on his bad side if I was anyone else but me. I get it. Wasn't your place to tell. And out of respect for you and them, I'll wait until they tell me themselves before I start hounding you with questions on how you factor into their world. I don't want to risk you getting hurt."

"Thanks," she says.

We sit in silence for a while, just watching the stars out in the backyard of this crappy place. I'm not sure how much time had passed but I think I drank like five of those coolers.

"H-ey," I hiccup. "Can I have more of these?"

"Oh shit," she says, her eyes roaming over my face. My eyes are hardly open, so she looks blurry to me. "You're drunk, aren't you?"

"Me, drunk? Nah, I'm feeling good. Really good. You know what else would be good? Sex. Sex with Hunter. But nooo," I say, waving my mostly empty drink around, causing whatever is left inside slosh out. "I'm good enough for his fingers to fuck, but not his monster cock." I turn to Andy. "Oh my god. Have you seen his cock? It's big, like I'm talking elephant trunk big. How does he fit it in his pants? And the piercings! If he was buried on the beach and a treasurer hunter came looking for stuff, their metal detector would be going off like fucking crazy."

"Ray, babe, you're fucking smashed. You are 100% a light weight."

"Awww," I say, putting my hand on my heart. "You're so sweet. I was feeling a little extra chunky from all the cake."

"Alright, you're done for the night," she says.

"You're no fun! I still feel things." I pout.

"Sorry, but I'm not gonna let you die of alcohol poisoning. That would get me killed too if your guys found out."

"This birthday sucks!" I whine. "Happy eighteenth birthday to me."

"I'll plan something fun for us okay?" Andy says.

"Come on," I say as I struggle to get up out of the chair.

"Where are we going?" she asks.

"I'm hungry and want some candy. Let's go find a house and ask for some," I say, as I start to stagger into the house.

"What? Ray it's like ten p.m., trick or treating ended an hour ago," Andy argues as she rushes to keep up with me.

"I'm sure some people have leftovers. If they say no, I'll get my boyfriends to kill them." I nod matter-of-factly. Bet they would give me all their fucking candy then.

"God," Andy groans.

"Hey, you," I yell, looking at the group of guys from before. "Look at me like that again, and I'll get Black Venom

Crew to kill you." I grin. Their eyes go wide as they visibly pale.

"Calm down there, Harley Quinn. Let's not summon the Joker," Andy teases, grabbing me by the arm and steering me out the front door.

"I don't feel so good," I whimper as the world starts to spin the moment we step onto the grass.

"Fuck!" Andy says as my belly starts to roll. And then everything I drank came back up and all over my feet and the lawn. I don't like feeling like this. I wanna cry, cuddle up with my guys and have them take care of me. I'm never drinking again.

TRAVIS

"We should be with Raven. It's her fucking birthday," I mutter as I clean up the last of the fucker we just killed. Normally, we leave that to the clean up crew, but Link seems to be on edge today and things got a little messy.

"Well, we're done here now. I'll let Link know and then we can go home," Taylor says, taking off up the stairs. I head inside the club, the music blaring as everyone gets trashed on Halloween. I fucking hate that Raven doesn't know who we really are. I'd love to bring her here to dance, drink, and just let loose. But instead we always have to leave her at home. I hate leaving her behind. Every second I'm away from her, it makes my fucking skin crawl.

"Hey," I say to Hunter as I step up to the bar. Poor fucker

really messed up, and he's never looked so miserable. He doesn't say anything, just gives me a grunt of acknowledgment as he takes a drink from his glass. "We're heading out. You coming?"

"No," he rasps. "I'm getting shit faced, then sleeping in the office."

"Again?" I ask.

"If I'm at home, I'm tempted to see her. She doesn't wanna see me. She made that clear this morning. I would bust into her room and demand her to forgive me, but why should she? What I did was fucked up."

"Once she knows, she's gonna forgive you. You know Ray."

"I really fucking hope so. God, I feel like a lovesick fool, but the idea of her hating me... it makes me wanna shoot everyone in here."

A few people go quiet around him, eyeing him warily. "Don't worry. He's joking," I tell them.

"No, I'm not," Hunter grumbles as he downs his drink.

My phone rings. Reaching into my pocket, I see Andrhea's name flashing on my screen. Brows furrowing, I answer. "What's up?"

"Hey," she says, sounding weird. "By any chance did Ray tell you we were going out tonight?"

My body tenses. "No," I curse, letting out a sigh. "Where are you?"

"We went to a party. She didn't wanna stay at home alone for her birthday. I thought she was going to be spending it with you guys, so I didn't ask her to do anything.

She called me, and of course, I jumped at the chance to be with my best friend on her birthday."

"We had a job," I sigh, not liking that we had to leave Raven. We had a good morning. Lunch made me feel like everything was normal again, even if it was only for an hour. Then to see the disappointment on her face when we had to bring her home and leave, fucking gutted me.

"Anyway. Raven is still bummed about the whole Hunter thing."

"She told you about that?" I ask, looking at the man in question who's already half done with his next drink.

"She tells me a lot of things. Like I said, we are besties. And as her bestie, I'm calling you guys, her *boyfriends* for help."

I don't deny the boyfriend part when I answer her. "What do you need help with? Is she okay?" I ask, stepping away from Hunter so he doesn't hear. He's drunk and will do something stupid if prompted.

"She got drunk. Like really trashed. And now she's puking on the front lawn of the house we're at. I tried to move her to my car, but she just ended up puking again."

"Fuck," I curse, worried for my girl. She's never drank before. God, she's going to feel like death tomorrow. "We're on our way," I say, hanging up. Taylor approaches me. "Come on," I tell him, rushing toward the exit.

"What's going on?" Taylor asks as he joins my side.

"Ray went out with Andy. I'm gonna kill that fucker for not calling us and letting us know," I snap as we get to our Jeep.

"Who, Andrhea?" Taylor asks as he slips into the passenger seat.

"No, not her, Quinton," I clarify as we peel out of the parking lot. "Text Andy and get the damn address."

Taylor does, getting an answer right away. It doesn't take us long before we're pulling up. "This wouldn't have happened if she was fucking with us, where she belongs," I mumble, getting out of the car and slamming the door shut.

"I'm ready to say fuck Link and just tell her everything."

"Me too, brother, me fucking too." My heart drops when I see my girl laying on the grass crying.

"What the fuck, Andy!" I snarl, getting in her face.

She steps back, raising her hands. "I'm sorry. I didn't know she would get so drunk. She only had a few coolers."

"She's never had alcohol before," Taylor chastises, kneeling down next to her. "Foxy Girl," he says, lowering his voice as he moves the hair away from her face. "How are you doing, baby?"

"Make the world stop spinning," she sobs. "My head hurts so much. So much puke."

Looking around, I grimace. *How can so much fit in such a little thing?* "Hey, Dove," I try. "How about we take you home, clean you up and then we can all cuddle?"

She looks up, blinking her pretty hazel eyes at me. "Please." Her voice sounds so sad and pathetic.

"Anything for you, Dovey." Not caring about the puke, I scoop her up in my arms and bring her to the Jeep. "You drive," I tell Taylor as I toss him the keys. Once we're in the back, Raven laying on the seat, there's a knock at the window.

"Here," Andy says, handing me a bucket. "I use it for trash, but just in case she needs to puke."

"Thanks," I say. "Get home safe. I'll keep this from Link, because the fucker didn't check in yet again. But don't let this happen a second time. We're all for Ray going out and having fun, but you know the drill."

"Won't happen again, boss." She nods.

"Good."

The drive back is silent, the windows all down so that the cool breeze keeps Raven from feeling sick. She's passed out cold, her head in my lap. "My sweet Dove," I sigh. "Soon, baby girl. Soon you'll be ours. You already are, but soon we can let the whole world know."

"I knew she was a heavy sleeper, but she slept through a shower and getting dressed," Taylor chuckles as he lays her down in her bed.

"You know how hard it was not to poke her with my fucking boner as we washed her naked body? I'm dying to sink my teeth into the soft skin of her hips," I groan.

"Shut up, fucker. Now I'm hard," he mumbles as we climb into bed with her. "I hate seeing her like this."

"So do I." I sigh, looking down at her sleeping face. Brushing the hair from her forehead, I rub her cheek softly with my thumb, her thick lashes brushing against the tip. Her pink lips are parted as she softly breathes. "How did everything get so fucked up?" I ask, looking up at my twin. "Things were going fine. Life was good."

"Then she started to push our limits. She knew what she wanted, and was tired of waiting for us to make a move. She tried to get us to, and... well, here we are because we can't say all the things we want to."

Raven bolts up right, her face going deathly pale. "I'm gonna puke," she whimpers.

"Fuck," Taylor hisses, quickly grabbing the bucket we placed near her bed.

Gathering her hair, I hold it back as she gets sick. Taylor rubs her back, telling her everything is going to be okay as she starts to cry. Raven hates puking. She would always cry any time she did it when she was younger. But we were always there for her, holding her hair, her hand, and anything else she needed us for.

And it kills me that she thinks we don't want her that way anymore. Taylor and I have been trying but she's gonna give up on that part of us, so we've been extra clingy. We're pussy whipped, and we don't give a single fuck. She's our world, and I can't hold back much longer.

When she's done, Taylor cleans up the bucket as Raven snuggles into me. Taylor comes back with a cold wash cloth, placing it on Raven's forehead, and a bottle of water, which he puts on her night stand.

"Never drinking again," she murmurs into my chest, still sounding drunk.

"I'll remember that," I tell her, rubbing up and down her back as I kiss the top of her head.

"Why did he do it?" she asks, her voice sounding small and vulnerable. I look over at Taylor, my heart breaking. "Why doesn't he want me? Why don't any of you want me?"

"We love you, Ray," I tell her. "You're our best friend."

"But I want to be more," she whimpers, softly crying. "I love you dummies so much. Why are you all so stupid?"

"I don't know, baby. I don't know," I sigh, really fucking hating life right now.

"If it's because you're Black Venom Crew, I don't care," she murmurs, and my brother and I go stiff.

"What did you say?" I ask, making sure I heard her right.

"I saw," she mumbles, sounding like she's about to drift off to sleep at any moment. "I saw you all covered in blood in the warehouse. I saw you take lives. I don't care because I know you would never hurt me." The last word was barely audible as she passes out on my chest.

"Fuck," I breathe, looking at my brother, who's staring at our girl with wide eyes.

"How does she know?" he whispers. "We've done everything we can to make sure no one told her."

"Does it matter?" I ask him, a smile finding my lips. "You heard her. She doesn't care. She still wants us, even knowing what we do. This changes everything."

"It does?" he asks, looking up at me with furrowed brows.

"Yes, because other than Link's controlling bullshit, the only thing that kept us from claiming her the way we want was telling her what we do behind closed doors. Now, it's no longer an issue." I'm not stupid enough to think she's 100% in based off some drunk ramblings she may not even remember in the morning, but the fact is, she knows and she's still here, upset about us not wanting her. Which is utter bullshit because I fucking adore her.

"So, if something happens like it did with her and Hunter, we just ... go with it?" he asks.

"Yeah. We don't pull away, we tell her point-blank that she's ours, and we show her. Again and again until she can't talk or walk." I give him a wicked grin that has him chuckling.

"Deal."

Fuck Link. He can stay away all he wants, but if something happens that's going to put us in the same position Hunter was in, I'm not pulling back. I'll deal with the consequences. I won't let her hurt like this again.

CHAPTER 19

RAVEN

I'm officially eighteen now. It didn't really sink in until a few days after the dumpster fire that was my birthday.

Not that I remember anything. I blacked out, and the last thing I remember was taking a drink that Andy offered me. She filled me in the best she could. Told me I was very sharing about what I knew with the guys being Black Venom Crew. And apparently, I gave her details on Hunter's dick. I mean, the thing is impressive. Then she said I got sick, so she called the twins to come get me. I don't remember a single minute of it.

But I don't think I embarrassed myself too much because the guys haven't given me any funny looks or mocked me.

"Are you going to forgive him anytime soon?" Andy asks me in a hushed whisper from her desk next to me.

"What?" I whisper, looking up at her from my math text book. She nods her head, and I look in that direction.

Hunter is staring at me with a hardened look. He looks like a fucking creeper, contemplating on how he's going to kill me and bury my body. Weirdo. Grabbing my phone out of my book bag, I put it under my desk so my teacher doesn't see and text him.

> Little Mouse: Stop fucking looking at me like that. You're creeping me out.

Hitting send, I wait a moment. He looks away from me and down to his phone. Unlike me, he doesn't bother to hide it from the teacher. Now, I get why the guys could do whatever the fuck they wanted and the teachers didn't do anything. They knew who the guys were and didn't wanna risk getting hurt. I still don't know where they would draw the line when it comes to killing someone. I guess, as long as they weren't innocent, I wouldn't make a big deal over it.

> Hunter: I can't stop looking at you. Impossible, Little Mouse. You're too fucking stunning.

Biting my lip, I both love and hate his words. He talks to me like this, yet acts like he did that night in the tent. I don't get it.

> Little Mouse: Well fuck off, or I'll kick you in the balls.

Okay, so it's not the most mature response, but I do have the urge to do it.

> Hunter: Now, now, Ray-Ray. Don't promise me a good time. ;)

A giggle bubbles up. *Fuck, I miss him.* I don't forgive him, and I won't forget what he did anytime soon. Not until he mans the fuck up if he ever does plan on doing it. But he's my best friend, and I miss him. Maybe a few weeks is long enough to freeze him out.

> Little Mouse: Fucking crazy bastard

> Hunter: But you love me anyway.

Yeah, I do and that might be the problem. Not knowing how to respond, I put my phone away and keep working on the assignment. I can feel his eyes on me for the rest of the period.

I'm in a good mood today, and it has nothing to do with my guys. Last night, I spent an hour getting everything ready for my new job. That's right bitches, your girl is about to make some green. The cam world will know me as 'Peaches' and I'm so damn excited.

Some might think exposing your body on the Internet for money is gross and tacky, but I don't. Who fucking cares? It's my body, and I can do whatever the fuck I want with it. And if that means playing with sexy toys, giving myself some orgasms in front of people I'm never going to see in real life then so be it. And it's not like they're going to know who I am anyways. I stole one of the guys' ski masks, and I'll wear it whenever I'm on cam.

If they don't want to enjoy my body, someone else will, and I'll get paid a pretty penny for it. Win-win.

This is one of the times that I'm hoping all the guys have to 'work' because I'd like to start tonight. The sooner I start, the sooner I can earn money, and I can stop relying on others.

After math class, it's gym. My least favorite subject. And of course the catty bitch squad gives me dirty looks.

"What do you want to do?" Andy asks me when the gym teacher says we can choose what we want. They split the gym up into three different sports. All the guys chose basketball, most of the girls chose volleyball, and well, I don't want to play with any of them so I'm choosing badminton.

"Badminton?"

"Sounds good to me. I'll go grab some rackets and the birdie," Andy says before running off to the equipment room.

Sitting on the bench, I wait for Andy. My eyes find Hunter just as he rips his shirt off, putting his tattoos on display. His whole fucking back is one giant skull face, and it's hot as hell.

And I'm not the only one who thinks that because all the damn girls in the room are now staring at him. Anger fills me as my jealousy flares. *He's mine!* I don't give a shit if I'm pissed at him, he's still mine, and if any other bitch wants to try me, I'll be more than happy to kick their asses.

Andy comes back with the stuff we need, and we start to play. I suck, missing every throw because I'm too distracted by the girls trying to get the attention of the guys playing basketball, including Hunter.

Something hits me in the face, snapping me out of my own head.

"You good?" Andy asks with a laugh. "You look ready to kill everyone in this room."

"You're not far off," I sigh, "I'm done with this. I just wanna go home." Thankfully, it's our last class of the day on Thursdays.

Once class is over, everyone goes over to the bench to grab their water bottles and talk amongst themselves.

After I put the rackets away, I walk back out to see that bitch Lindsay standing next to Hunter. She's got a big flirty smile on her face as she talks to him. He's still shirtless, and she's loving it.

I feel my anger start to boil as I watch her lift her hand to place it on his arm. And that's when I snap. No one touches what's mine.

Before I know what I'm doing, I'm charging over to her. Grabbing her arm roughly, I pull it off Hunter, making her stumble back.

"What the fuck?" she shouts, but she's cut off as my fist meets her nose.

Grabbing her by her shirt, I pull her close as she starts to cry, clutching her nose. "Touch him again," I say in a deadly low voice. "And I'll cut your fucking tits off."

"You're fucking crazy!" she sneers, pulling out of my

hold and running off. I'm fuming, adrenaline taking over. Looking at the other girls who are standing there with shocked and horrified expressions, I give them the same warning. "That goes for all of you. I didn't think you would be so fucking stupid as to touch what's mine, but clearly, you are. Any of you try the shit she just did, I'll make every one of you bleed."

"Fuck me, Little Mouse," Hunter's deep husky voice has the anger melting away, replacing it with a hot flash of need. "Watching you go all crazy jealous is so fucking hot. I don't think I've ever been so hard in my life." He steps up behind me, pushing the proof right into my ass.

Sucking in a shaky breath, I enjoy it for a moment before spinning around. "Fuck you." I glare at him. "I'm still pissed at you."

"I know," he says, his hand reaching up to cup my cheek. "I deserve it."

"You do," I say, my words having less bite.

"I'll make it up to you. I promise," he vows, his eyes telling me it's taking everything in him not to kiss me right now.

"I hope you do," I tell him. We hold each other's stare, more emotion than either of us have shared in a long time.

"Ray," Andy laughs as she comes over to us, breaking the moment. "Did you really punch Lindsay in the face?"

I give her an unashamed grin and shrug. "She deserved it."

"I love you. Like I'm obsessed with you. Marry me?" Andy jokes. Hunter growls, gaining both of our attention.

Biting my lip, I hold back a smile as he gives Andy a look that says if she wasn't my best friend or a girl, she should worry about her safety. Ugh, I love that he's jealous, even over Andy, someone he never has to feel that way about.

Hunter reluctantly heads to the guys locker room while Andy and I go to the girls. Once we're showered and changed, we head toward the exit.

Turning around the corner, I end up bumping into someone. "Sorry," I say, until I see who it is.

"Watch where you're going," Jeff, the school man whore, sneers.

"Or what?" I ask with a grin. "You gonna hit me? Threaten me? You can't do shit to me. Just like you couldn't get me alone long enough to fuck."

His eyes widen before he schools his shocked expression. "I don't know what the fuck you're talking about, crazy bitch."

"I'm sure you don't. You don't have enough brain cells to comprehend much. One too many hits to the head, I'm assuming."

"Watch your mouth," he warns, taking a step toward me, but Andy is in front of me in a flash, a blade pressed up against his neck.

"Fucking touch her, and I'll slice that baby carrot in your pants that you sadly call your cock," Andy's voice is low and dangerous, and if I was into girls, I'd totally pull her into the locker room to fuck her right now, because that was fucking hot.

Jeff looks over at me. "Can't even fight your own battles.

Fucking pathetic," he spits before spinning around and taking off the way he came.

I can't believe I thought of pretending to have a fling with that jackass to make the guys jealous. Can I claim I was mentally unstable? Fucking creep.

"Come on, babe. Better get you out to your boy toys before they come in here looking for you. I'm sure they would love to take a crack at Jeff too."

We finally make it outside, and there they are, waiting for me in the parking lot. I grin as I take them in. They are too fucking good-looking for their own good. Travis is in black jeans and a black t-shirt. He's leaning against the car, his arms crossed, making his muscles bulge. He's tracking my every move as I walk over to them. His face is blank but as I step up to him and give him a smirk, he can't help but crack a smile. "Waiting for me, are you?" I ask them.

Taylor hops off the hood of the car and over to me. He pulls me into his arms, and I go willingly. "Have a good day, Foxy Girl?" he asks against the top of my head. I wrap my arms around him, shoving my face into his chest and inhaling his scent. *Is that weird? Would running my hands through his wavy black hair be weird?* Fuck, I really wanna be weird right now.

"It's school. So, no?" I say.

"She got into a fight," Andy tells them with amusement from behind me. I forgot she was there for a moment.

"You did?" Travis growls. "What happened?"

"Some bitch," I mutter, not looking them in their eyes. "She was talking to Hunter." I shrug.

Taylor laughs, earning himself a glare. "You went all scrappy bitch over him talking to another girl? That's my girl."

"No. Not just talking. She was flirting and touching his arm. I didn't like it. And there was no scrapping, the bitch didn't stand a chance. One punch and she was running home to cry to her mother."

"Fuck me, Dove," Travis groans. "Hearing you be all possessive and shit, that's better than porn."

"You're my best friends. No one is good enough for you," I say. *No one but me, that is.*

"Very true. None of them ever stood a chance," Travis says, his blue eyes looking deep into my soul as he tucks some hair behind my ear. I swallow hard and really try not to let my mood go now. I've been excited all day.

After saying goodbye to Andy, I hop in the Jeep with the twins. "So, we hate to drop you off and run again," Travis starts.

"It's okay," I tell them. "I'm tired anyway. I think I'm going to grab something to eat, then watch some TV before going to bed early."

"You sure you're okay?" Taylor asks.

"Yup. Go work, fix them cars and make that money," I tease. They both look at each other, having one of those freaky twin conversations. I'd love to know what they're thinking right now.

When we get home, the guys don't get out of the car, saying goodbye with a kiss to the forehead like always before I hop out. I wait until they've pulled out of the driveway before quickly grabbing my phone to text Hunter and see if he's going to be coming home after school or not.

As I pull up his name, I see he already texted me saying he's been called into work, and he will be home later.

Grinning, I turn around and race inside. All the moms are going to be at work for another few hours and Leah is on the floor below me in a room on the opposite side, so no one should hear me... *working*.

I'm nervous but excited. To get to pretend to be someone else, to explore something that excites and turns me on, is enticing. I can't remember the amount of times I've imagined the guys taking me in front of other people, showing who owns them and what others will never have. It's one of my kinks that I really hope they're okay with. That's if I ever fucking get with them at this point.

In a way, this is kind of like that. I'm taking my own pleasure and showing people what they will never have, no matter how much they want it. And the bonus is, I'm getting paid to do it.

I'm practically vibrating when I get to my room. Making sure my bed is made, I grab my box of toys. There's not much because I'm still a virgin and the only cock that's going to be splitting me open and stretching me wide is one of my guys, not some fake silicone dick.

I have things like vibrators and nipple clamps but I know once I finally start having sex, I wanna try everything.

Draping a waterproof blanket over the bed, I put the toys and mask on one side table and pull the other one to the edge of the bed to hold my laptop.

When I'm happy with my set-up, I pick out what bra and panty set I'm going to wear. The nice thing about the ski mask is I don't need to bother with doing my hair and the only makeup I'm going to be wearing is eye shadow and mascara.

Stripping out of today's clothes, I put on a cute peach color set I got when I was out with Andy. It's fitting for the name.

Crawling onto the bed, I sit cross-legged as I log on to the site. My plan is to do a live stream first, draw some people in, and after a little bit I'll start taking private chats. I'm going to be playing on the virgin thing so they don't ask me to do anything too crazy. I watched a few cam girls do their thing, but from what I've seen, everyone does something different. It's my channel so I'll do what I want if it works for me. The worst that could happen is I don't make any money and have to find another job.

Grabbing my mask, I slip it on. Taking a deep breath, I click the live button. Here goes nothing.

"Hey there, everyone. I'm Peaches..."

LINCOLN

As I wash my hands, the water runs red, then pink before going clear. Another day, another sick vile fucker taken off this earth by my hands.

I'm still a little wound up. I'm hoping hitting the gym for a while will help; if not, I'll just wait until Raven is sleeping and pay her a late night visit.

Unlike my little brother, I'll make sure she's fucking asleep before I do.

I love him, he's my family, but it took every fucking thing in me not to put a bullet through his stupid head. I can't believe he fucked with Raven like that.

When Hunter said she ran off after what they did, after I was done bitching him out I took off to find her. She was, thankfully, safe at home and in her bed. I stayed there, watching her sleep until the sun rose. I didn't want to leave, but I didn't want her to see me there. I'd have to lie and that would only fuck things up more.

Hunter's lucky that the only one she was pissed at was him, rightfully so. She didn't pull away or avoid the rest of us. Hunter looked like a wounded puppy, but he brought that shit on himself.

Raven seems to be coming around. I don't think she's forgiven him yet, but she can't stay mad at him long. She loves him too much.

The guys are pissed off at me because I'm forcing them to stick to the plan we agreed to years ago. But I didn't put it in place for the fun of it. They need to understand that Raven needs this year filled with as much freedom and normalcy she can get. If we break the plan, it's all over. She wouldn't get a moment to herself. I would own her, fuck her, consume her. I'd never be able to let her out of my fucking sight. She would be mine in every way possible. I'm possessive and selfish when it comes to my Little Bird, and I have no fucking care in the world what anyone has to say about it.

She's not ready for me. Ready for my level of darkness.

I'm sick in the head for all the things I dream of doing to her. I live for the day that I can wrap my hand around her pretty little throat and squeeze until she fears she's going to die. To hold her life in my hands and have her know that I'm the reason why she's still living. Why she will always stay standing. Her life is in my hands and even though I'd never take it from her, she will know that I have the power to do so.

The others might be ready, but I'm not. And even then, it took Travis and Taylor years of fucking useless holes to get their little sick and depraved fantasies out.

That's the reason why they've slept with other girls while my brother and I haven't. They're just as dark and fucked up in the head and thought by using other people to get that part of them out of their systems, they wouldn't feel the need to be that way when we take Raven as ours. They fear that Raven will hate them, see them in another way and not want anything to do with them if she knew just what gets them harder than stone.

Me? Well, I couldn't give a shit about what Raven thinks. I'll be embracing every part of me, showing Raven just who I really am. Just how sick and twisted I am.

Hunter... well, he's just happy as long as he's with Raven. He's been the best for her out of all of us. Don't get me wrong, when it comes to taking another's life, Hunter is a little psychopath. But with Raven, he's just a fucking weirdo.

Killing the rapist who I just got done with was satisfying and all, but my skin still itches with something more. I'm wound too tight.

Leaving the bathroom, I walk through the club level toward the back stairs to get to the gym on the floor above us when I pass some of my men.

"God, that body. So creamy and smooth. I'd love to run my tongue over every inch of her," Ringo groans.

"She's too fucking sweet. A virgin with a body like that, I wouldn't be able to keep my hands off her. And that birthmark just adds to her sweetness. It's like a little heart."

That has me stopping. Something is yelling at me to look at their phones, to see what the hell they're watching.

Stepping up behind them, I look over their shoulders. "Oh, hey boss," Marty says, looking up at me.

"What are you watching?" I ask.

"Oh, a new cam girl. She just started today, and I think I'm gonna subscribe to her channel. You can tell she's new, but god, them tits."

"Well, show me," I grunt. He holds up his phone, and my whole fucking world stops. On the screen is my Little Bird. She's got a ski mask on, so I can't see her face, but I'd know those hazel eyes anywhere. I'd know that sinfully stunning body anywhere. Even if I didn't, the little heart birthmark on her shoulder is the same one Raven has.

Question is, why the fuck is my woman on a porn site doing live cam shit for any fucking pervert to see?

I'm pissed and seeing fucking red. Grabbing the phone out of Marty's hand with a savage snarl, I smash it on the ground. They don't flinch and know better than to get pissed. "If I find out anyone of you ever watch her on that site again, I'll fucking gut you like a pig. Understand?" I snarl.

Understanding flashes on their faces, but they keep their mouths shut and nod. There's only one girl in the world that could get this kind of reaction from me. The whole fucking world knows Raven is mine. All but her. But she will, soon.

With my chest heaving, I take off into my office, no longer wanting that work out. I need to find out what the fuck is going on with Raven. *Is this some way to get back at us? Another one of her stunts to get under my skin?* I'm gonna fucking ring her neck.

Throwing myself in my office chair, I open my laptop and type in the site name in the search bar.

Clicking on the cam girl part of the site, I search her name. When I find it, I click on it only to have it tell me I need to make a damn account to gain access to this feed.

Letting out an annoyed sigh, I quickly make one, paying whatever they ask for and search her name again. "Twenty bucks to see her live," I mutter, clicking on the pay button.

It takes a second to load before my girl shows up on the screen. My cock thickens by the second as I take her in. She's in a ski mask and a peach bra and panty set.

My eyes trail over the swell of her breasts as her chest heaves, a small vibrator between her legs as she plays with herself, leaning back into a mountain of pillows.

My hand reaches into my pants to pull out my cock, ready to jack off to the cries of her pleasure when I remember who's on the fucking screen.

Leaving my cock hard and out, I go over to the corner of

the screen and click on the private chat request. The minimum I can offer is $100 for ten minutes. Or I can make a special request to heighten my chances at being bumped up to the top spot.

"There's no amount I wouldn't pay for you, Little Bird," I say to myself as I type in a grand and hit send.

"This has been fun," Raven giggles. She's lucky she was playing with herself over her clothes because I would have gone home and reddened her ass right fucking now. But my kinky little bitch would have liked that too much. "If you guys want to see more next time, be sure to subscribe, and I'll make it worth your while." She winks, getting on her hands and knees to crawl towards the camera. "Now, let's take some private requests. I can guarantee there will be more to see than on my live feed," she giggles.

Her eyes roam over the screen, and I know the moment she sees my request. "Holy shit," she whispers. "Well, VenomousKing, I must admit, I'm honored. I'd love to chat with you. I'll see you in there. Bye everyone, see you soon."

The fuck you will. Hope everyone enjoyed the show my Little Bird put on, because that's going to be the last they ever see. I'm so fucking pissed that she did this. That she's showing strangers what belongs to me, to my brothers.

"Alright, Little Bird, let's see what you got."

RAVEN

A thousand bucks for ten fucking minutes! This is a joke, right? I'm being fucked with. Who the hell would pay that much for me? I've only been on this site for forty minutes, and half that time I spent talking to viewers before giving them a show of me playing with myself over my clothes.

I am having fun though. The nerves went away after I started talking. But I wanted to give them a little something to keep coming back. I knew right away after I hit that live button that I wasn't going to dive right in, I wasn't ready for it. And because I'm playing on the whole virgin thing, it was for the best. The comments I was getting, the praise of how my body looked, how my voice sounds, it filled me with pride. I loved it all.

And even though I wasn't ready to do much for the people who were watching, I thought I'd try my luck at a private chat. I sure as hell didn't expect to see someone by the name of VenomousKing offering a grand to talk to me.

The live feed ends as I let my finger hover above the accept button. *Should I?* I mean it's a lot of money. Looking down, I see I have five other requests for a private chat, but they're all the minimum one hundred dollars.

It's ten minutes, why the hell not. My finger presses the button to accept. The screen changes into a chat room. My cam shows up in the top right hand corner, but it says VenomousKing has his cam off.

"Playing shy, I see," I say, smiling at the camera. "Well, hi. I'm Peaches. I'm happy to see you wanted to chat."

> VenomousKing: Hello, baby doll. You're a pretty little thing, aren't you?

"Thank you." I giggle, playing the part of a blushing

virgin. "I'm new here, and I don't really know how to start this. Is there something you want me to do for you, or would you like to just talk?" I ask, playing with the edge of my hair. It's not a lie. I have no idea what to do. I never paid for a private chat with the cam girls I looked into, I didn't have that kind of money. And you can't really look this kind of stuff up on Google. I mean, I tried but didn't get much.

> VenomousKing: Here's the thing. I'm a man of few words. So I'm not interested in chatting. I like what I see, and I want it. But the thing is, I don't like to share.

My brows furrow in confusion. "I'm not sure what you mean? This is my job. I'm here to share my body online with viewers like you, who would like to watch."

> VenomousKing: Not anymore. I'm gonna make you a deal. I'll pay you two thousand dollars for every private video chat.

My eyes practically bug out of my head, and I have to blink a few times to see if I'm reading this wrong. "That's a lot of money, Sir."

> VenomousKing: To me, it's nothing. You're worth every penny. I'll pay you two thousand dollars per chat, three times a week. But, there's a catch. You only private cam for me, and you no longer do live streams.

Holy fucking shit. Is this man for real? He wants to give me... I do the math on my phone real quick and almost stop breathing when I see the price. Twenty four thousand dollars a month. A fucking month!

"You can't be for real? Why on earth would you be willing to pay that much money for me? I'm sure there's tons of other women on here worth that. I'm sure as hell not," I say, still in shock.

> VenomousKing: That's where you're wrong. It's quite the opposite to me. None of the other women on this app, or even in this world, would ever be worth that amount. I can't let the opportunity to have a pretty birdy like you all to myself slip away.

My mind tries to process everything he's offered. I just started this job, am I willing to just quit now and only cam for him? I've been excited to start this job for a long time. A way to explore my body while making money. But this is more money than I ever expected to make with this job. I never planned on this being a long term thing, just something fun to do to make some quick cash. I knew the moment the guys admitted their feelings for me, there'd be no way I could continue doing this. Not while I'm in a relationship. I wouldn't want anyone but them to see my body.

I reread the last line of his last message over and over. Pretty birdy... why does my mind keep focusing on that. It sounds a lot like... no... no fucking way. He's not.. He can't be!

But he can. He has the money to pay this price. The whole wanting me to himself and no one else. I mean, who else would pay that insane amount for a girl they just saw for the first time today?

Link calls me Little Bird. VenomousKing called me pretty birdy. Maybe it's one big coincidence. Or maybe it is Link behind the computer.

A rush of excitement fills me as my belly flutters. *If this really is Link, do I act like I don't know and have one hell of a time with him?*

The whole point of this job was so I could pay for things myself and stop letting the guys spend their money on me.

Is this cheating? I mean, I'd still be working right?

I need to know more before I agree. I need to test this man, if it even is a man, to make sure it's Link. And I need to do it fast because we only have three minutes left.

"I don't know. I mean, it's an amazing amount of money, but I've been pretty excited to start this job. I already had a few people subscribe to my channel. To end this so soon, how would I know you won't just do a few chats with me and then ghost me, making me have to start all over again? Asking me to be only yours is a big deal."

There's a few moments before I see the dots on the screen, indicating he's typing.

> VenomousKing: I don't want anyone else seeing that gorgeous body of yours. Only me. The idea of anyone else touching themselves to you... well, let's just say it's not pretty. You will never want for anything with what I'll pay you. And there's no way I'd leave you. Don't be a fool, Peaches. I'm not asking you, I'm telling you you're mine. Now stop holding back and accept my offer.

I try to hold back my smile because he is failing badly at not being obvious. If I were anyone else and he was talking to them like this, all demanding when you just met the person... yeah, they probably would have blocked him after their time was up.

This is Link, it has to be. If the nickname wasn't enough to have me convinced, the way he talks, the chosen username of VenomousKing, and the fact that he's in Black Venom Crew does.

"Alright. I'd be crazy to give up that kind of money. I have a few rules, though. I won't put anything inside me. The virgin thing isn't an act. And I want the first thing inside me to be one of the men I'm in love with. I'm willing to go full nudity. No butt stuff. And I will not pretend to be anyone but myself. If you want me, you get me. Not your mother or sister or anything like that. Also, I can't guarantee a time. It's got to be when I'm available. I have school and other things. And no, we can't ever meet in person. This is an online only thing. Before you ask, yes, I'm eighteen. If you're fine with all of that, then I'm more than happy to agree to your terms."

I know half of that wasn't needed, but if he was anyone else, those would be my terms. Link would think I'm foolish if I blindly agreed to what a stranger wanted.

> VenomousKing: Smart move, Peaches. I can't wait to play with you.

I hear an engine outside my window, followed by the chatter of Hunter and the twins. *Fuck.* The first thing they're going to do is come up here to see me. "I gotta go. Your ten minutes are about to be up anyway. I'll make sure not to change the settings when we meet again. It's nice doing business with you, VenomousKing." I wink and press end before giving him a chance to hang up.

Laughing, I slam the laptop shut before hopping off the bed. I'm buzzing with this giddiness as I grab the box for my toys, tossing them all inside. Ripping off my ski mask, I add it to the box before hiding it in the closet. I'll clean the toy I used later, right now I need to get this room back to the way it was before the guys find out what I'm doing.

Grabbing the waterproof cover, I hide it in the closet as well.

I can't believe that really happened. It's not like camming was my dream job, and sure, I was excited to explore that part of me, but now I get to do it for Link, one of my guys. *God, I really fucking hope it's Link and I'm not thinking too much into it.*

If it is, I know he knows it's me; there's no way he wouldn't recognize my voice.

Pulling the bedside table back in place, I look around the room to make sure everything is good to go. My eye catches myself in the mirror, and I realize that I'm still in my bra and panties. "Shit," I hiss, running over to my laundry and grabbing the first thing I could find.

"Ray?" Taylor calls my name through the door as he knocks. "You in there? We got off work early."

"Hey," I say, tossing the door open, sounding a little out of breath. "What's up?" *Yeah, because that doesn't sound suspicious at all.*

"Ahhh..." Travis says as all three of their eyes look me over. "Nice fashion choice."

"What?" I ask, brows furrowing as I look down. *Fucking hell.* In my rush to get dressed, I didn't notice I grabbed PJ pants and a one of my see through crop tops, that I'm sure is giving them a nice view of what's underneath.

"You sound flustered. You look it, too. What were you doing in there?" Taylor asks, giving me a mischievous grin.

"Oh shit," Hunter chuckles. "Did we catch you in the middle of having some fun *alone* time?" He grins, too.

"Wait... were you really masturbating in there?" Travis questions, his brows rising.

Rolling my eyes, I huff. "So what if I was? If I wanna finger fuck myself, I have every right. Now, let me get dressed, and then you three can feed me all my favorite things. I've worked up quite an appetite" I say, giving them a wink before closing the door.

All three of them curse, making me giggle as I put on a better outfit.

Once I'm ready, I open my door again to find them all still waiting. "Well, let's go. I'm starving."

"So are we," Hunter mutters as I walk ahead of them.

Silly boys. I could satisfy all your hunger needs if you just asked.

The whole ride to the restaurant, I'm on cloud nine. I'm still on a orgasm high, going to get something to eat at one of my favorite places, and my sinfully sexy best friend, who I'm madly in love with, is paying me out the ass to play with myself on cam for him.

When we get to the restaurant, I'm taken by surprise to see that Link is sitting at a table, waiting for us. "I thought I'd try inviting him," Hunter says from behind me. "Surprised to see the fucker actually accepted."

Link looks me up and down before licking his lips. My eyes lock on Link's as my heart starts to violently thud in my chest. The way he's looking at me, I just know it's him behind that account.

I'm hoping he gives the guys more jobs so I can get alone time again soon. I really want another cam session.

Life is fucking grand.

CHAPTER 20

LINCOLN

I've never been so sexually satisfied and frustrated in my whole fucking life than I have in the past few weeks. I have my girl, my Little Bird pleasuring herself at my command. Doing everything I tell her like the good little slut she is.

When she walked into that restaurant after the first time we talked as VenomousKing and Peaches, we locked eyes and there was no denying that we both knew. But neither of us brought it up.

My naughty girl likes to pretend, likes to play this game. I'll allow it because it's so fucking hot to watch her laying on her bed, her pupils dilated, her chest heaving as she pants for breath.

I'm doing this to myself, testing my fucking limits. I know I should have just kept my distance like I've been doing. Okay, that's a lie. I've been sneaking into her room every night since Hunter did his little fuck up. Partly because I was worried she would run when no one was watching. After I realized she didn't want to go anywhere, I stayed to watch her sleep, letting my fucked up fantasies run wild.

I am closer to my breaking point than I would ever admit to anyone, not even the guys; I almost give in, ready to break the plan, every single day. Hell, just by looking at her I have to resist the urge to claim her. So watching her come undone for me, my name on her lips as she topples over into ecstasy, it's heaven and hell rolled into one.

Right now, it's about to be the real test of my will power because this is going to be the first time I tell her she's going to be naked for me while she pleasures herself. I've given her enough time to get used to being on cam. Now I need to see all of her when she shatters for me.

Closing my office door behind me, I make my way over to my desk and open my laptop. The first thing that pops up is the site with her channel, ready and waiting for me.

I look at her number of subscribers and I'm surprised it's gone up to three hundred. She hasn't been doing any live shows per our agreement, at least none that involves showing her body.

But she's taken it upon herself to chat to people fully clothed. She explained why it was short-lived but was willing to talk on live for anyone who wanted to just chat.

She's still making money from it too, a bunch of sad men who just want someone to listen to them. And of course my girl has a fucking heart and hates to see people hurt.

As soon as my ass hits the chair, I jump up as I feel something poking me in the ass. "What the fuck?" I hiss as I look down to see a little pink duck sitting in the middle of my chair. "Fucking Hunter," I mutter as I toss it on the desk.

Something tells me he wouldn't come in here to hide *just one*, and I'm right when I look around, finding tons of little colorful ducks around my office. On the bookshelf, filing cabinet, and there's even one spilling out of the decorative skull's mouth that may or may not be real from one of my past victims.

"Fucking childish asshole," I snarl, moving around the room and aggressively snatching all of them up. I don't have time for this bullshit, I have a meeting with my girl, but I'm not risking my men seeing them all over my fucking office.

I'm about to toss a handful of them in the trash but stop. Letting out an annoyed sigh, I add them to the bottom drawer with all the other ones he's previously left. Fucker does this any chance he gets. He just loves to get under my skin. He's lucky I love his punk-ass.

Annoyed, I finally sit down and see my girl is online and waiting. Making sure my cam is off, I send her a video invite. She answers almost immediately.

My cock hardens so fucking fast the moment I lay my eyes on her. She's dressed in nothing but her bra and panties, this time they're black lace and see through. Her silver nipple piercings poke through, making me groan. Fuck, when she flashed us her tits the day she got them, I wanted to throw her on the hood of the car and suck them into my mouth.

"Hello, VenomousKing," she says, giving me a smile. She always wears the black ski mask, and I oddly think it's sexy. "What would you like me to do for you today?" she asks, moving to lay back on the bed against the mountain of pillows behind her.

> VenomousKing: Hello, my Peachy girl. I've been looking forward to this all day. My cock is fucking stone, dripping with pre cum, and all for you.

She takes a moment to read what I said and smiles. "I'm glad," she says in a breathy tone as she widens her legs. I curse my cock, pulsing in my jeans, as my eyes dart down to watch her fingers rub over her lace covered pussy. "Because I'm so damn wet. The thought of you stroking your hard, thick cock as you watch me cum, just for you, has me dripping."

I'm a man of few words, and I don't want to waste our time together talking. So I'm going to get to the point because my cock is aching, and I need some relief.

> VenomousKing: Are you ready to take things a little further this time? I've been dying to see everything, nothing left to mystery. Touch yourself today with nothing hiding your sexy little body from me.

Her eyes light up as she bites her lower lip and nods. "Anything for you, my king," she purrs, and fuck me, if I don't enjoy being called that.

She moves to sit up, bringing her arms around her back to unclasp her bra. She pulls it off her arms and tosses it to the side. I groan as I start to undo my pants and pull my cock free. It's heavy and warm in my hand, pre-cum beading at the tip as I watch her heavy breasts fall free.

Then my naughty Little Bird turns around, getting on all fours so that her plump ass is facing the camera. She looks over her shoulder, giving me a sultry grin as she uses one of her hands to pull down her panties.

"Fucking hell," I hiss as I grip my cock, giving it a firm stroke as my eyes lock on her glistening cunt.

"This is all for you, my king," she says, moaning as she dips two fingers into her pussy.

Releasing my cock, I type out a command.

> VenomousKing: Suck your fingers clean for me, Peaches. Taste your sweet juices for me.

She reads what I say, and her eyes go heavy-lidded. She rolls over onto her back, getting into the position from before. "Fuck's sake," I growl as I look at her laid out there for me like a feast, just waiting for me to eat every inch of her. I'm gripping my cock so hard it's borderline painful.

"Like this?" she asks, taking another swipe at her pussy before bringing her fingers to her face. She opens her mouth, sticking her tongue out, and places her fingers on her before sucking them in. She moans as she cleans her juices off, and it has me thrusting up into my hand as I work myself slow and hard.

Prying my hand off my cock, I type out my next demand.

> VenomousKing: Such a good girl. You
> listen so well. What do you taste like?

"A little sweet, a little salty. But I think you might enjoy it more than me." She grins. I know I would. Her cunt would be the best thing I've ever tasted. "Too bad you can't have any." She pouts.

I snarl as I type again.

> VenomousKing: No need to be a little
> brat, Peaches. Teasing is naughty. Now,
> you're gonna make it up to me. I want you
> to take your bullet vibrator and you're
> gonna hold it to your clit until you cum
> hard. I expect you to squirt for me, baby,
> and scream my name as you do it.

"Yes, sir," she breathes out. Grabbing the vibrator, she turns it on and places it on her clit. She doesn't need foreplay because she's already desperate for me.

Raven cries out at the contact, her back arching off the bed as her eyes roll back. So fucking beautiful. My Little Bird is everything.

I don't bother typing out any more orders, she won't see them. She's too lost in her pleasure.

Leaning back in my seat, I widen my legs as I grip my cock again. My breathing picks up with each stroke. My eyes never leave the screen. I take everything in, wanting to memorize it all. The way her body quivers when she shifts a certain angle. How her breasts rise and fall with each panting breath. How she moans and whines as her pussy quivers, begging to be filled by my cock.

When she cums the first time, she screams my name, her body shaking, but she doesn't squirt like I told her to. It's too much, her clit too sensitive that she eases the pressure of the vibrator.

With heaving breaths, I type.

> VenomousKing: You need to hold it there, Peaches. I know it might seem like it's too much, that you can't take the pleasure, but you need to push past that feeling... I promise it will be worth it.

She reads what I have to say with heavy-lidded eyes, still blissed out from her climax, her breathing still fast and labored.

"I don't know. It's a really weird feeling. What if I pee myself?"

> VenomousKing: You won't, I promise and oh well, if you do. You're gonna look so fucking sexy doing it, I'll be blowing my load in seconds.

She smiles softly and giggles. "Fine. Only for you."

That has me preening as I take my cock in my hand again. My balls are throbbing, the need to cum makes me feel feral. My hand isn't enough as I watch her start round two. Her whimpers and whines, my name on her lips as she works herself over.

Fuck, I'm so close to breaking. I'm about to stand up and leave, to go over there and pin Raven down and feast on her cunt until she can't breathe before fucking her until she passes out but I can't, not yet.

Raven lets out a sob, her body writhing on the bed, her head thrashing back and forth as she holds the vibrator to her clit. A savage snarl rattles in my chest. I need to cum so fucking bad, my balls are ready to burst any damn moment and I need to see her shatter while I do. She still hasn't done what I fucking asked her to do. If I was with her right now, I'd tie her to the bed and hold that damn vibrator to her swollen clit until she soaked me and the bed.

Letting go of my cock for a quick moment, I type.

> VenomousKing: Fuck me, Peaches, you look so fucking gorgeous when you cum. But you still didn't squirt for me. One more, and then I'll let you go for the night.

She's sweating and panting, shaking her head back and forth after she reads what I said. "No," she cries. "I can't. I'm too tired. My body doesn't have it in me."

I do what I have yet to do... I send her a voice memo.

"Do as you're told, Peaches. Be a good girl, and cum for your king one more time. One more fucking time, and I want you to soak that fucking bed. You can do this. Play with your nipples, imagine my cock deep inside that greedy little cunt and cum for me one more time," I growl.

When she sees my voice memo pop up, she shakily shifts to press play. Her eyes widen as she listens, and I chuckle as I hear her whimper. "Yes, my king," she breathes out.

Raven moves to lay back down again, but she doesn't use her vibrator this time. She uses her fingers, dipping them inside her before pulling them out and rubbing her cream all over her pussy. "Fuck," I grunt, gripping my cock in a vice grip. "That's it, my Little Bird. Fuck your tight wet pussy with your fingers. Squirt for me, my little slut, my balls are ready to burst. God, you have no idea how fucking stunning you are. You can bring any man to his knees. Maybe even me one day," I growl, talking to myself as I watch my queen.

Pre-cum is leaking from the tip of my cock, dripping down to my hand. I use it as lube as I stroke myself harder, faster, chasing the oncoming orgasm I feel deep in my fucking bones.

"Take my fucking cock," I snarl, watching the screen as Raven plays with her clit, her eyes on the screen, her breasts heaving as she works on bringing herself to the edge again.

Her sounds of ecstasy are fucking perfect, like the sounds of an angel. The song of a siren. And they're all for me. I grunt and snarl as I feel my balls tighten and my whole body tingles.

"I-I'm going to cum," Raven pants out, her voice straining as her shaking fingers rub her clit faster while I jerk myself at the same pace. "This feels so weird, gah," she cries out, and holy fucking shit my girl does it. Her body locks up as she lets out a loud sob, her body jerking as she squirts like a fucking water gun. As I watch her pussy spasm, drenching the bed below her, her whines and whimpers coming through the screen.

I'm done for. "Fuck!" I roar, thrusting up into my hand as my cock violently spasms, cum shooting up over my hand and onto the floor.

"Did I do good?" Raven asks, her head lolling to the side as she gives me a sleepy smile. *Fuck, why do I want to pull her in my arms and praise her until she falls asleep?*

Without even letting go, I lean over and type.

> VenomousKing: You did so good, Peaches. I'm so proud of you. Now, get some sleep. You've earned it.

She smiles and nods, getting up weakly. "Bye," she says softly before turning off the cam.

"You might wanna stick to over the clothes stuff," Quinton says with a chuckle.

My eyes shoot over to see him standing in the doorway of the office.

"Fuck off," I snap, my breathing still ragged. As amazing as that was, it wasn't enough. I'm still fucking vibrating, the urge to go over there and fuck her for hours, days, is riding my ass. I need to kill something or at the very last beat the shit out of someone.

"I'm just saying, you're torturing yourself," he says, his eyes taking in my state.

"It's fucking worth it," I grumble as I tuck myself back

into my pants and slam the laptop shut. "Maybe you should stop torturing yourself."

He narrows his eyes at me before correcting himself, knowing better.

"You know, I don't just fuck any chick who tosses her pussy my way," he says, running a hand over his face.

"Then go find a nice fat cock to fuck you in your uptight ass." I give him a savage grin.

"Not gonna happen and you know it. Not that there's anything wrong with it, but I'm not gay. I like ass play, sue me. There's not many girls who would be willing to put on a strap-on and fuck a guy in the ass." He rolls his eyes.

"Hey, girls can be freaky little fuckers. You just gotta find the right one." Like my Little Bird. God, just thinking of all the things I'm going to do to her has me getting hard again. "Anyway, I'm still pent up and seconds away from starting shit with our own people just to feel the rush of pounding my fist into someone's flesh."

"I thought as much. It's why I came to check on you. With every one of these video calls, you've been more testy than normal. Our guys are afraid to even look at you the wrong way in fear of getting shot over it." he gives me an amused grin.

"Smart men I'd say," I grind out as I push past him. "Because they're probably not wrong."

"You need to get laid," he says.

"Not unless it's my Little Bird," I growl.

"I know, but are you really going to be able to hold out

until June?" he asks me as we make our way down the stairs to the bottom level.

Outside of my brother and the twins, Quinton is the only one I trust, maybe even with my life. He's been a part of Black Venom Crew from the very start and has been by my side through some heavy shit throughout our lives.

He's the only one I trust with Raven outside the twins and my brother. He's been in her life almost as long as we have, she just doesn't know it yet. I wonder how she would feel if she knew I always have someone watching her from the shadows. Not that I give a fuck. All that matters is she's safe, and if one of us can't be there with her, Quinton is the next best thing.

But fuck, maybe he's right. All I really want is Raven. I'm starting to see why the guys are slowly breaking down, because I might not be too far behind. That woman, my queen, she's not someone I can resist much longer.

"I'm taking my bike, I can't be confined in a car right now." I say, throwing my leg over the seat of my bike.

"I'll make some calls and have someone waiting for you at the gym," he says.

"Then get your fucking ass back outside Safe Haven. The guys are coming to work on some cars for once."

Raven thinks that every time we're away from her that we're here working on cars, but that's only true maybe twenty five percent of the time. We love it, the feeling of grease under our fingers nails, the purr of a well tuned engine but we much more prefer it be blood under our nails as the last screams of scum leaves this earth.

I speed to the gym, tempted to turn onto Safe Haven's street as I pass it and go to my Little Bird. But I find the fucking will of God or some shit and pass by.

When I get to the gym, I find one of my men waiting for me. "You got someone for me to play with?" I ask as I pass him, going around the building to the back.

The gym is a legit gym. At least the top level is. People of Black Ridge come to work out, lift weights and go a few rounds in the boxing ring, but down below is something much more to my liking. A place where the only rule is, try to survive.

"It was short notice, so try not to kill him please." Ricky says with uncertainly in his voice. I shoot him a glare and he swallows hard. "Or not. Fuck."

"Would anyone miss him if he happened to disappear?" I ask as I jog down the stairs and to the basement.

"No, not really," he says as he follows after me.

"Perfect because I can't make any promises," I say, swinging open the door. Sitting in the middle of the ring is a man bound and gagged to a chair, the spotlight shining down on him as if I'm being shown my prize.

A feral grin slips onto my lips as I lock eyes with him. He pales, true fear showing in his eyes and rightfully so. Sometimes we need to make sacrifices and because my Little Bird isn't quite ready for me, he will be mine.

"Show time."

CHAPTER 21

RAVEN

Life has been amazing the past few weeks. Things between Hunter and me have been getting back to normal. School is going as well as to be expected. The girls still shoot me nasty looks, but no one has said a word to me since the gym incident. I've been hanging out with Andy less because any free time I have, I've been camming with Link.

After a week of turning her down to hang out, she cornered me at school and demanded I tell her why. Because we're friends and she's one of the few people I trust, I told her everything. Well, not all the dirty details but enough. After that, she understood, but told me not to let all the hot cam sex go to my head.

It's kind of hard when it's so fucking good. I've never cum so hard on my own than when I'm performing for Link. I thought it might be weird doing this with him when he hasn't admitted his feelings for me yet, but it's not because in a way, this is his way of telling me, isn't it? I mean, who would pay that kind of money for someone you don't love or want?

I've made a crap-ton so far to the point that my bank called me, asking if something was going on. Nothing like telling the bank teller... *yeah, everything is fine, just got a new job pleasuring myself on a porn website, no biggie.*

I do plan on reinvesting most of my money into helping Safe Haven or other charities. With Thanksgiving and Christmas coming up, I want to do something big for the homeless in the next town over. Maybe I can talk to my mom about setting something up to help people get on their feet by getting them homes.

If I'm going to be making this much money, then I want to make sure I make good use of it. I don't need this much for myself.

Right now, I'm laying in my bed, panting from the three orgasms Link demanded out of me during our session. It was amazing, my body is still buzzing. But I'm not sure how much more I can take of just messing around with my fingers and vibrators. I always end these sessions feeling satisfied, but also a little empty, needing and wanting more.

I want him to be the one to touch me, to make me cum on his tattooed fingers and his deadly tongue. To have him wrap his hand around my throat as he fucks me savagely into the bed, or wherever he chooses to take me. For him to force me to gag on his cock while I'm on my knees for him, tears streaming down my face as my pussy clenches for more.

Ugh, I need to shut my mind off because now I'm fucking horny again, and Link had to go. I wonder if he's actually fixing cars or taking lives. Yeah, I'm going to go with the latter.

As I lay there with my skin coated in a sheen of sweat, my body spent, my phone starts to ring.

Groaning, I roll over onto my belly and reach for it on the bedside table. When I see it's Andy, I almost laugh at her timing. "Hello," I answer.

"Hey, bitch. You done fucking yourself for my boss or what?" Andy asks, amusement lacing her tone.

"How did you know?" I ask, huffing out a laugh.

"Well, you sound out of breath. But all the guys are here... working and Link was missing, when he walked into the club he looked like one sexually frustrated man. Don't worry, he went down into the basement with the others, I'm thinking it's safe to bet he's going to go take his pent-up energy out on someone else. If you know what I mean."

"Stop, I'm already horny, that's not helping," I part groan, part laugh.

"Ah, what a kinky little bitch you are. Are you telling me you weren't satisfied afterward?"

"I was. Until I let my mind wander. Andy, I know I said I'd take a step back about trying to use their fucking words and get the truth out of them, but I know who Link is and that's a big change. It's just, not enough. I don't want just one of them. Call me selfish or a slut or whatever the fuck these bitches out here are calling me behind my back, but I want them all. All for me and only me."

"Well, you know my stand on this. Just tell him. Walk up to them and say, yo, I'm in love with you, and I want to be your naughty little whore. I'll let you do anything you want to my body, and I'm ready to do the same," Andy says in a fake swooning voice.

"Fuck off." I laugh.

"Nah, but I think you already did," she sing songs. "Now that I know you're free for the rest of the night, you should come to a party with me."

Flashes of the night I got trashed and puked my guts out come rushing back, making me gag. "I love you, girl, but I can't drink. And there's no way I'm going to a party like before sober."

"It's not going to be like that pathetic excuse of a party," she promises. "This party is in Hill Ridge, two towns over. It's where the rich bitches live. Remember that hot girl who did your nipples? She's friends with the people throwing the party, so we have an in. You don't have to drink, but there will be music and other fun shit. They even have a pool!" Andy sounds excited about it, and I know how much she likes Angie.

At first it was just texting, but as of a few weeks ago, she's been starting to hang out with her, and they seem to have hit it off. I'm happy for her.

"Come on, please? You owe me for blowing me off to get your freak on with killer Daddy."

I burst out laughing. "You did not just call him that."

"He totally gives off Daddy vibes," she says.

"True." I sigh wistfully.

"Ohhh, you're gonna make him your daddy, aren't you?" she teases.

"His eyes do get heated when I call him that teasingly," I admit. "Alright, you're right. I miss your sexy face. Give me an hour to shower and get ready."

"Yes!" she cheers. "We're gonna have a good time. Give you a party that's worthy to knock off that bucket list of yours."

"I almost forgot about that," I tell her.

"Yeah, too much dick on the mind. It's okay, I might be gay but those guys are fine as fuck. And those tattoos! Oh, that reminds me, I gotta see if my girl will give me my matching one."

"Matching tattoo?" I ask.

"Yeah... you know, the skull and snake. The symbol for... you know! The one all four of your guys have."

Holy shit. How have I never put that together? I just thought they had gotten matching tattoos because they're best friends and shit. I didn't think it was the symbol for Black Venom Crew. Although, I didn't even know what it looked like anyways.

There's a lot I guess I still don't know. I plan on making the guys tell me everything they've left me out of for all these years. No more secrets once this one comes out.

"Right," I say, like I knew what she was talking about. "Anyway, I'm gonna go get ready. Then we can go crash some preppy rich person's party," I tell her, getting up off the bed.

"That's my girl! See you soon."

We hang up and I start getting ready. Once I'm done showering off all the evidence of my fun with Link, I dry my hair. I end up going with loose curls, jeans and a long sleeve maroon crop top. It's the best I can do to keep me from sticking out at this party like a sore thumb and still feel like myself.

Pairing it with an adorable pair of Timberland boots I bought, I add a little bit of makeup, nothing too heavy.

By the time I'm done, there's a honk outside. Rushing over to my window, I see Andy sticking her head out the window. "Get in bitch, we're going to party!" she says laughing.

Grinning, I grab my phone and shoot Hunter a quick text. He seems like the one who would be less likely to get pissed I'm going out. I don't think anyone's going to see the text any time soon though.

"Where are you going?" my mom asks as I get to the bottom of the stairs.

"Out with Andy," I say, stopping to give her a quick kiss on the cheek. "Don't worry, no drinking. I'm never touching that shit again."

"That's good to hear," she laughs. "Have a fun time. Be safe."

"Always. Love you," I say before heading out the front door.

Sliding into the passenger seat, I put on my seat belt.

The moment it clicks in place, we're pulling out of the driveway and taking off down the road. Andy turns up the music and shoots me a grin.

"Tonight is gonna be unforgettable." She laughs.

Little did I know how right she was. In more than one way.

"This place is packed," I say as we drive toward the house. The street is lined on both sides with cars. "I think we're going to have to turn back," I tell her, leaning forward as I look for a spot to park but can't find any spaces. There's no other houses around from what I can see, so all these cars must be for the party.

"Nope," she says, popping the p. "I'll find us a place close by," she says as the house comes into view. My eyes widen as I take in the fucking mansion.

"Holy shit," I breathe, snapping my gaze over to Andy. "I've seen parties like this in movies, but I didn't know they were real."

Andy snorts out a laugh. "Ah, my sheltered friend. Just wait until you get inside." She grins. "Oh look. A place to park."

"Where?" I say, looking around and seeing no free places.

"Here," she says. The car jolts, making us bounce as Andy takes us up over the curb.

"Andy!" I laugh. "This is their front lawn. We can't park here."

"Why not?" she asks, putting the car in park. "Who's gonna stop me?" She gives me a devilish look.

"You wouldn't... you know... kill them would you?" I ask, blinking at her.

"God no." She waves me off like it's no big deal. "We have people for that."

I wonder if my guys are the only ones who've killed. I'm sure some of the other members have. I'm glad Andy hasn't... *has she?*

"Have you ever before?" I ask.

"Nope and I don't want to unless I have to," she says, getting out of the car. She leans back in. "Come on! There's only so long before your boy toys show up and ruin the fun."

"Good point," I say, getting out and joining her.

As we get closer, the music becomes louder. There's people all over the front lawn and... are those people jumping off the fucking roof?

"What the fuck?" I say, pointing up to the people cheering before launching themselves into the sky.

"Oh, the pool must be at the bottom," she says, pointing to the gate.

"I hope so and it's not just drunk people doing stupid shit."

"Could very well be." She shrugs.

When we get to the door, there's a guy standing there, blocking the entrance. He's big and sweaty and looks tipsy.

"Ten dollar cover charge," the guy says, looking at Andy. Then he notices me. "You can get in for free." He grins, licking his lips.

"How about we both get in for free, and I let you keep your shrimp dick," Andy counters, smiling up at him all sweet and innocently.

He snorts out a laugh. "I'm not afraid of you," he scoffs.

Andy pulls out her switchblade and flicks it open. "You should be."

He pales, swallowing hard. "Fine, go in, you crazy bitch," he whispers the last part, moving out of the way to let us in.

"My best friend is a bad ass bitch. It's hot," I say with a laugh.

"I know I am," she says, flicking her hair dramatically. "Now, let's check this place out."

We weave through the crowd of people as we move around the lower half of the house. I'm going wherever Andy takes me, otherwise I'd fucking get lost in this place.

When we break from the crowd, we end up in the back of the house. "Wow," I say, looking at the pool that looks like it takes up most of the backyard.

"Cannonball!" someone shouts before a person comes flying off the roof into the pool.

"Ahh, so it was people jumping into the pool. Not gonna lie, I'm kind of disappointed, there's not some pancaked people on the ground," Andy comments, watching the people in the pool.

"Andy." I laugh, gaping at her.

"What? You wanna get smashed and do stupid stuff, pay the consequences." She shrugs, looking up and watching the next person get ready to leap off the roof. "Much like this person. Oh my god he wouldn't..." I follow her line of sight, and my brows go up. There's a guy on the roof, but he's not near the pool. No, he's over by a trampoline. Below him are a group of people cheering on their dumb ass friend.

Cupping my hand to my mouth, I shout. "Do it! Do it!"

"Raven!" Andy snorts a laugh. "And you say I'm bad."

"Hey, you made a point. It's his own fault." We watch as this idiot jumps off and manages to land on the trampoline, only to have it send him flying up into the air, throwing him off the trampoline. He hits the ground hard, his leg bending the wrong way. The dude screams bloody murder. "Oh fuck, I think he broke his leg," I say, cringing as I see his friends move him, his leg most definitely not in the right position.

"Hey!" some girl comes outside screaming at the guy and his friend. "Get your buddies and leave. I will not have this party ruined by any ambulances. Get the fuck out of here."

"Rich people are scary," I say. "Come on, let's go do something normal."

"Wanna dance?" Andy asks me.

"Fuck yeah!" I say.

Andy and I head back inside and find a spot on the

dance floor. A song comes on that I know and we both start singing as we grind against each other. For a moment, I let myself forget about stupid guys and just enjoy another new experience to knock off my bucket list. It might not be a fun and exciting one, but it means something to me. So far this school year has been good. And it's only the start.

We get about three songs in before I start to get sweaty, the heat of all the bodies and lack of food from today makes me dizzy.

"I need some air!" I scream over the music.

"Okay! Go out back, I'll grab us a few bottles of water."

Nodding, I start making my way through the crowd. "Fresh air," I sigh as I take a deep breath in when I get outside.

Moving out of the doorway, I pass a group of girls, making my way to an empty cluster of lawn chairs and taking a seat.

"I can't believe she's here," someone says close by. I pay them no mind as I take my phone out to check it.

"Maybe she got tired of being low life trash and wanted to see what it was like on the other side of the tracks" someone else laughs.

"I don't think that's gonna help. She might be their best friend, but that's all she will ever be. I see how she looked at them in the restaurant. As if the fine as hell twins would actually want her."

That has my ears perking up. "Are you sure? I mean they seem pretty close. They're always hanging off her."

"I'm sure. Because Travis and Taylor were both at my house last Saturday," a girl giggles.

My belly flips as panic starts to take over. Looking over my shoulder, I see the girl who was hitting on Travis in the restaurant when the twins took me out. So she is talking about my guys.

No shit, she's talking about your guys, how many sets of twins around here share the same names?

"You're kidding right? Both of them, at the same time?" her friend asks in awe.

"Yup. And when I tell you, the size of their cocks," she fans herself. "I'm still walking funny," she giggles.

I know she's lying because the twins were with me the whole fucking weekend. Unless they slipped out to go fuck her while I was sleeping, even then when I got up to pee, they were asleep in my bed. I even took a photo because I thought it was adorable how they were cuddled in together.

"We have plans to do it again soon. As much fun as both of them are, I'm going to have to pick one. I hate it, because it's going to break their hearts." she pouts.

That has me snorting loudly, gaining their attention.

"Oh, it's you," the dumb blonde bitch snarks.

"How do you breathe?" I ask her, cocking my head to the side.

"What?" she asks me, brows furrowing.

"How do you breathe?" I ask again.

"Are you drunk or just fucking stupid?" she scoffs. "What the hell are you talking about?"

"I asked because I'm surprised you're not drowning in

all the bullshit that's spewing out of your mouth right now."
I laugh.

She curls her lip at me, taking a step forward. "Look, it
was all cute, you pining after your best friends, but, honey,
if they wanted you they would have had you by now. I
think you need to take the hint that they're just not interested in you. You can't get mad at me that I have something
they want that you don't." She gives me a fake pitying
smile.

This fucking bitch. "What, like chlamydia? Umm,
honey, that's not something to be proud of."

"You stupid bitch," she shrieks, and I get to my feet.

"How about you stop spreading lies just to make yourself look good. I know Travis and Taylor weren't in your bed
last Saturday because they were with me, the whole fucking
time." I pull up the photo and click on the details. "As you
can see the time and dates of each of these," I say, scrolling
through the other photos we took that night. "They were
with me the whole time."

"Listen, here you–" I cut her off with a slap across the
face.

"No, you listen here," I say in a dangerously low tone.
"I'm getting really fucking sick and tired of stupid bitches
like you saying they fucked my best friends, when most of
the time it's a fucking lie. I'm sure there are some of you girls
out there that managed to get lucky enough but not all of
them and definitely not you. So give it the fuck up. Because
I'm sure you know who they are, right? Like who they really
are?" Her face goes pale while she cups her sore cheek.

"Thought so. Keep lying and they might have to silence you. Permanently."

I'm not sure what their rule is for killing girls, but I don't think lying about sleeping with them would warrant her death. But she doesn't need to know that.

"Also," I say, grabbing her red drink. "White doesn't look good on you. Try a splash of color." I toss the drink on her white dress, watching it drip down before soaking in.

"What the hell!" she screams as her friends all crowd around her to help. She's fucking lucky that's all I did. The only reason why I didn't do more is because of all the witnesses.

I'm annoyed, and it sucks because I was starting to have a good time with Andy. Maybe the party scene isn't for me. I'm not a fan of big crowds or strangers. I know no one except Andy, and people giving me nasty looks all night is not my idea of fun. As cool as this house is, I'm ready to leave.

"Here," Andy says. Spinning around, I take the bottle of water from her. "You okay?" she asks, brows furrowing as she searches my face.

"Just some stupid girls lying about fucking the twins. What else is new," I huff, cracking off the top of the water bottle. "Thanks," I say before taking a few long drinks. "I'm going to go search for the bathroom."

"We can leave if you want after you get back," Andy offers.

I feel like a shitty friend because I have been using all

my friend time for Link. And if I'm not having hot, sweaty orgasms with him, I'm with one of the other guys.

"We can stay," I say. "Plus, Angie is coming, isn't she?"

"Yeah." Andy's face lights up. "She just texted she's almost here."

"I wanna get to know her better, I'm sure this party will be a lot better once she's here," I tell her.

There are too many people on the ground floor, so I'm not even going to be wasting my time trying to find a bathroom down here. I search for a staircase. It takes me pushing my way through most of the house to find one. Once I get to the next floor, there's thankfully less people.

I really have to pee now, and I'm desperate to find which door leads to the bathroom. I let out a sigh of relief when I see someone walk out of a room and when I look behind them, I see a toilet. "Excuse me." I probably push the dude out of the door as I slip past him, quickly closing it behind me.

I walk over to the sink and splash some cold water on my face before quickly peeing.

Sitting there, my mind is in overdrive. I know I said after

the whole thing with Hunter that I'd only be their friend, but that's bullshit. I love them. I want them, and I won't give up on them that easily.

And I'm really fucking close to telling the twins I'm gonna chop their cocks off if they fuck around with another girl again because I get it, we're not together, they're older than me, they can do whatever the fuck they want, but I'm sick of this shit. I don't know how many people they've actually slept with at this point because I don't know who is telling the truth and who is lying.

Needing to get back to Andy, I wash my hands and leave the bathroom.

As I'm walking down the hall, a door next to me opens. I don't even have enough time to register what the hell is going on when I'm pulled into the room. The door shuts, and I'm slammed against the back of it.

"What the fuck!" I scream, my mind taking a moment to recognize who has me pinned to the door. "Jeff?" *What the fuck is he doing here?* "What do you want? Fucking let go of me!"

"Or what?" he slurs, his alcohol laced breath wafting in my face, making me scrunch up my nose. "You going to get your boy Hunter to come punch me in the face again?" he laughs. "Sorry, sweetie, but none of your boys are here to save you now."

"Let me go," I snarl, fear and anger rising up inside me. How fucking dare this asshole touch me.

"I don't think I will. You see, you made me lose money. You were supposed to be an easy lay, easy money. Then your stupid fuckboy had to go all psycho on my ass. I don't like being made a fool in front of my friends, Raven."

"Why? It's so fucking easy to do," I spit.

"Shut the fuck up!" he shouts. "Your little crazy friend is busy. The place is loud with people and music. No one will hear you as I take what I'm owed," he says, giving me a sleazy grin. "Just be a good girl and don't fight me. I promise I'll make it good."

CHAPTER 22

TAYLOR

"Is it odd for me to say I'm glad we ended that douche's life faster than normal?" I ask Travis as we wash the blood from our hands.

"No, because I feel the same. I just wanna get home to Raven. I can't wait until we tell her everything so we can just bring her with us," Travis says, grabbing a towel to dry his hands.

"Let's go check in with Link, then we can get out of here."

We head up to the club's floor, spotting Hunter at the bar. "Hey, you coming home to see Ray?" I ask. I'm glad to see his glass is full of soda and not alcohol. He was hitting it pretty hard when Raven was giving him the silent treatment. They're not back to their old selves yet but they're getting there.

"No because Raven isn't home," he says, not looking too happy about that.

"Where is she?" I ask, brows furrowing.

"Got a text that her and Andy are going to some rich bitch party a few towns over. Don't worry, Quinton is there, watching from the shadows as always."

"I don't like that she doesn't know. Quinton has to watch her from the background. What if something happened inside, and he's not there to see or hear about it?" Travis sighs, running a hand through his hair. "Someone should be with her at all times."

"She's with Andy," Hunter counters. "She's BVC. She knows how to handle herself, and Raven has a good right hook." He grins. Fucker's been rubbing it in how Raven punched a girl and threatened others over him.

"We know she can handle herself, but with who we are, who knows who could be stupid enough to try and fuck with us," Travis argues.

"Hey," Link says, coming to stand behind me. "What's going on?"

"Raven went to a party with Andy," I tell him, and he scowls.

"Why the fuck does she keep needing to leave the damn house and do shit," Link growls. "She should be home where it's safe."

"Isn't the whole point of us waiting until graduation so that she can live as normal of a life as possible before we consume every ounce of her time?" Hunter asks his brother, raising a brow.

"She wasn't so adventurous until Andy came into the picture," Link grumbles.

"So you expected her to stay at home all the time because it's what she used to do?" I ask him with a smirk.

"Yes. She doesn't need Andy, she has us," he says, crossing his arms as he gives me a hard look.

"Yeah, you do know she's not going anywhere. She's Raven's best friend now too."

"We'll see about that," he says, looking over my shoulder. "What?"

Looking behind me I see Jamie, one of our men, approaching us with some papers.

"Hey, boss. So, these just got faxed in from our men in the PD. I thought you might want to see them right away. The dude goes to school with your girl," he says, handing Link the papers.

"Thanks," I tell him, nodding his dismissal. "Who's it about?" I ask.

"I knew it," Link snarls. "I fucking knew there was something up with that little sleaze ball, but there was no documented proof."

"What?" Hunter questions, on guard as he stands up to get a look at the paper.

Link grabs his phone, presses a button and puts it to his ear. He starts yelling over the phone as I read over what's been written.

Jeffrey Parson. *Wait... as in Jeff. The Jeff who Raven almost went on a date with?* My eyes scan the paper. The more I read, the angrier I get. He's been charged with raping three woman. They have all the evidence. But the moment I see that he's been released on bail, I full on panic.

"We need to get to Raven. Now." I don't know if she's in any danger, but until we can get our fucking hands on this creep, I don't want her out where he has access to her.

"What's going on?" Travis asks, on edge like me. But Link answers him.

"That fucking piece of shit who thought he had the right to talk to our girl is a fucking rapist, and he's out walking around. We need to get to her now. I'm going to fucking kill him," he snarls, his body vibrating as he takes off.

We're on his heels, adrenaline and fear rushing through me.

We're all bombs ready to explode, the car is filled with silence as we speed toward the party. *Why the fuck does it have to be so far away!*

"Where's Quinton? Is he with her?" Hunter asks.

"He was outside watching the party. He went in to find her. I don't fucking care what I have to tell her if she sees him, as long as she's safe. And if something happens to her, I will burn this whole mother fucking world down!" he roars as he punches the steering wheel.

I kill people for a living, I've laughed in the face of death as I bathed in blood, but I've never felt so scared as I do right now. Not knowing if my girl is safe guts me.

"Of all the fucking times my phone has to die," I say, my knee bouncing as I feel like a caged animal needing to be released.

"I tried calling her, and she's not fucking picking up!"

Link snaps. "I'm gonna redden her pretty ass when I get my hands on her."

"What about Andy?" I ask.

"Going to voice mail. She's gonna hear it from me too. She better be fucking dying, and that's why she's not answering. If not, she will be."

It feels like forever before we're pulling up to the house. Cars and people line the property as music blares from inside.

People scramble as the group of us charge our way into the house. We're all looking around for Raven, Andy, or Quinton.

We spot Andy, making out with some tattooed girl. As we reach her, Link yanks Andy off the girl. "What the fuck?" Andy starts to protest before going deathly pale.

"Where the fuck is she?" Link snarls, stepping into Andy.

"S-she went to use the bathroom a few minutes ago!" she says, looking a few seconds away from shitting her pants.

Link lets go of her and turns to us. "Check upstairs first," he barks.

We all take off running for the stairs. All I can think is my Foxy Girl better be okay or I'm right there along with Link with burning the world down.

RAVEN

"I'd rather die than let you touch me!" I scream in his face, bringing my knee up and ramming it into his crotch.

He cries out, dropping to the ground. "You little fucking bitch!" he groans as he cups his junk. I'm about to curb stomp his ass when the bedroom door bursts open.

Spinning around, I see all four of my guys pile in like a pack of feral dogs. Link looks at me, his eyes wild and crazed. They calm slightly when he sees I'm okay but charges toward me nonetheless.

I'm taken by surprise when he fucking pushes me against the wall, his hand wrapping around my neck. I gasp as he adds pressure, towering over me with his chest heaving.

"I hope it was worth it, Little Bird. All the teasing and the pushing because this is me at my breaking point. You have no idea what you got yourself into, but here it is. You are mine, Raven West. Mind, body, and soul. You don't know what all of that entails just yet, but you will. I tried to keep my inner demon locked up as long as I could, but it's all over now. I will consume this body whole. I will fuck you, worship you, but most of all, and understand this, I. Fuck-ing. Own. You."

His voice is low, husky, and oh-so-dangerous. I'm wet and a part of me wants him to fuck me against this wall right now.

I give him a savage grin as I struggle to breath. "About damn time," I choke out.

He growls, more like snarls, as he crashes his lips to mine. It's hard and bruising as he thrusts his tongue into my mouth before pulling back and taking my bottom lip into his mouth. He bites, hard enough that I cry out.

He yanks himself from my lips, panting. Without looking away from me, his gray eyes so intense I want to look away but can't, he addresses the others. "I need to get out of here before I shoot this place up. Hunter, grab the fucker, we end him tonight. Travis, Taylor, make sure our little brat comes with us," he barks before letting go of my neck and storming out of the room.

I sag a little, my hand going to my throat as I close my eyes, sucking in deep breaths. I'm still smiling and a manic laugh escapes.

"Well, well, Little Dove," Travis says, his voice low and husky. Opening my eyes, I find him in my space, in the spot where Link once was. He cups my cheek, brushing his thumb against it before sliding his hand behind my head. His blue eyes hold mine, his black hair falling over one of his eyes.

Grabbing a handful of my hair, he yanks my head to angle it up toward his. "You played quite the game," he murmurs, brushing his lips against mine. I whimper, desperate and needy for him, all of them. "And now, you won. I think it's about time you received your prize."

He tucks his face into my neck and inhales deeply. He lets out a strangled groan before licking up my neck, making me shiver and my knees buckle before he bites down hard. I moan loudly, making the others curse. "You're not just his, Dove. You're mine now too. All of ours. I hope you know what you got yourself into."

"I don't care. I just want you guys. Need you all," I whisper, my chest heaving.

"And now you have us. You always did. Now and forever, Dove. We're yours, and only yours." He sucks my earlobe into his mouth, letting it go with a pop before whispering. "I love you, my Queen."

A sob almost escapes me but I swallow it down. I have so many mixed emotions right now. Shock, relief, love, but most of all I'm so fucking happy that they are finally mine. A part of me thinks this is all a dream and I'm going to wake up in my bed and nothing has changed.

"Come on, man. We need to go before cops come sniffing around," Taylor pushes.

Travis pulls back, our eyes meeting for a moment with so many unsaid words before he tucks me under his arm.

Jeff is still on the ground, whining like a little bitch about his dick. "Fucking pussy." I laugh. "Your dick is so small, I don't think I hit you hard enough for you to even feel it. Here, let me try again," I taunt, lifting my foot and bringing it down hard between his legs. The guys laugh as Jeff starts to sob.

"Alright, buddy," Hunter says with a crazed laugh as he grabs Jeff and throws him over his shoulder. "You're coming home with us. Hope you enjoyed the party, because it's the last one you'll be attending," Hunter says, giving the guy a hard smack on the ass with a laugh as he carries him out of the room.

"Come on, Foxy Girl. You've been a naughty girl tonight. We'll deal with you later," Taylor says as he looks me over like he wants to eat me. He gives me a wink before clapping his brother on the shoulder and taking off after Hunter with a laugh.

As I walk through the crowd of people, Travis' arm is draped over me as if to tell the world I'm his girl. I feel powerful as everyone looks at us with a mix of fear and envy.

I have no doubt that Link is right. I don't know exactly what I got myself into, but what they don't know is... I don't care. They can bring it. I'm ready for any depraved fucked up shit they're into. Hell, it fucking turns my sick little mind on. Hope they are ready.

Tonight, my whole life changed, and it's about to get a hell of a lot more interesting.

To be continues in Venomous Queen- Black Venom Crew
Book 2

EXCLUSIVE PAPERBACK CONTENT

HERE ARE THE FIRST TWO CHAPTERS OF VENOMOUS QUEEN- BLACK VENOM CREW BOOK 2

CHAPTER ONE

QUINTON

Being Raven's shadow is the job I take the most pride in. I thrive to be on alert, to do the best I can to protect her while keeping myself hidden.

And for the most part, it's been a pretty easy job. But on nights like this, while being in a house full of people, it's near impossible to keep myself hidden.

For the past hour, I've been watching from the outside. Anywhere she goes, I'm watching from a window or back door. She's glued to Andy's side the whole time, up until now, when I hear her mention to Andy she's going to the washroom.

Raven slips inside the house and I curse as I lose track of

her in the crowd. If I have to break my cover and risk her seeing me, then so be it.

But before I go in there and follow her to the bathroom, I decide to look at the blueprints of the house on my phone.

Yes, as ridiculous as it might sound, we have access to every property within an hour's distance in every direction. I know the layout of the whole place by just typing in an address.

It's something we've been doing since Link started Black Venom Crew. Any time I was watching Raven, while the guys did their thing and she went into a building I wasn't familiar with, I'd pull up the blueprint, so I knew every inch of the place. I need that control, so I can get to her no matter what. It doesn't happen often because Raven didn't leave the house much without the guys, not until she became friends with Andrhea.

Taking a quick look at the blueprints, I see that the bathroom window is in the backyard. Moving from my spot behind where Andy and Raven were, I make my way over to the window, praying to God that this is the one she would go to. All the others are on the main floor and most likely have a line. This is my best bet.

Just as I step around one person, another person bumps into my arm, sending my phone flying out of my hand and into the fucking pool.

"Fuck!" I shout, running a hand over my short strands of hair in frustration.

"Sorry man," the dude says.

"Screw you," I snarl. His eyes widen as he takes a step back.

I don't have time for this shit. I'll worry about my phone later. Link is going to be fucking pissed if he calls me and I don't answer.

Abandoning the phone at the bottom of the pool, I continue to make my way through the crowd of drunk dumbasses.

As I walk around the outside of the house, the music starts to fade as I stand below the bathroom window. I'm starting to worry if Raven is even in there or if something happened to her on the way there, but when I hear her talking to herself I let out a low chuckle. Sounds like she's having a full on conversation with herself. It's not the first time I've overheard her talking to herself. She's an oddball, but it's one of the things that I like about her.

Not that I know much. For years, I've just been in the background. There's only a handful of times I've actually talked to Raven. I'm hoping now that she knows who the guys are she will say something to them and then she can start coming around the warehouse. It would be nice to get to know her for real.

Straining to listen to Raven, I hear the sounds of the music within the house make its way into the bathroom. She must be leaving. Needing to make my way back to where Raven left Andy, I start to walk away when I hear a door slam shut.

"What the fuck!" Raven screams. My heart starts

pounding in my fucking chest as my body breaks out into a full body sweat.

"Let me go!" she shouts again.

That has me moving. Running around the house to the side entrance, I throw open the door as my blood pumps adrenaline through my veins. I can only think about getting to Raven and make sure she's okay.

Thankfully, there's a set of stairs as soon as you get inside. I run up two steps at a time.

Just as I make it to the top of the stairs, I see a group of guys sitting there.

"Move!" I bark. All of their heads snap up to mine. They jump to their feet, but they don't get out of my fucking way.

"I said, move!" I snarl, not giving a fuck anymore as I try to push my way through.

They fucking have the nerve to grab me, stopping me from getting to Raven.

I start to fight them, managing to elbow one in the face. He screams as he falls backward, tumbling down the stairs.

"I'm going to fucking kill you!" one of them shouts as he tries to take a swing at me. My hand finds my gun in its holster on my hip. Pulling it free, I take a shot at the fucker hitting him in the thigh. There's no bang thanks to the silencer and he drops to the ground like a rock.

The other two back away from me, raising their hands. I take a moment to memorize their faces, vaguely wondering why they're in my way before taking off down the hall. Fuck! Why does this place have to be so fucking big?

I have no idea what hall leads to the room that Raven

was in. As I try to remember the direction I took and the way the stairs were positioned, I chance going to the right.

I'm usually a hell of a lot better at my job. The main reason why Link chose me to watch Raven when he or the guys couldn't was because of how focused I am, and how I can make snap decisions with a clear mind.

But never has Raven's safety been threatened.

After bursting into every room, I finally found the bathroom. That means the room she is in is right next to it.

Stepping inside, I don't see anyone. "Fuck!"

"Did you see the smug as hell look on her face as she walked out of here on Travis' arm?" A girl comments as she steps into the hall.

Hearing Travis' name, I pause, blood pounding in my ears as I try to listen to what they're saying. "Looks like they officially claimed her," she pouts.

What... so Link... the guys? Striding over to her, I grab her by the shoulders, giving her a little shake. "Did you see Raven?" I ask the girl.

She startles as she shrugs her way out of my hold. "Ahh, yeah, she just left with the twins, Link and Hunter." she rolls her eyes. "Lucky bitch."

Thank fuck, she's okay.

Pushing past the girls, I ignore them calling me rude as I race down the stairs. I just need to see with my own eyes that she's okay. As long as Raven is safe, I don't care what Link does to me.

When I step out the front door, I scan the lawn and find Andy standing there with her girlfriend as they look at something across the lawn. Following her line of sight, I see the guys and Raven walking toward their car. Squinting, I see someone tossed over Hunter's shoulder.

"Fuck." I hiss as I book it down the stairs, passing Andy and head toward the guys.

Link looks over his shoulder as I get closer, and a wave of true fear flushes over me as I see the venom in his eyes. He sneers as he turns around and starts charging toward me.

I stop and wait, knowing it's only going to make things worse if I say anything at this moment.

I'm not surprised when I see his fist flying toward my face. He punches me in the jaw, making my head snap to the side. Pain splinters through my jaw as a ringing starts in my ears. I can taste blood as I turn my face to look at Link. He grabs me by the throat, squeezing hard enough that it cuts off my air supply.

"Tell me why I shouldn't put a bullet through your fucking skull right now," he snarls, his face less than an inch from mine.

"I'm sorry," I choke out. It doesn't even begin how I'm feeling right now, just useless words that change nothing.

"She could have been hurt. If we didn't get there when we did, that piece of fucking shit would have raped her!"

"Hey," Raven says, stepping up to us, looking back and forth between the two of us. "I have no fucking clue what's going on. Or where the hell Q came from. but umm. hello, don't just assume he would have done anything to me. You saw that I had him on the ground when you got there. And I wouldn't have just stopped there. If you didn't show up when you did, you would be dragging a dead body out of there," she says, raising a brow as she crosses her arms. She's so sexy when she's sassy, but now is not the time.

"Little Bird. Shut the fuck up right now." Link is dead serious and I'm glad Raven can see it because she lets out a breath, giving him an eye roll but says nothing else.

Link turns his attention back to me. "What the fuck happened, Q? I'm giving you one chance to convince me not to end your life right fucking now."

He lets go of me. Sucking in a breath, I cough a few times and spit out a mouth full of blood before answering him.

"I had my eye on her all night and when I didn't, it was never more than a few seconds. I've been watching her from the outside and when she had to go to the bathroom, I lost sight of her. I should have gone inside and risked her spotting me, but instead, I looked at the blueprints and found the most likely of the bathrooms she would have gone to. It wasn't one of my smartest moves."

"What if she didn't go to that bathroom, Q? What if she went to a different one and you had no fucking clue where she was!" he shouts in my face.

"I know. I fucked up and I'm really fucking sorry." I look at Raven, regret bright in my eyes. "I'm so fucking sorry, Raven. He shouldn't have been able to get anywhere near you."

"No, he fucking shouldn't have!" Link roars, grabbing his gun and pointing it at my head. I'm trying not to shit my pants because even as close as Link and I are, he would kill me in a heartbeat when it comes to Raven. If I die right now, all that matters is Raven is safe. That's all that has ever mattered.

RAVEN

"Wow!" I shout at Link. "What the fuck? You can't kill Quinton." I say, looking at my crazy boyfriend. Wait... is he my boyfriend now? He did say I was his. Fuck, I'm his now. Holy shit. I'm all of theirs.

Focus, Raven!

Right.

"I very much can," Link growls.

"I have no fucking idea what's going on right now, but please, for me, don't kill him," I ask Link.

"I know it doesn't change the fact that I wasn't there, but fuck, Raven, I really am so fucking sorry," Q says with pleading eyes.

"Sorry for what? What is going on? Someone better start talking." I turn to the other guys. Travis and Taylor are standing behind the car, arms crossed with guarded looks as they wait to see how Link lets this, whatever this is, play out.

"Hold, please," Hunter says, holding up one finger before opening the trunk and tossing Jeff in there like he's his fucking gym bag or some shit before slamming the trunk shut. He hops up to sit on it and gives me a big goofy smile that I can't help but return. "Carry on."

Shaking my head, I let the smile fall and get serious

again. "No more lies. Everything out on the table right now." I look at all of them, giving them my best pissed off glare.

"You're so fucking cute when you're annoyed," Hunter says with a sigh as he leans forward, his chin in his hands as he looks at me dreamily.

"Fuck off." I flip him off. "Stop distracting me."

"God, my cock is so hard." Hunter groans, letting his head hang.

It's so hard to keep a straight face with these guys. "Start speaking," I say, looking at Travis and Taylor, hoping one of them fills me in on this because Link is really near the edge and Hunter seems a little too playful right now. It's like he's all hyped up for his kill.

Still crazy knowing that these guys are killers. Sexy killers. And they're all mine. Fucking finally.

The twins give each other a look before Tay speaks. "You know we're Black Venom Crew." I give him a firm nod. "And I don't mean we're a part of it. We *are* Black Venom Crew."

"I know," I tell him.

Hunter's head snaps up, his eyes going wide. "Since fucking when?"

"Yeah, Little Bird, I'd like to know that too," Link growls, still holding the damn gun to Q's head.

"Would you put that damn thing down?" I ask Link. But it's pointless. He doesn't move, cocking a brow at me. "Fine. I snuck out of the house one night a few weeks ago. It was getting a little ridiculous, the weird hours you all had to 'work.' Like, come on, who needs their car worked on at 1 in the morning?" I snort out a laugh.

"It's not impossible," Hunter adds, and I give him an eye roll. "Someone's car could break down."

"And it needs all four of you to fix it in the middle of the night and not wait until morning? Look, I'm not a fucking genius, but I'm not stupid."

"No one ever thought you were, Little Dove," Travis says.

"Really? Because all these secrets you've been keeping from me sure makes me feel like you think I'm too young and dumb to know anything about your life. We're all best friends. I thought we meant the world to each other."

"We. Do," Link snarls. "There's a lot you don't understand, Ray."

"And I can't wait to hear all about it. But to answer your question, I snuck out and went to the warehouse one night. I got inside and looked around a bit. Found you four in the basement with a few guys strapped to some chairs. And well, you were there, you know what you did," I say, shivering at the memory. Not the killing, but the way they looked so fucking sexy covered in blood.

"Are you fucking kidding me?!" Link snaps at Q, shoving the barrel of the gun harder into his forehead.

"Why are you getting mad at him? He didn't do shit!" I try to argue.

"That's where you're wrong, Foxy Girl. Quinton here has been your shadow for years. When one of us couldn't have eyes on you, he was there. You couldn't see him, but he was there making sure you were safe."

"And was doing a pretty fucking good job up until tonight. And maybe not just tonight. You knew she came to the warehouse?" "Link asks.

"Yes, I followed her there," Q says as I gape at the two of them.

"And you still fucking let her go in? You didn't even let me know," Link snarls.

"No matter what I say right now, you're going to want to kill me." Q is trying to hold it together, but I know he knows his friend is unstable. It's normally hot, but I'm really afraid he's going to shoot Q. I don't know the man well but he seems chill, someone I'd vibe with.

"Wait, what?" I say, brows furrowing. "We'll circle back to the whole stalking thing later, but you were sitting back and watching as I snuck in?"

"I wasn't stalking, I was protecting." Q mutters, giving me a side eye.

"Holy fuck!" My eyes light up. "You're the mystery dude who helped show me how to get in. This is fucking awesome."

"You what?!" Link growls.

Shit.

"I mean... ahhh." I've got nothing. I fucked up.

"I'm sorry, but I've seen how she was hurting from all the secrets you guys have been keeping from her. I know you guys wanted to protect her, to give her a normal life but you should have given her the benefit of the doubt. You left her out of something massive without thinking about how it was going to affect her in the end because you wanted to keep her safe. And it worked until it didn't."

"First off, it's not of your fucking business how we chose to do things when it comes to our girl. And do you think we enjoyed hurting her!" Link screams in Q's face. "It fucking killed me."

"Really?" I ask, sounding way too vulnerable for my liking, but Link slipped up and I'm seeing a small, very small, glimpse at his cold black heart. Link says nothing, not bothering to look at me while his jaw ticks.

"Of course," Taylor says. He steps up to me, taking my face into both of his massive hands. "We love you, Raven. With every fiber of our beings. You're ours, always have been, and always will be. And now that all this shit is out, we're never letting you go," he says, leaning down and capturing my lips with his.

I let out an embarrassingly loud moan as I grip his shirt, sagging into him as he parts my lips with his tongue, before slipping it in and over mine. Holy fuck, I think I'm creaming my panties right now. Someone pinch me because I'm starting to be convinced I'm dreaming.

Scratch that, don't wake me, never wake me.

"Fuck off," Link snarls. "You're making my cock hard and it's not the time for this shit."

"It's always time for a hard cock," Hunter says with amusement.

Pulling back, I blink up at Taylor, who has a cocky but soft smile on his face. "I'll be expecting more sounds like that later."

"Okay," I breathe out, still high on that kiss. I'm never going to get used to this. "But I'm going to need more of that."

"Any time, Foxy Girl. These lips are yours." He brushes his thumb against my bottom lip and I shiver.

"You can't shoot him," I say, turning my attention back to Link.

"Yes, I can," Link says. He's not going to kill him, because if he was, he would have done it already. Link doesn't seem like the kind of guy who hesitates. He's just really fucking pissed right now.

"Nope. Because he got bonus points," I tell Link as I step toward them.

"What?" Link asks, looking at me with confusion.

"He knew I had the right to know what you guys did, and he helped me find a way to gain that knowledge. So, I like him. He's earned bonus points in my book. Also, the stalker thing is kind of hot." I grin and Link snarls.

"Not a stalker," Q mutters, letting out a sigh.

"Whatever you say, stalker boy." I wink at him. Ah, I see it! The smallest hint of a smile. Grabbing Link's wrist, I do something that could be a very stupid move, but I can't let him kill Q. I might not know him well, but if Link trusted him enough with my life, he must be good people. "Put the gun away. All of this fighting is ruining our night. We have a skeezy perv in the trunk that you all were excited to play with just moments before." I remind him.

"You really need to stop with this shit." Link glares down at me.

"With what?" I ask, blinking up at him innocently.

"Making me look weak in front of people." He licks his teeth but puts his gun away.

"Nah, big guy. The Queen is the most powerful player on the chess board. But I'd be nothing without my Kings. You're anything but weak. But neither am I. You just need to see that with your own two eyes and stop handling me with kid gloves."

His hand shoots outs, grabbing me around the throat. I moan again, my eyes fluttering half lidded as he brings his mouth just a millimeter away from mine, his lips moving against mine as he speaks. "You're going to be the death of me, woman," he growls before his lips crash to mine in a bruising kiss. It's quick and dirty, all teeth and tongues, as he has me panting like a bitch in heat. He pulls back, biting down on my lip hard enough to make it bleed before sucking it into his mouth, his tongue lapping away the blood.

In a flash, we went from kissing, to him tossing me over his shoulder. I let out a giggle as he takes me to the car.

Using my hands, I push myself up against Link's back to see Q standing there with a grin. "You're welcome, stalker boy!" I shout. "You owe me one."

His face falls at his new nickname, making me grin like a mad woman.

I think this might end up being one of the best nights of my life.

CHAPTER TWO

RAVEN

The energy in the car is electric. There's this stupid smile engraved on my face right now and I don't even care that the muscles in my face are hurting.

Or the fact that there's a screaming guy in the trunk.

"Let me out!" Jeff screams as he pounds on the roof of the trunk.

"Eat shit and die!" I scream back, making the guys chuckle. I don't even feel bad that he's going to die tonight. Link told me that he's been charged with raping a few girls, and that's only the ones who came forward. Who knows how many he's hurt. And now he's out on bail? How fucked up is that?

Jeff screams some more and as much as I love the fact that he's terrified by knowing what his fate is, I don't wanna listen to him anymore.

Needing something to drown out his noise, I lean over the middle armrest, reaching forward to turn the radio on. "Is this linked to your phone?" I ask Hunter.

When he doesn't answer me, I look over at him, finding his eyes glued to my tits that are practically hanging out. "Hunter!"

"What?" he asks again, his eyes flicking up to mine. He gives me a devilish grin. Not at all sorry for ogling.

"Is this hooked up to your phone?" I ask him again, raising a brow as I grin back.

"Oh. Yeah, it is."

Nodding, I go to search through the songs for the one I want when I feel a sharp pain in both of my ass cheeks. "Ouch!" I shout, head snapping around to look over my shoulder, finding the passing streetlamps shedding light on to two identical smirks. "Did you two just bite my ass cheeks?"

"Sorry, Foxy Girl. You can't just present us with this perfect treat and not expect us to take a bite," Taylor says with a chuckle.

Grinning, I shake my head as I go back to picking a song, but I can't hide the thrill that runs through me at their touches.

Finally, I find *Bangarang* by Skrillex and blast it. The sound drowns out Jeff's screaming as the whole car starts to vibrate from the bass.

Moving to sit back down, I'm dragged on to Taylor's lap. He glides his hand to the back of my head, grabs a handful of my hair, and grips it tightly as he crashes his lips to mine. I moan as I part my lips, letting him in. I want all the kisses they have to offer me.

"I fucking love you," he says against my lips before kissing me again. My body starts to tingle, my lower belly heating with every passing second. I'm about to adjust myself to straddle his lap, needing to grind against the hard cock under my ass, needing some friction against my throbbing clit when Link turns the music down. "Put her back in her seat and buckle her the fuck in. Risk her safety again, and I'll kick your ass," he growls at Taylor.

"Interrupted again," he sighs and I pout as I move back to my seat and Taylor buckles me up.

"You suck," I mutter to Link as I shift in my seat. "It's not nice to get me all worked up and leave me wanting."

"Welcome to our life," he murmurs. "Travis."

"Yeah?" Travis answers.

"Take care of our girl," Link demands, sending a shiver down my spine.

My breathing starts to pick up as I stare forward out the front window. We've just reached a stretch of highway, so the car is pitch black. I am unable to see his face but I can feel his warm breath as he leans in, his soft lips brushing against my neck, making my skin prickle with pleasure before he places a kiss on my neck. "Need help, Dove?" he murmurs against the sensitive skin below my ear.

"Please," I whimper as he sucks and nips at my neck. I suck in a sharp breath as his hand lands on my thigh, giving it a squeeze.

"Anything for you," he says, sucking my ear lobe into his mouth before biting down. My eyes flutter shut as his hand creeps up my leg, closer and closer to the one place I need him.

Travis kisses my neck with little nibbles, driving me wild as he cups my pussy, pressing the heel of his hand against my clit.

"Oh fuck," I moan, my hips bucking against his hand.

"Such a good girl," Taylor rasps as his hand finds one of

my breasts. He pulls down my top, letting my breasts fall free. "God, I can't wait to fuck these perfect tits," he groans. I whimper as he sucks my nipple into his mouth. The feeling of his hot wet tongue against my piercing feels so good.

Together, the twins work me over. Taylor sucks and nips at my nipple as Travis does the same to my neck. Travis moves the heel of his hand in a circle, adding the perfect pressure and movement over my clit, giving me the friction I desperately need. My heart is pounding, my breathing coming in short little pants as my body lights up like a Christmas tree.

"Are you going to cum for them, Little Bird?" Link's rough voice has my eyes slowly opening. I meet his in the rearview mirror. He stares at me in challenge, daring me to say no.

Letting out panting breaths, my mind is buzzing. I feel like I'm dreaming. Just this morning, these fuckers were avoiding their feelings, driving me mad. And now, they're working together to demand my orgasm.

With a moan, I nod my head in answer to Link's question.

"Words, Little Bird," he growls.

"Yes!" I shout as Travis moves a little faster, finding the perfect rhythm as Taylor bites down on my nipple. "So close. Please, don't stop."

"Never, Little Bird. We wanna hear you scream. Cum for them, for us," Link demands.

"Right there," I pant, my hands shooting out to grab both

twins' legs. My nails dig in, making Travis groan in my ear and Taylor against my breast. "Fuck, fuck, fuck!" I chant as the pressure builds to a boiling point.

"Sing for us, Little Bird. We wanna hear your sweet sounds," Link chuckles. And then I'm free falling over a fucking cliff. My eyes roll back as I scream out my release. My pussy pulses around nothing and I almost sob at the empty feeling as wave after wave crashes over me. I can hardly hear the guys cursing and groaning in response over the buzzing in my ears.

"Fuck," Hunter groans. "I really don't need to cream my fucking jeans before killing someone."

I huff out a laugh as I try to catch my breath. "Save it for later," I say, and Hunter turns around to look at me. I can see the hunger in his eyes as the moon shines through Link's window, lighting up Hunter's face.

"Why's that, Little Mouse?" he asks.

"Because I want all your cum for myself." I grin back, loving how none of this feels weird or awkward. Even though we've officially crossed the friendship line, I'm reminded that we've always been so much more.

All the men curse, making me grin wider as I tuck my boobs away.

"Feeling better, Foxy Girl?" Taylor asks, his voice sounding smug as fuck.

"Yes and no," I say.

"Why no?" Travis asks.

"I feel better now that I've gotten some relief, but it wasn't enough."

"What else do you need?" Hunter asks.

"To be fucked within an inch of my life sounds good right about now," I say casually.

"Fuck me," Travis groans.

"Or she could fuck me," Taylor says.

"She's not fucking either of you just yet," Link snaps.

"Sorry, boys, you know how this is going to go," Hunter says in a cocky tone.

I shiver at the idea of being with one of them. But I have a feeling about who gets to taste me first. I can't fucking wait.

"Let's get this fucker dealt with. I need a drink," Link says as we pull into the garage parking lot. He drives over to the gate that leads to the warehouse. It opens a second later and Link moves forward, driving the car inside.

No one speaks for a few moments and I use the moment to think. Travis and Taylor just touched me, kissed me, and made a mess of me. A smile slips onto my face. Yup, so far, the best night ever.

When the car is parked, we all get out. Hunter goes around to the back and opens the trunk.

"Please, please, let me go. I'll give you anything you want." Jeff begs the moment the trunk opens.

"Anything I want?" Hunter asks as I step up to stand next to him.

"Yes! Anything." Jeff sobs.

"I'll take your life then." Hunter chuckles and Jeff starts to blubber harder.

"Do you think he heard me back there?" I ask, looking up at Hunter.

I try to hold back my grin at the look of murder on Hunter's face, at my words. Hunter lifts his foot and slams his heel into Jeff's face, his nose breaking and sending blood bursting from his nose. Jeff groans in pain as Hunter grabs him and throws him over his shoulder before storming off toward the warehouse. Link follows after him as Hunter huffs and puffs to Jeff about him listening to me orgasm, like he had any choice in the matter.

"You love getting us all worked up, don't you, Dove?" Travis asks, chuckling. He tosses his arm over my shoulder, leading me around the car and after the other two.

"Maybe." I shrug, a grin forming on my face.

"Well, we like getting you worked up too," Taylor says. Looking up at him, he winks, but I see the heat in his eyes.

"You know everything has changed, right?" Taylor asks me.

"I know. That's the whole point, though, isn't it?" I ask.

"No, Dove. You don't understand. Sure, we're still going to be best friends, as close as before. But now? You're ours. To fuck when we want, to kill for, to please, to love, and everything else in between. Your life doesn't belong to you anymore. We own you."

I know I should tell them to fuck off, that I'm my own person and no one owns me. But I don't because they're right. I'm theirs in every way possible. I want them to own me, to control me. Doesn't mean I'm going to make it easy for them, but the idea of owning them as fully as they own me sends a chill down my spine and right to my clit.

"Keep talking. I'll stop you when you say something I don't like," I tell them as we walk into the building.

"Fuck me, Ray. We really had no reason to keep you out of the loop this long, did we?" Taylor asks.

"Ah," I say, snapping my fingers. "Now you're getting it."

"Brat," Travis growls.

"Yes, but I'm your brat," I grin up at him.

"Damn right, you are," he says, grabbing me by the back of my head to pull me into a soul crushing kiss. We pull away, panting. "You ready to watch us play?"

"Yes, but can I step out if it gets too bloody?" I ask. "As hot as you all look covered in blood, if there's guts, I'm gone."

"Alright, Dove." he chuckles.

As the twins bring me down the stairs to the bottom floor, I can't get what we did in the car out of my mind. Travis has his arm around my shoulder, his fingers rubbing against the top of my arm, and Taylor holds my hand, his fingers locked with mine. It's like they can't keep their hands off me and I fucking love it. Is it bad that I want one of them touching me at all times? Like they could bend me over and fuck me anywhere they want and there would not be a peep out of me regarding a protest.

"Sounds like they got started without us," Travis says as screams below us ring out. I squeal in surprise as Taylor scoops me up and starts jogging down the stairs. Wrapping my arms around his neck, I laugh wildly as I bounce with each step.

I feel so light and carefree for once. No stress, no worries, just anticipation of what comes next with me and my guys. *My guys. My mother fucking guys!*

"Couldn't wait, could you?" Travis asks as we burst into the door.

My laughter dies as I see Link and Hunter shirtless, standing in front of Jeff, who is strapped to some kind of cross. *Wait, is that a Saint Andrew's cross?* Wonder if they have another one around here we could use?

"You got some drool there, Foxy Girl." Taylor grins down at me as he wipes at the corner of my mouth.

"Fuck you. You guys know you're all dark gods. Damn right I wanna lick every inch of you." I grin back. His eyes flash with heat as a low growl erupts around the room.

"You can lick, suck, fuck anything on us that you want later on, Little Bird. Right now, we have work to do," Link says, cracking his wrapped knuckles.

"Sit here and watch," Taylor says, placing me on a chair that's against the wall.

"Remember. Once there's a lot of blood or guts, I'm out!" I shout as the twins go over to a table next to the cross.

Brows rising, I cock my head to the side as I try to get a look at what is on the table. Travis holds up a blade, examining it, as Taylor picks up what looks to be pliers.

I grimace as I wonder what the hell they're going to do with those. Never mind, I don't want to know.

Thankfully, Jeff has some sort of gag in his mouth to drown out some of his screams and sobs as the guys do their thing. I'm glad because he was starting to give me a headache.

I'm entranced as I sit and watch them in their element. I don't even pay attention to the person who won't make it out of here tonight. No, my guys hold my eyes as I take in the way Link's arms flex with each punch he gives. The way Hunter's face lights up with his manic laughter. How Taylor pulls off his shirt to use it to wipe the sweat off his face, putting his sexy tattooed body on display for me like the others. And Travis, fuck me, I never thought veins could be so hot, but how they bulge in his arm and hand as he slices up Jeff's body, so fucking sexy.

By the time Link says my name, I'm a horny little mess.

"Little Bird!"

My eyes snap up from where I was tracing Hunter's V. "Ah yeah, sorry, what?" I ask, blinking up at him.

He grins something wicked as he shakes his head. "Things are about to get bloody now."

"Oh," I say. Well fuck, I was enjoying the show.

Link turns back to Jeff. "Take a good look at our girl." Link grabs Jeff's face roughly. "It's the last time you're ever going to see another woman. Because your time hurting innocent girls ends tonight. We have so many fun things planned for you. Normally we would end your life a little sooner, but seeing how you thought you had the right to touch our girl, to lay your dirty hands upon her body, we're going to make sure you feel every bit of pain." Link's grin is something out of a horror movie. I should be afraid, I should take off running, but I'm squirming in my seat, resisting the fact I want to climb him like a tree and seat myself on his cock.

"Hunter," Link says, directing this attention to his brother. "Take our girl here up to the apartment. You've earned the right to have her first. You're going to fuck her, make her feel the best she's ever felt, because after tonight, she's fair game for the rest of us." Link looks at me with a different cruel smile that has me whimpering with need. Fuck me.

Hunter turns to look at me, he's blood free, but his body is covered in a sheen of sweat. A slow, hungry grin takes over his face as he starts to stalk over to me. "It would be my fucking pleasure." His low, husky voice lights me on fire. "Come on, Little Mouse. I'm fucking starving."

ALSO BY ALISHA WILLIAMS

Emerald Lake Prep

Book One: Second Chances

Book Two: Into The Unknown

Book Three: Shattered Pieces

Book Four: Redemption Found

Blood Empire

Book One: Rising Queen

Book Two: Crowned Queen

Book Three: Savage Queen

Silver Valley University

Book One: Hidden Secrets

Book Two: Secrets Revealed

Book Three: Secrets Embraced

ONGOING SERIES

Angelic Academy

Book One: Tainted Wings

Book Two: Tainted Bonds

Black Venom Crew:

Book One: Little Bird

Book Two: Venomous Queen

STANDALONES

We Are Worthy- A sweet and steamy omegaverse.

We Are Destiny A steamy omegaverse (2023)

If You Go Into The woods- Steamy MF Shifter Novella

A Mid Nights Bloody Dream (TBD)

Knot Going Anywhere

CO-WRITES

Solidarity Academy

Knock 'Em Down: Book One

Take 'Em Out: Book Two (TBD)

Lost Between The Pages

Mad For The Sea Witch

ANTHOLOGIES

Jingle My Balls : A Gay & Merry LGBTQ Charity Anthology

In The Heat Of The Moment: A Charity Anthology

Ours to Keep: A Why Choose Anthology Romance (September 2023)

SHARED WORLDS: A NIGHT OF RAPTURE AND PRIDE

Naomi (Dressed to Kill)

ACKNOWLEDGMENTS

As always, I'm beyond grateful for Jessica, Jennifer, Cassie, Mylene and Amy. You ladies are family more than anything! Thank you for all the time and energy you put into all my books. And a big shout out to Tamara. Thanks for being there for me, and helping me with everything you do, you're the best wifey!

Many thanks to my Beta and ARC teams for your time and efforts in help each of my books be the best they can be!

ABOUT THE AUTHOR

Writer, Alisha Williams lives in Alberta, Canada, with her husband and her two daughters. She has three crazy kitties who she loves. When she isn't writing or creating her own graphic content, she loves to read books by her favorite authors.

Writing has been a lifelong dream of hers, and this book was made despite the people who prayed for it to fail, but because Alisha is not afraid to go for what she wants, she has proven that dreams do come true.

Wanna see what all her characters look like, hear all the latest gossip about her new books or even get a chance to become a part of one of her teams? Join her readers group on Facebook here - Naughty Queens. Or find her author's page here - Alisha Williams Author

Of course, she also has an Instagram account to show all her cool graphics, videos, and more book related goodies - alishawilliamsauthor

Sign up for Alisha's Newsletter

Got TikTok? Follow alishawilliamsauthor

Printed in Great Britain
by Amazon